RICHARD HINE

PUBLISHED BY

amazon encore

The characters and events portrayed in this book are fictitious. Any similarity to real persons, living or dead, is coincidental and not intended by the author.

The *Publishers Weekly* quote on the back cover of this novel refers to the manuscript reviewed as part of the 2009 Amazon Breakthrough Novel Award contest. For more information, visit www.amazon.com/abna.

Printed in the United States of America

Published by AmazonEncore
P.O. Box 400818
Las Vegas, NV 89140

ISBN-13: 9781935597148
ISBN-10: 1935597140

For Amanda

"I often wonder what future historians will say about us. One sentence will suffice to describe modern man: he fornicated and he read newspapers."

—Albert Camus, *The Fall*, 1956

CHAPTER ONE

New York City, Fall 2006

"I'm still asleep," says Sam.

It's the kind of thing she says on a morning like this. When she feels me lying in bed three minutes after I've silenced the alarm. When she senses me, curled next to her, mimicking her shape without actually touching her. She doesn't want to move in case it encourages me.

Another minute goes by.

I put a hand on her hip, wiggle myself an inch or two closer. She sighs. I kiss the back of her head, savoring the smell of her coconut conditioner.

"Get off me," she says.

She slides out from under the comforter and makes her way to the bathroom. I don't get up. I wait. The toilet flushes, and as she pads back to bed I catch a glimpse of her: slightly tangled, shoulder-length hair; baggy purple T-shirt; a flash of white cotton panties. She slithers into her former position, adjusts her head against her pillow.

"Can't we just cuddle?" I say.

"There isn't time. Don't you have a meeting? I haven't brushed my teeth."

I know better than to argue any of these points. Sam and I have been together more than sixteen years, married for nearly thirteen. I don't remind her that in our early days together finding time for sex was never a problem. Or that I've survived being late for dozens of meetings. Or that once upon a time even morning breath possessed certain aphrodisiac qualities.

I roll away, sit on my side of the bed. My mind feels foggy, my vision is blurred. I grab my glasses and walk, head down, to the bathroom.

I shave slowly, cutting through the foam with one of those disposable triple-bladed razors. Sam used to hang out with me in the bathroom some mornings and tell me how sexy it was to watch me shave. I can't remember the last time she did that.

I do remember the last time we had sex. Twenty-five days ago. One of those unsatisfactory occasions where I came and she didn't and it was my fault for not holding on long enough and whoever said love means never having to say you're sorry was proved wrong again. Despite that failure, I'd be happy to try again. I'm willing to practice more. To try and do it right next time.

Twenty-five days. Nearly four weeks. I'm not supposed to be keeping tabs anymore. But so what if I do? Days without sex is an important statistic—the kind that used to matter to Sam as well as me. Before we were married, even when we lived six hundred and fifty miles apart during senior year, we had an agreement never to let more than a month pass without having sex with each other. Whenever necessary, we each drove six hours to meet halfway at a roadside motel just outside Harrisburg. We'd make love in the shower, on the armchair, on the bathroom counter, on the bedroom floor. We'd drink beers, eat shortbread cookies and inspect each other's bodies for crumbs. We'd sleep on the gray-white sheets, go out for pancakes, then head back to the room to take full advantage of the hours and minutes we still had left. When we parted, I'd drive home weak but elated, listening to the Pulp album that reminded me of the semester we'd shared in London. Every time I unpacked my bag, I'd find a piece of Sam's clothing stuffed inside—panties, a bra, a single white sock. I kept these items in my bedside drawer.

Our relationship was easier to navigate then: a twelve-hour roundtrip came with a built-in guarantee. Nowadays, even though we sleep just inches apart, our love life requires far more elaborate maneuvers. Sex has become something we build up to slowly, not something we do on a whim. For Sam, things have to happen in a certain yet inexplicable order. It's as if she's got the whole thing choreographed in her mind, but every time I put a foot wrong the music stops and the whole dance has to begin again.

I step into the shower stall and blast myself with water that's hotter than I usually like.

I towel off and stand naked in front of the bathroom mirror. I'm thirty-seven years old. My eyesight sucks. In the blurred reflection of my upper body I see the face of a cartoon dog—my nipples make two eyes above a round, belly-button nose and jowly, hanging cheeks. I put my glasses back on, hoping to make the face disappear, but the effect lingers.

I walk back into the bedroom.

"Do you think I'm fat?" I ask Sam. Now that I've showered and am focused on getting out the door, she can allow herself to display more signs of consciousness.

"No," she says. "Of course not." We both know that using the F-word can damage a relationship.

I pull back the curtain, trying to find some socks that will match the pants I plan to wear. I make the mistake of giving Sam a side view of my gut as I bend over.

"I just think you should work out more," she says. "I worry about your health."

That's a good one. The worry-about-your-health angle never fails.

"Would you want me more if I lost some weight?"

"Jesus, Russell," she says, turning away from me, pulling the comforter tighter around her.

I never ask Sam what she does after I leave each morning, but my working assumption is that once I kiss her on the head she drifts gently back to sleep for at least another hour.

The F-train is crowded, but there's a middle seat no one wants: an orange sliver between two passengers whose ass sizes exceed the MTA space allowance. I wedge myself between them and pull my newspapers from my messenger bag. It's a small gesture. But whenever I'm surrounded by iPod listeners, BlackBerry users, Sudoku addicts and anyone looking to either shake me down or inspire my religious conversion, I immerse myself in a newspaper. Not just to create a barrier between me and my fellow commuters. Not just to fly the flag for the company that employs me. I happen to think a newspaper is a convenient, wireless, handheld device. On a good day it might even tell me something I don't already know.

I conceal my *New York Times* inside the first section of the *Daily Business Chronicle* and start reading. It's my way of reminding any media planners who might get on the train that the *Chronicle* still exists, even if its readership among the under-forty crowd is in sharp decline.

The news is all bad. Our future's in the hands of scoundrels and fanatics. I skim the headlines, searching in vain for signs of hope for subway riders, New York City dwellers, American citizens at home and abroad, the entire God-fearing Christian world, people of all religions, agnostics, atheists, the planet we all must share. I read about the rescue effort underway halfway up an Oregon mountain. Three overconfident climbers are stranded. They ignored the weather forecasts and now about twenty people have to risk their own lives trying to save them. I imagine myself as a rescue worker, being lowered from a helicopter, buffeted by chill winds in the blinding snow. I can't resist the urge to slap the face of the first man I reach: "Fuck you, you stupid fuck!" I scream. "Look at all the trouble you've caused. I could be at home in my mountain lodge right now. Relaxing with a nice hot chocolate. Feeding my faithful St. Bernard. Tiptoeing around my gorgeous but indifferent wife."

I fold the paper and reflect for a while. I'm not sure what motivates mountain climbers anymore. It's either heroism or idiocy or both. It's not as if the mountains haven't been conquered before. And we already have all the business metaphors we need.

Three years ago, when my company still spent money on such things, Jack Tennant, our division's president, hired a mountaineer to talk to us about "Peak Performance." Her claim to fame was that she was the first one-armed woman to climb Mount Everest.

She stood alone on the stage of our company's auditorium talking about the teamwork required for such a complex expedition. She paced backwards and forwards against a backdrop of projected images from the climb. She told us all about the planning, the preparation, the different kinds of expertise required to achieve the ultimate goal. Until she held it up, it was impossible to tell which was her artificial hand. Reaching base camp was relatively easy, she said. The gang was all there. Tents were set up. You had plenty of supplies—food, clothing, medical equipment. But when the time came, she, the leader of the expedition, said good-bye to the team and, with only a trusty Sherpa to carry her camera and flag, set out alone for the final push.

"Aim high," she said as her final, twelve-foot-tall image was projected on the auditorium screen. "Reach for the top. Dream big dreams. Set yourself unattainable goals. Because with teamwork you can transform the unattainable into the achievable." After her speech we clapped enthusiastically and then lined up as she signed leftover copies of her once best-selling book. We weren't expected to read it, but I did spend ten minutes looking at the pictures. There were three pages devoted to the surgeries, rehabilitation and technological advances that made her arm so functional. But I wanted to see what the Sherpa looked like. The only place I could find him, he was partially obscured in a group shot.

I emerge from a side exit at my midtown subway stop, and as I wait for the light to change, I raise my eyes to study the impressive high-rise building where I work. People still call it the Burke-Hart Building, even though Burke-Hart Publishing—the company that founded the *Daily Business Chronicle*—is now only a small division within the Ghosh Corporation.

I cross the street and walk across the mini-plaza that creates a public space in front of my building. This plaza is swept and hosed each morning to erase all traces of the tourists, skateboarders, lovers and bums who congregate here at different times during the day and night.

I pass through the revolving doors and walk toward my elevator bank. Two workmen on ladders are adjusting the four-foot-tall letters suspended on barely visible wires behind the main reception desk. These letters are new. They spell out G-H-O-S-H in the eye-popping purple and yellow logotype that serves as a reminder that our company name—and the name of the Ghosh Corporation's founder and CEO—should always be pronounced "gauche," never "gosh." This hanging logo is just one part of the worldwide corporate rebranding being executed at all of the old Burke-Hart offices.

I like the new logo and the change it signifies. I'm not one of those old-timers who grumble about the fact that our heritage is being subsumed by a ten-year-old company known for its arrogant business dealings, aggressive outsourcing and love of bright, childish colors. These old-timers recall how the company used to be like family. People in senior management would walk around the floors. They would stop and chat. They would even remember your name. At meetings, speakers would routinely stir up corporate pride by saying, "We bleed green blood," in reference to our original corporate color and their pride in a heritage dating back to 1923.

Now our green logo is gone from the lobby. We read in our own and other newspapers how Larry Ghosh intends to return Burke-Hart Publishing and its flagship publication, the *Daily Business Chronicle*, to a new era of profitability. We read in management memos that we are looking to change the

DNA of our division. We witness the influx of new managers, consultants and free-floating strategists—people who seem to speak a different language than we are used to and who measure success by different metrics.

There's no fighting change. And it's not just our logo. The heart of our company has been transplanted. We aren't supposed to bleed green blood anymore. People who do are out of touch.

CHAPTER TWO

My personal base camp is a two-windowed, north-facing office on the twenty-fifth floor. At first glance it's a total mess. Every conceivable surface is covered with stacks of file folders, bound presentations, newspapers, magazines and assorted papers. The overall effect is chaotic, random-looking. But appearances can be deceptive. In reality, despite its dumping-ground appearance, my office is the visual manifestation of a highly alert, productive, creative and well-organized business mind.

Lucky Cat waves at me from the windowsill. I walk over to him between the piles of work that rise from my floor. At the start of each day, I rub Lucky Cat's paw and make a wish. Lucky was a gift from our Japanese design intern, Kiko Soseki. On her first day in the office, Kiko presented me with a gift-wrapped box and a note that read, "Dear Mr. Wiley, Please enjoy traditional Lucky Cat and special rice crackers from Japan, bringing happiness and good fortune." The wrapping paper looked more expensive than the plastic object inside. I pulled the cat's head off and tipped the crackers out of its stomach. They were dry and stale and I threw them away immediately. But there was something that drew me to the black shell of the cat itself. I played with it for a while, removing and replacing its detachable head, studying how the glued paper aligned when its face and colorful belly were put back together. I imagined that Lucky Cat possessed special powers. At the very least, I thought perhaps I could absorb something good from his hollow, manufactured cheerfulness. I found a spot for him on the windowsill, among my commemorative lucites and discarded promotional items. And that's where he stays, opposite the door to my office, smiling at everyone who crosses my threshold, his paw permanently raised in welcome.

"Please, no more than three interruptions before lunchtime," I whisper today.

I've found it's best to manage my expectations in regard to Lucky Cat's powers.

I sit at my desk and scan my emails to confirm there's nothing super-urgent to deal with. I launch my web browser and log on to the Ghosh Corporation intranet. Before starting the day's climb, I like to make sure the mountains haven't moved—that no one important has been fired and none of our business units has been sold overnight. Everything seems in order. So I swivel around to my actual desktop and try to reacquaint myself with the logic behind the mass of overlapping papers in front of me: mail, documents, file folders, sticky notes and paper scraps.

The top layer of the pile relates to the Livingston Kidd account. It's the biggest project I'm working on. Livingston Kidd is our largest financial advertiser. The partners who run the firm are the kind of old-school clients we like: people who actually read the *Chronicle*. For years they've renewed their advertising schedule with scarcely a question. But Livingston's going through a transition of its own. They recently hired a slick, super-confident marketing team from Citigroup. And their new guys are looking to do things differently from the people they've come in to replace. According to their media agency, they intend to "bring the Livingston Kidd brand into the twenty-first century." Which means moving more money online and limiting newspaper advertising to just one title. The Livingston team has invited a *Chronicle* delegation to their New Jersey headquarters next month to present a "partnership review." It will be our one and only chance to save the business. My boss, Henry Moss, the vice president of sales and marketing, will be making the presentation himself.

The *Chronicle* can't afford to lose Livingston Kidd. Financial advertising is the category we rely on most. Over the past several years, as most of our clients have shifted large chunks of their budgets to the internet, it's the one area that's held up best. Losing the Livingston Kidd business would be a huge psychological blow. In business terms, it would transform a year of moderate decline into a complete disaster.

"Hey, pal," says Henry. "What are you doing at lunchtime?"

"Nothing," I say. "I was hoping to make some headway on this Livingston Kidd proposal. I don't have anything to show you just yet."

"That's good. That's good." Henry sounds far away, distracted. He has me on speakerphone. I wait a couple of seconds.

"Did you need me to do something at lunchtime?" I ask.

"Yeah," says Henry. "Let's have lunch. I'll see if Ellen can get us into Fabrice."

"OK. Do I need to bring anything?"

"No. No," he says. "Don't bring anything."

"Great," I say. "I'll see you at lunch."

Another long pause. I wait in case Henry wants to say more. I don't hang up till I hear him humming softly to himself, tapping an accompanying rhythm on the surface of his uncluttered desk.

Focus.

I need to focus on the job at hand. It's the only way to get anything done. As the *Chronicle*'s sales development director, I have only one mission: to help our salespeople sell more advertising pages. I need to create presentations that convince advertisers that the *Chronicle*, the fourth-largest national newspaper, is the only place to be. Forget the top three titles. The *Chronicle*—smaller and cheaper, with a waning but still powerful influence—offers the kinds of advertising efficiency you just can't get from the *Journal* or the *Times* or even *USA Today*. OK. Maybe that's not true for *every* advertiser. But right now I only have to make it sound believable to one. I need a story that will convince the skeptical new team at Livingston Kidd. There's no reason I should be worrying about Henry. Who sounded weird. Or Sam. Who doesn't want me to touch her anymore. Or the problems in the newspaper industry. Which can't find enough new readers to replace those who are dying off. Or the asinine way our company is structured. Which puts our print sales team in direct competition with our online division. Or the way our online sales team gets treated like heroes every time they convince a big print advertiser to run fewer ads. Don't get me started.

Focus, Russell.

Don't think about that job offer from Google you turned down six months before their IPO. Selling print is what you're good at. Anyway, what else could you have done? Henry had just promoted you. Even upped your bonus target. You were loyal. You kept honing your skills in the newspaper business. You stuck it out in the land of dead trees even as those huge-but-nimble digital fortresses were being built all around you. You thought newspapers still had a role to play: helping us make sense of the world at least once every twenty-four hours. But then you woke up. Google had taken over the world. Digg.com—a company with fourteen employees—was getting more page views than the *New York Times*. Newspapers didn't make quite as much sense anymore. Not in a high-speed, 24/7, continually updated, RSS-fed, screen-based, downloadable, do-it-yourself, read-listen-watch-for-free world.

Focus, Russell.

Just read the Livingston files. Review the client history. Assemble the key points from our audience research. Make a list of all the reasons why Livingston Kidd should continue to advertise in the *Daily Business Chronicle*. I wonder if this is how carriage drivers felt when they first noticed those Model-T Fords overtaking them a hundred years ago. What did carriage manufacturers do in those days? Build better, more expensive carriages? Make the seats more comfortable? Pioneer the use of rearview mirrors?

Focus, Russell.

Close the door. No more extraneous thoughts. No distractions. Remember Peter Drucker. The effective executive focuses on his number one priority. And nothing else.

Interruption #1: Barbara Ward, Departmental Assistant
"Excuse me, Russell, but I just have to ask you. Have you seen what Angela is wearing today?"

I didn't hear her knock. But when I look up, I see Barbara is already inside my office, holding the door almost shut behind her. She's a small, religious woman, speaking in a stage whisper intended to alert me to the scandalous nature of the news she's conveying.

"To tell you the truth, I haven't," I say. "And I'm really quite busy right now. But I will pay close attention when I see Angela later."

Barbara is one of those people I never quite know what to do with. She's worked here since 1975 and seems not to have updated her wardrobe or her job skills since then. Because jobs at my level no longer justify full-time assistants, Barbara is supposed to support my entire department. But beyond the fact that she sometimes answers my phone and offers to transfer people into my voicemail, I simply don't have any work I can give her with confidence. According to Sam, whenever she calls me at the office, Barbara is more likely to connect her to someone called Katie Krieger's voicemail than she is to my own mailbox. Despite all that, Barbara has taught herself the skills she needs to upload digital photographs of her grandchildren and email them to her friends and family around the world. She is also, I'm told, an expert at placing last-minute bids in online auctions for a certain kind of collectible porcelain figurine.

"I'm not sure she's wearing a bra," says Barbara, looking at me as if she thinks this is my fault. "Everything seems very tight and transparent."

I pause to contemplate the kind of conversation Barbara would like me to have with Angela Campos, the beautiful high school senior who is interning with us this semester. She's one of fifty such kids who are scattered throughout the company. It's an initiative launched by Burke-Hart's new CEO, Connie Darwin, to provide valuable work experience to gifted but economically disadvantaged public school students. Henry, of course, insisted I sign up. He's probably the only one in sales and marketing who hasn't noticed the commotion Angela's presence has created.

"I thought you had already spoken to her about what's appropriate for the office," says Barbara.

"Yes, yes," I say, not sure what else to add. I haven't actually spoken to Angela directly, and it seems the telepathic messages I sent didn't get through.

"Let me have another word with her later," I tell Barbara. "I just have to finish what I'm doing here. Could you close the door?"

"I'm not the only one who's noticed," she says.

"Absolutely. Understood. And thank you for bringing this to my attention."

I wish one of the women on my staff would deal with this. Maybe I could zap Meg an instant message and ask her to talk to Angela. Scratch that. Take a lesson from Congressman Foley. It's not a good idea to send IMs about teens and undergarments.

Focus, Russell.

Forget Mark Foley. Remember Peter Drucker. Angela's clothing is not a priority. Livingston Kidd is your only priority.

Interruption # 2: Martin Hopkins, Creative Director

"How old do you think I am?" says Martin. He's standing on a patch of carpet that gives him just enough room to twirl. He's wearing the trendster uniform he adopted at the start of the week: tight black T-shirt tucked into black jeans, ankle boots with a one-inch heel. He thinks this new wardrobe makes him look younger. In reality it draws attention to the fact that he's a middle-aged straight guy trying just a little too hard and acting a little too gay.

"Wasn't my door closed?" I ask him.

"This isn't business. It's personal. I'm coming to you as a friend."

I give him my grudging attention, and he twirls again.

"Forty-six," I say. "Careful. Don't knock those files over."

"You think so?"

"You've told me a hundred times."

"OK. But if you didn't know. Just based on looks. How old would you think I am?"

"Did I tell you how busy I am right now?"

"Russell."

I stand up, walk around my desk, look at him more closely, noticing the wisps of chest hair curling around the shallow V of his T-shirt. Martin used to dress in a more standard mid-forties-divorcé uniform: badly ironed, open-at-the-neck, button-down shirts, mismatched with pleated slacks or khakis. His hair—previously a shaggy, long-at-the-back, almost-mullet-like disaster—is now buzzed short to reveal the exact topography of his male-pattern baldness. He's started working out too. But it's early in the process—too early to give his T-shirt something firm to cling to. His upper body is still lumpy in a way that makes his new clothing choices seem ill advised.

"I don't know," I say. "You probably look about..."

I'm playing with him. I know exactly what he wants to hear.

"Tell me," he says.

"I guess you could pass for thirty-eight."

"Really?"

"Absolutely. No shit. Could you just sit down and stop touching your stomach?"

Martin, smiling now, does what I ask. "I read that article you gave me," he says. "That guy made some good points."

"I told you, Finchley's one of the best thinkers out there. Gladwell and Bing had better watch out."

"When he says thirty-eight is the new twenty-five, he's so right. It's all about experience. We can't expect twenty-five-year-olds to have all the answers or know how to run a business."

"I'm glad you liked the article."

"It really opened my eyes to what I need to be doing for myself. I've decided that thirty-eight is not just a number, it's a state of mind."

"That's cool."

"I'll tell you, Russell, I've got a whole new attitude. I've taken my graduation year off my résumé, and I'm only listing jobs that go back fifteen years."

"Shit. You're looking?"

"Not looking. Just opening myself up to new possibilities."

I peer a little closer at Martin's wrinkled features. "How long do you think you can keep this thirty-eight thing up?"

"I told you, it's a state of mind. And it's working. I bumped into Barney Barnes yesterday. He told me to call him."

"Shit. Don't tell Henry you're talking to Barney."

"Cross-divisional dialogue, baby," says Martin, getting back up. "Isn't that what Connie wants to see more of?"

"OK," I say. "I'm just looking out for your thirty-eight-year-old ass."

Martin floats out of my office. I'm glad that the Christopher Finchley article I gave him had such a big effect. But still, knowing how important loyalty is to Henry, I'm worried that Martin's even talking to Barney Barnes.

Or I *could* be worried. But I don't have brain space to worry about Martin. Martin is not my problem. Livingston Kidd is my only problem.

Interruption #3: Cindy Lang, Sales Development Manager

"So Roger is going out on medical leave," says Cindy. She's the last person I want to see right now. But she knows something I don't.

"I didn't realize he had announced it yet."

A couple of months ago, Roger Jones told me he had finally topped four hundred pounds and was thinking of getting his stomach stapled. But he didn't mention it again. I assumed he had backed away from the plan.

"He's telling people he'll be out for up to six weeks. I'm a little concerned."

I don't like being blindsided by internal news, especially from within my own department. But I try not to let it show.

"I'm sure he'll be OK," I say. "It's quite a common procedure these days."

"I'm concerned we don't have a plan. Roger and I were working together on a few projects." Cindy is standing on the other side of my desk, arms folded. She's that kind of skinny, gym-toned person whose head looks too big for her body. When she tilts it to the side, it puts an alarming strain on her neck muscles.

"Really?" I say. "I thought I asked you and Roger to work on completely separate assignments. Sit down. Let's take a look."

Cindy sits and, referring to her leather-bound notebook, reels off a list of projects she and Roger are "collaborating" on. She's wearing a crisp white blouse with a pearl choker around her neck. I jot down the client names she mentions. Each one falls squarely within the categories Cindy is supposed to be covering by herself. She should have had no need to get Roger involved.

As far as my department goes, I made a big mistake when I hired Cindy four months ago. Right from her first day, I realized she was something less than the hardworking, quick-thinking, creative-yet-analytical, perpetual-motion productivity machine she had claimed to be when I interviewed her.

As the weeks have turned into months, she has done little more than repackage the work produced by my other managers or joined teams that allow her to skate by without making any kind of visible contribution to a project. Cindy's corporate skill set doesn't get activated until after a project is completed. That's when she displays her special talent for presenting herself as the mastermind behind the finished work. While her other team members don't have the luxury to pause between projects, let alone reflect on their successes, Cindy invests most of her time in making sure management—Henry in particular—is aware of what's being accomplished. In just a few months, her relentless self-marketing has convinced Henry that she's the only one on my team who knows how to get anything done. Within the pressure cooker of my department, Cindy has created the kind of simmering resentment that usually takes years to blow the lid off. My whole team hates her. They're practically begging me to fire her before the end of her six-month probation period. But as long as Henry loves her, my hands are tied.

"OK," I say. "Anything else you're working on?"

Cindy starts running through a second list of projects. These are assignments I know are being handled by either Meg Wilson or Pete Hughes. Clearly, Cindy is preparing to attach her name to as many projects as possible over the next couple of months. There's an impressive amount of work going on. I remind myself that I—as the boss to Cindy, Meg, Pete and Roger—should be receiving more credit for it all.

"Wow," I say. "You've taken on a hell of a lot. Tell you what, though. While Roger's out, why don't you just devote yourself a hundred percent to that first list? I'll crack the whip with Meg and Pete on the rest. Clearly, I need to do a better job supervising everyone's workload. Make sure everyone's doing their fair share."

I notice a flash of fear in Cindy's eyes. But then she steadies herself. "OK," she says, then nods, clenches her jaw, and gets up to leave.

"Hey, Cindy," I say. "Thanks so much for bringing this to my attention. Could you pull the door closed behind you till you hear it click?"

It's only ten fifteen. But it's already been a three-interruption morning. I look over at Lucky Cat. He's smiling inscrutably at the closed door, challenging me to put him to the test.

I stare at the papers spread out on my desk.

Focus, Russell.

But what if Lucky Cat lets me down again? If I lose faith in him, what will I have left to believe in?

At 10:17, I gather up my files and head to the small conference room. It's a quiet spot where I can hide out undisturbed till lunchtime.

CHAPTER THREE

Fabrice is Henry's favorite hangout. It's the signature restaurant of New York chef du jour Fabrice de Monbrison, the gathering place for the power people in the media industry. Along with its food, Fabrice offers an appropriately sumptuous setting in which relationships can be nurtured, alliances formed and deals struck.

Henry surveys the room as we're led through. Connie Darwin, the CEO of Burke-Hart Publishing, is at a window table with her boss—the boss of us all—Larry Ghosh.

Ghosh looks several years older than the pointillized version of his face that still appears frequently in the *Wall Street Journal*. The drawing dates back to the days when he made his first billion in the grocery cart business, with the infamous Ghosh Guarantee. The plan was simple. Its execution inspired shock and awe. Under cover of night, a network of sales reps dispersed. At first light they descended on the purchasing departments of major retailers to promote Ghosh Carts with an unprecedented lifetime wheel-alignment warranty. The orders flooded in. Ghosh's competitors never knew what hit them.

Larry Ghosh was hailed as a business genius. And he didn't stop there. After winning the grocery cart wars, he really went shopping. Within twelve months, Ghosh Corporation established a significant presence in media and entertainment, acquiring a host of second-tier radio, film, TV and music assets. Another year later, drowning in debt, he sold the original Ghosh Cart business.

Just in time. Ghosh got out of grocery carts right before his cheap wheels began seizing up and his old customers started hurling lawsuits.

Ghosh was condemned as a charlatan and a con artist. But luckily for him, the general public was less outraged by unsteerable grocery carts than they were by the Enron, Worldcom and Martha Stewart scandals.

By the time it was all over and settlements had been reached, Ghosh was ready for his next big act. Murdoch beat him to MySpace. The Google guys beat him to YouTube. So Ghosh did something different. Instead of paying a premium price for a company with a big future, he looked back in time and bought a business that was priced to sell: Burke-Hart Publishing.

Not the most exciting acquisition, perhaps. It didn't even make our own front page. But it signaled Ghosh's quest for legitimacy as well as profits. And it made the *Daily Business Chronicle* the jewel in his media crown.

Henry tips his head as we pass Ghosh's table, but he and Connie are engrossed in conversation. Neither gives any sign they've noticed us. I can't quite understand why, after all the company's recent belt-tightening, Henry thinks it's a good idea to be seen in the same restaurant as Connie Darwin, let alone Larry Ghosh.

We're seated at an inconspicuous table against the back wall. I take a slice of rosemary-infused sourdough from the selection of breads I'm offered. Henry waves the bread away. He's still freaked out by carbs. He tries to limit them in solid form in order to justify a more unrestricted approach to consuming them via beer and wine. Henry's rules regarding liquid carbs: When alone, personal consumption is allowed only after five o'clock. When in the company of clients, liquid carbs may be taken at any time the client deems appropriate.

"You see that?" says Henry. "Larry Ghosh wants people to see him with Connie. It's a clear signal."

"Right."

"A public acknowledgement of the trust he has in her."

"Or maybe he wants to show how hands-on he's being," I say. "That it's really him who's calling the shots."

Henry looks disturbed. But the waiter appears before he can speak again. He orders mineral water for the table and asks for "the usual." The waiter nods and makes a note. I ask for the hamburger with fries. It's the restaurant's signature dish. A sixty-dollar concoction perfected by Fabrice de Monbrison himself using imported beef and specially grown organic herbs. It has been taste tested on national TV and photographed exotically in several magazines.

Henry spreads his napkin across his lap and surveys the restaurant one more time in a faux-casual way.

"That's Patrick Moncur," he says. "In the corner, in the hat, that's Anna Scrupski."

I nod as if I'm impressed, though the names mean nothing to me. The maître d' appears at Henry's side, whispering in his ear, apologizing for the fact that the waiter is new, asking him to clarify his order.

"Cobb salad, no avocado," says Henry.

We sip our mineral water. Henry is acting in a self-conscious way, as if he feels people's eyes on him from all over the room. In reality, no one has given us more than a passing look since we came in. It's obvious to everyone else that we're only minnows in this pond. The only eyes on Henry are mine. I'm wondering why he brought me here, what it is he wants to discuss. He seems slightly more coherent in person than he did on the phone.

"How long have we worked together?" Henry asks, leaning toward me.

"Four years and a couple of months."

"We're a good team, Russell. I can trust you, can't I?"

"Absolutely."

"I can tell you things in confidence."

"Anything you tell me, Henry, goes straight into the vault."

"Loyalty's important."

"I know that."

It's true. Henry is one of those executives who values loyalty even ahead of competence. It's a trait that becomes more dangerous the higher he moves up the food chain, dragging deadwood like Jeanie Tusa, our finance director, with him. Like all of Henry's loyal lieutenants, Jeanie's now in a position where she can really screw things up.

Henry sips his mineral water and dabs his lips with his napkin in a slightly effeminate way. A thought flashes through my mind that he's about to confess something of a personal nature. The chatter at the other tables seems artificially loud.

"Just between you and me, Connie's planning a major restructuring within the next six months." He pauses to allow the significance of this revelation to sink in.

"Makes sense," I say, reaching for Fabrice's famous unsalted, hand-churned butter.

"She has to get everything done within twelve months of the merger. The voluntary retirement program came first. Next we'll have the first round of layoffs. After that, a company-wide restructure."

"Why so fast?" I say, biting into a chunk of buttered bread.

"Wall Street," says Henry. "In the first twelve months, all merger-related costs can get rolled up into a single accounting charge. Won't affect earnings. Connie's set herself a BHAG of reducing expenses by two hundred million."

I'm chewing, but I nod to show him I understand. Connie's built her career by adapting the best ideas from business books and making them her own. She's a big believer in the BHAG concept—the setting of Big Hairy Audacious Goals.

"My guess is she'll merge the business and lifestyle groups. Why does a company our size need two separate print divisions?" Henry leans forward again, even further this time. "If she does that, Jack's out and Yolanda will be running things. You and I could end up working for Barney Barnes." Henry can't say Barney's name without his lip curling in a sneer. Years ago Barney worked for Henry in the business group before quitting to join Yolanda Pew—Jack Tennant's counterpart—who heads the lifestyle group.

My first thought is it would make far more sense to keep the business and lifestyle groups separate and get rid of the dopey Mark Sand, who heads Burke-Hart Online. That way

Jack and Yolanda would get full control of their respective brands both in print and online. And the *Chronicle* would have at least a chance to shape its multimedia destiny.

My second thought is that, even if Henry is right, working for Barney Barnes wouldn't be such a bad thing. Barney's smart and confident. He's won the trust of Connie and Yolanda. He's launching new magazines like *Flip*, *Posse* and *Heel*, and he's hiring new people all the time.

Henry's view of things is sometimes impaired by his history with Barney, the fact that Barney never paid a price for walking out on him or Jack. In fact, Barney's treachery paid off big. He's one man in our company who's really going places. He recognized early that the traditional, male-dominated parts of our business were stagnating. He embraced the new, feminine side of Burke-Hart just as our lifestyle and specialty fashion titles were really taking off. Last year he produced a hugely successful conference on "The Future of the Sleeve."

I chew some more bread and butter, thinking about having Barney for a boss. Not such a bad idea. Still, as Henry says, loyalty's important.

"So," I ask, "what can we do to help Jack in all this?"

Henry fixes me with his most serious expression. Then he looks away suddenly, as if affected by a poignant memory. A muscle in his cheek twitches.

He looks back at me and says, "I love Jack. I really do. You know how much I love Jack."

And I stare back at Henry, knowing that what he really means is "Fuck Jack. Jack's dead. This is all about me now. And if I don't have Jack to protect me anymore, I need to be working on another plan."

We eat. I listen. In case you're wondering about my burger: Good. Tasty. Interesting herbs and seasonings. But let's be real—it's for expense accounts only. No burger's really worth sixty bucks.

By the time our cappuccinos arrive, Henry has spelled it all out for me. He thinks he has six months to prove himself to Connie and Yolanda. And proving himself requires two things:

1) Cutting costs. Henry has decided to fully embrace what Connie describes to Wall Street as her "clinical approach to squeezing cost out of the system."
2) Thinking big. He wants to come up with a new business idea that will eclipse anything Barney has done.

"You'll have to be ready to let people go, Russell," he says. "Right now, we can only afford to keep our A-players. I wish we had a few more like Cindy Lang at a time like this."

Henry has no idea of the problems Cindy is causing me. But now's not a good time to get into it. I need to limit the damage to my department when the layoffs come. So I say, "My whole team's working flat out. I think you'll be impressed. In fact, I'd like to sit down with you next week and take you through some of the work they've been doing."

"Let's not get too granular," says Henry. It's one of those expressions he picked up at last year's leadership retreat. It's where he learned that leaders are "Unicorns." They need to think big picture and articulate a vision for their teams. Unicorns are not supposed to act like Horses. They don't pull carts or get sucked down into the weeds. They don't soil themselves with the realities of actual work.

"We need to think big picture," says Henry. "That's why I've hired a new consultant to come in next Monday. Judd Walker. Great guy. Great credentials. You'll meet him."

"Do we really have time for that?" I ask him. "I just read a pretty negative article about consultants. Maybe you saw it in *Vicious Circle* magazine. Written by Christopher Finchley."

Henry gives me his what-the-fuck look, then says, "Judd knows he'll have to work fast. His job is to help me articulate a vision. I'll need you heavily involved, Russell. Just you and Jeanie. Let's not loop anyone else in just yet. And don't let it slow you down on the Livingston Kidd presentation."

"No problem," I say. "You know, because timing is so important, you might want to look at some of the concepts I've been putting into my product development file. There are one or two that could be really interesting to explore."

"We can't afford to spin our wheels. This is too important. I've already briefed Judd on the project I want him to look at. We're going to need to keep him focused. Let's see what he comes back with."

I don't press the point. I know Henry can't process too many ideas at once. When he's under pressure, his style of leadership is to grasp at straws, pick one, then stick with it till the bitter end.

"Is there a code name?" I ask. Henry loves code names for his secret projects.

Henry nods, looks around the restaurant at the other midlevel executives trying hard to be noticed.

"D-SAW," says Henry. "Don't say a word. Until we get a green light, this project will be ultra top secret."

Henry sits back and steals a glance over at Connie's table. She's getting up to leave, laughing at something Larry Ghosh is saying.

"We're a team, aren't we, Russell?" Henry says, still gazing in Connie's direction.

"You bet," I say.

He turns back to me with fear glistening in his eyes and says, "And this is going to be fun, right?"

There's a limousine waiting outside the restaurant to take Henry directly to his next appointment, so I walk a few blocks back to the office alone.

My lunch with Henry has confirmed what I already knew. Things will be ugly for the next few months. Even with Larry Ghosh's backing, the *Chronicle* is in decline. Like each of our daily competitors, we are struggling to formulate a new "transformational" strategy that will position us for continued growth at a time when our traditional newspaper business is slowing much faster than our online business is growing. Nobody, least of all the Burke-Hart management team, knows what to do. The standard short-term approach to any crisis—cutting costs, letting people go—is all Connie is left with. But longer term, Connie won't be able to cut her way to growth.

Meanwhile, Henry seems more out of touch than ever. He seems oblivious to the fact that mass media are being replaced by media created by the masses. In this fast-changing world, Henry's a holdout: an old-school print guy, blinded by internal politics, with one foot stuck firmly in the past. He's the kind of executive who will be tolerated only as long as the numbers in his Rolodex connect to living, spending customers. Worse, he's starting to carry about him the stink of desperation. If that takes hold, nothing good will happen. Desperate people don't make good decisions. Desperate people take others down when they fall.

CHAPTER FOUR

I ride up in the elevator with a couple of loud women from accounts payable who get off on twenty-two. I'm alone when the doors open again. I start to step out, then realize this is not my floor. The artwork on the wall is wrong. I'm on twenty-four, not twenty-five.

I hear a voice outside and step back quickly. A hand reaches around to hold the door an extra second. It's a small and elegant hand, one that fills me with an impossible desire. The hand belongs to Erika Fallon. She wraps up the conversation she's having, then steps inside the elevator. She sees me pressed against the back wall and smiles.

"Hey, Russell Wiley."

"Hey, Erika Fallon."

Erika Fallon has picked up on the fact that I always address her by her first and last name. Now she does the same to me, as if it's some kind of cute game.

We rise to the next floor in silence. As the doors open, I'm concentrating so hard on not looking at Erika Fallon that I can't help staring at the number twenty-five emblazoned on the inside of the elevator shaft. It's as if the building wants to mockingly remind me of the number of days I've gone without sex. Erika Fallon exits the elevator and turns left to head to her side of the floor.

"Later, Russell Wiley."

"Take care, Erika Fallon."

I hurry back to my office and sit down to collect myself. To me, using Erika Fallon's first and last name all the time isn't cute. It isn't a game. It's a form of self-defense. Using her full name reinforces the fact that she is not someone I can get close to. I must treat her as a fictional character from a play or a movie, not a real person. Erika Fallon petrifies me. I fear she may destroy me. Even brief, casual encounters like this one make it difficult to stop thinking about her face, her voice, her perfume, the back of her head, that sliver of ear poking through her hair, her blue suit, her gray suit, the chocolate brown turtleneck she wore three times last fall, her fingernails, the wireless headset she wears when she's on the phone, the aura I sometimes see around her late in the afternoon, the shape of her calves and her intimidating pointy shoes.

It's not simply a question of beauty. Beauty I can deal with. It's like art. I appreciate it and move on. Erika Fallon is in a separate, more disturbing category.

Maybe it's chemical. Maybe it's just the way her pheromones mix with mine.

Whatever it is, it creates a sensation that I like and don't like. A feeling that even if I take a step back, part of me stays where it was, hovering outside my body. Being in the presence of Erika

Fallon makes me experience a yearning to rethink every aspect of my existence. It makes me realize that the various pieces of the life I have constructed don't fit together in the proper shape. I've sculpted something that bears no relation to my original vision. Erika Fallon makes me understand that for thirty-seven years all I've done is make one choice after another without ever being a hundred percent certain what the hell I'm doing. Every time I've chosen one door over another, the opportunity to go back and find out what was behind that other door has disappeared. And every door I go through reduces the number of choices I get to make in the future. My life is contracting, not expanding. After all the choices I've made, after all the doors I've closed behind me, this is where I've ended up: in a twenty-fifth-floor office, surrounded by meaningless papers, with a dopey black cat waving its plastic paw at me, spending most of my waking hours working for a company that wants only to squeeze me a little harder so I can help it monetize a fading asset for at least a few years more, dealing with an endless line of people trooping in to tell me the latest petty nonsense that's troubling them, and a boss who spends more time worrying about his corporate viability than he does attempting to solve our most pressing business challenges. And if I do my job well, the only reward I get is the chance to come back and do it all again on Monday and the next day and the day after that. And tonight when I go home craving some affection, needing to sense a simple human connection that will help me transcend all this and simply feel warm and comforted and loved, I can't even be sure of that. There's a good chance my wife won't even touch me.

"This is it. I've had it. I can't take this place for one more fucking second," says Susan Trevor.

"Give it to me," I say, glad to be snapped back to petty, nonsensical reality. I can always tolerate Susan in small doses. She's a complainer, but her grievances often reveal a depth of passion that is somehow inspiring. After eighteen years at the company, she remains devoted to her job and outspoken in her opinions, especially on the topic of our senseless senior management. Up till now our senseless senior management has tolerated her because they have no idea how she does what she does, which is to head up our advertising services department. Susan's the person who makes sure all the ads appear where and how they are supposed to in the paper each day. Outsourcing her function to India has not yet surfaced as an option.

"Have you seen this?" she says, brandishing a sheet of paper.

"What is it?"

"The agenda for Monday's Henry meeting."

"Oh good. An agenda for once."

Susan's six years older than me. Married with two kids and living out on Long Island. She's half Italian and—except for the times when she goes on a strict diet, loses several pounds, buys new clothes, and undergoes a personality change that makes her think she's a teenage sex kitten—she's attractive in a curvy, Mediterranean way. Her diets are extreme, but they never last long, and the weight always comes right back. That's OK with me. I like her more when she's heavier, with her curves hidden behind a more conventional and demure work wardrobe. I lean back in my chair, wondering how much of her passion Susan manages to save for when she gets home. Even with the pressures of family and a long commute, I can't imagine she and her husband allow a week, let alone twenty-five days, to go by without satisfying their wildest conjugal desires.

I look at the agenda she lays on my desk in front of me.

"That's exciting. A new consultant."

"What is it with this fucking place? Henry can't even take a piss without an MBA to hold his dick for him."

"You know how it works. It's not just Henry. Everyone's too scared to decide anything without an independent perspective."

"What are we going to find out now? That we don't know how to do our jobs or manage our own business?"

"That's not the point. Most companies think their problems can only be solved by outside experts. You know that writer I was telling you about, Christopher Finchley?" I reach into my drawer, pull out a file folder that contains several stapled copies of an article I've saved specifically to share with others. I hand a copy to Susan. "Check this out. Maybe it will make you feel better."

Susan reads the headline aloud: "'Fool's Gold: Is Your Consultant Practicing the Deceptive Art of Rainbow Painting?' What the fuck does that mean?"

"It's actually pretty interesting. This Finchley guy talks about the pressures companies are under to find big ideas to reinvigorate their businesses. But because their employees are so overworked, underpaid, burnt out and frustrated, management can't trust or value the ideas they come up with anymore. So they go out and hire consultants to study the big picture for them. The consultant's job is to sit back, chew on a piece of grass, understand the landscape and then paint a rainbow on it. After that, the consultant leaves and the overworked, underpaid employees are sent off in a new direction, searching for a pot of gold they can never find because it doesn't actually exist."

"Like those last guys who told us we could cut our ad rates fifteen percent and more than make it up in volume?"

"Exactly. The Rainbow Painter's job is simply to keep management's hope alive, to convince them that the pot of gold exists. Legitimate facts to the contrary will not be admitted into evidence."

Susan talks for a while about the fiasco that ensued after our last consulting firm left us all holding the bag when they moved on to their next corporate victim. Within a month, year-over-year advertising revenue was down twenty-three percent and we had to revert to our former pricing model to avert a complete disaster. Maybe it's fun to relive this stuff for a minute or two. But suddenly, I'm bored. She's going on too long and I want her to stop. I begin offering nonverbal cues to signal that I'd like her to wrap this up and get the hell out of my office. I start by looking in my Livingston Kidd folder and scanning last year's proposal. Susan is unfazed. I pick up my pen and begin making notes in the margin.

I glance discreetly at my watch, wondering if I'll have time to make any real progress on my project before the end of the day.

Finally I start tapping out pithy emails to the managers on my staff.

Pete, GREAT WORK on that IBM proposal! You rock!!

Meg, AMAZING ideas for Audi! Let's discuss!!

Roger, LOVED what you did for Pfizer! I owe you one, buddy!!

Usually a few minutes of inattentiveness is all it takes for Susan to get the message.

"I've got to go," she says, standing abruptly.

"Sorry. God, I hate it when people multitask," I say. "Have I at least talked you off the ledge?" I ask.

"What do you mean?"

"When you came in you said you couldn't take this place for another fucking second."

"Yeah, I'm off the ledge."

"And you'll be here Monday?"

"I'll be here."

"And you'll read that article?"

"I'll read it."

After Susan leaves, I take a few minutes to reread the article I gave her and commend myself for introducing another reader to the extraordinarily perceptive work of Christopher Finchley.

There's one more thing I need to do today. I summon Angela into my office. She arrives clutching a reporter's notebook and pen.

"Hi, Mr. Wiley," she says in her whispery young voice.

"Russell's fine," I say. "Come on in."

Angela stands facing me across my desk. She's wearing a tight white T-shirt and low-front stretch jeans. Her skin is a deep, dark brown. Her lips are painted a glittery purple. Between her breasts, her T-shirt is decorated with a small gold star.

I gaze at her with studied impassivity, resting my chin on my thumbs, pressing my steepled fingers against my face. Angela seems to enjoy awkward silences as much as she enjoys every other moment of her day. I'm not sure she is aware how much she has stirred everybody up. As the executive supposedly managing her, I have already heard a litany of complaints from Barbara and other female colleagues who tell me she is:

"Not focused on her work."

"Spending all day on the phone."

"Flirting with the mailroom guys."

"Nowhere to be found."

"Leaving nothing to the imagination."

So far, none of the men have complained, though I sense an air of melancholy in some cubicles each time Angela—with all her youth and beauty and happiness and potential—passes by.

"I just thought I should check in with you," I say. "Have a chat. See how you're getting on."

Angela smiles, displaying perfect white teeth. "Everything's great," she says. "I really like it here."

"You're fitting in OK? We're keeping you busy?"

"Oh yes," she says. "Everyone has been really nice. I'm learning a lot."

I swivel from side to side in my chair. She sways slowly where she stands, a gentle rotation of the hips. Her eyes are incredibly round. She is breathing deeply through her nose. Barbara thinks it's my responsibility to inform Angela that she's a walking example of "What Not to Wear." But I don't quite see how I can bring the topic up without embarrassing either or both of us to a painful degree. Why the hell hasn't one of the women in the office taken Angela aside and told her to cover herself up? What's wrong with everyone? Why is everything left to me?

"You don't find it cold in here, do you?" I ask.

"Not at all. It's always too hot at my house. I love it here."

"That's great. Perhaps you could make me two photocopies of each of these presentations?" I ask, handing her a stack of documents. "It's just that the photocopier on this side is acting up."

"No problem, Mr. Wiley."

"Russell," I say again. "No rush. Monday will be fine."

"Anything else...Russell?" she says, in a way that makes me appreciate how great men are sometimes brought low by the folly of lust.

"That's all. Thanks." I watch her walk to the door, then blurt, "In case it does get too cold, you'll notice a lot of the women here like to keep a sweater on the back of their chair."

CHAPTER FIVE

Sam's in the shower when I get home. I sit on the couch, skimming through the mail, studying the charges on our joint credit card. As usual, she has spent several hundred dollars at local stores and various online merchants.

"Are you getting changed, or are you going like that?" She's standing with one towel wrapped around her body, another around her hair.

"We're going out?"

"Jesus, Russell. It's Shila's birthday. We're going to Magnolia with her and Judy, Zoe and Max."

"Oh, right. Sorry. I forgot." I stand up, walk to her, open my arms to hold her.

"Don't touch me with all your subway germs," she says. Her face is shiny with moisturizer.

I head to the bathroom, wash my hands and face, roll on some deodorant, brush my teeth as well.

In the bedroom, Sam's sitting on her stool at her makeup mirror, plucking. I nuzzle the side of her neck, holding her through the towel. Gently. Innocently. Below the breasts. She waits for me to finish, tweezers hovering in midair.

I step away, strip to my underwear, lie back on our bed. "What time do we have to go?" I ask.

She positions the mirror to look at me without turning. "Soon," she says, giving me the magnified eyeball.

I heave myself back up and reach into the wardrobe for my jeans.

At dinner, she hangs her cardigan on the back of her chair. She's wearing a sleeveless dress, drinking wine, laughing more than anyone at Max's feeble jokes. There's a candle on Shila's dessert and we all sing "Happy Birthday." As a group we treat Shila to her meal. Sam's and my share tops two hundred bucks.

At home, she says the wine has made her woozy. She's tired and needs to sleep. She undresses in the dark, slipping into her purple T-shirt before turning on the light to hang her dress.

While she's at the bathroom mirror, I reach around her, grab the floss and rip off a section. Something from the credit card statement has been nagging at me all night.

"You spent fifty-nine dollars at Classmates.com?"

She spits toothpaste and grabs the edges of the sink. "Jesus, you're so fucking cheap sometimes. It was a three-year subscription. It's the best deal they offer."

"I'm just asking."

"This is why I need my own credit card. I'm sick of you scrutinizing everything I buy."

I could tell her to get her own credit card and a separate checking account to go with it. I could also suggest a pay-as-you-go budget amendment that puts a limit on her monthly spending. Instead, I retreat to the living room. I floss slowly, waiting for her to leave the bathroom. I wrap my floss in a tissue. I stretch my arms above my head, then reach over my left shoulder to massage the achy spot on my upper back. Sam turns off the bathroom light and heads to the bedroom. The clock on the cable box counts off two more minutes. I wait for her to switch off the light on her side of the bed. I wait a minute more before heading quietly into the bedroom.

"Ow! What are you doing? Stop that. What time is it?"

"Come on," says Sam. Having thrown open the curtains, she's now pulling at the comforter. "It's the one day we have together. We need to go to the greenmarket, then the grocery store. And I want you to get the laundry done by twelve so we can get to Bed Bath & Beyond and back before we go to Julie and Fergus's."

Our apartment's on the top floor of an elevator building. Our bedroom faces the back. Lying in bed, when I take my forearm away my eyes, it's possible to look through the lead-paned glass and see nothing but sky.

"Can't we do Bed now and Bath and Beyond later? Like you said, it's our one day together."

"Don't start. There isn't time."

"What do you mean? It's not even eight yet."

"We've got a lot to get done. My head is pounding. Work with me, OK?"

I stretch out diagonally across the bed, then prop myself on my elbows. Sam is undoing the buttons of the comforter cover so she can throw it into the laundry pile. "You know what makes Fergus jealous?" I say. "The thought that you and I can luxuriate in bed together on a Saturday morning. No screaming kids. No diapers to change. No 'Blue's Clues Nora Squarepants' to watch."

"We still have a lot to do, Russell."

"I just thought you should know how Fergus imagines us. He thinks we're just two young lovers without a care in the world. Taking advantage of a relaxing Saturday morning. Enjoying a slow journey of mutual exploration through the exquisite contours of each other's bodies."

"You think talking like that's going to help?"

Sam's already dressed for outdoors. A blue T-shirt, khaki shorts, sneakers. She reaches in a drawer for her Boston University baseball cap, puts it on, and clips it so her short ponytail pokes through the space in the back.

"What do we need at Bed Bath & Beyond anyway?" I ask.

By three o'clock we are on Fergus and Julie's doorstep. They live with their son and daughter in a small two bedroom on a quiet side street in Cobble Hill.

Fergus opens the door with his three-year-old girl perched on his elbow.

"Hi, Beryl!" I say enthusiastically. "Haven't you grown? Where's your big brother Angus?" I want to emphasize for Fergus's benefit that I have memorized his kids' names like a best friend should.

While Beryl buries her face in his neck, Fergus gives me a one-armed hug and Sam a peck on her cheek. Beryl was an ugly baby, but she seems cuter now—a miniature humanoid who may eventually grow up looking OK.

Julie shouts from the bedroom, telling us to sit down, she'll be right out. We join Angus on the sectional couch. He's a roly-poly looking kid with a round head and straight brown hair cut in pudding-bowl style. He's dressed in soccer gear, twiddling the knobs of an Etch-a-Sketch.

"Hey, Angus. What you drawing, buddy?"

"I'm not drawing," he says. "I'm sulking."

"Just ignore him," says Julie. "Wow. You look fabulous." She's talking to Sam, who is looking fabulous, wearing her hair down, doing her best Winona Ryder in a retro-looking cotton print dress. Julie adds, "Of course, I'm still a giant tub of lard."

"Stop," says Sam, in place of a more definitive contradiction. She hugs Julie, which only reinforces their physical differences. Julie used to refer to herself as big-boned even before she had kids. These days she's a particularly imposing figure. Heavy but solid looking, Julie carries her bulk better than Fergus does his. Fergus has had a history of sympathetic weight gain during, between and since Julie's two pregnancies. Fergus was always smarter, stronger and better looking than me at school. Now he seems to have settled into a premature middle age, with not much thought given to working out.

Sam presents Angus and Beryl with the gifts she's brought: a remote-controlled car for Angus and a cuddly monkey for Beryl.

"Thank you," says Angus, giving Sam a sulky kiss. He takes his new toy into the corner of the room.

"Look, Mommy," says Beryl before tossing the monkey aside and walking over to see what her brother is doing.

Fergus goes to boil water for herbal tea.

We sit with our teas and the plate of assorted cookies Fergus also serves. In the corner of the room, a cartoon movie plays on the TV screen, the sound turned unintelligibly low. Before long, Angus has his car whizzing around the floor, crashing into table legs and adults' feet. He seems to have stopped sulking. Beryl chases the car for a while and after that decides to run around in random spurts making high-pitched shrieks until she collapses on the floor and starts pushing the beeping buttons of a battered electronic toy.

Once the antics of the children become too boring and repetitive to be worthy of our encouragements or commentaries, Sam and Julie take fresh cups of tea into the master bedroom so they can chat. Fergus and I reminisce about things we did half a lifetime ago, recollecting youthful stupidities and congratulating ourselves for living in the pre-MySpace-Facebook era. In our college days, we had no means to create embarrassing online profiles or post photos, videos and blog entries of our escapades. If we had, those best-forgotten moments would surely, we agree, haunt us still.

There's a break in our conversation. I sense our minds drifting in different directions, like our lives did after college. We look over at Angus, who is instructing Beryl to stack some building blocks on a small stool.

These days Fergus is assistant editor at the monthly magazine *Vicious Circle*. Because of its erratic editorial content—which includes a mix of liberal commentary, anti-globalism rants and video game reviews—the magazine has always struggled to find either an audience or a solid base of advertisers.

Fourteen months ago Fergus interrupted a similar lull in one of our conversations by asking me if I wanted to write an article for him.

I did. I produced a gripping, reality-based, names-changed-to-protect-the-innocent account of the dramas that ensued after Henry announced we were consolidating office space by forty percent. Fergus added the headline "Cubicle Size Matters." Then he offered me a byline and a monthly column.

And that's how Christopher Finchley was born.

I write the column for fun. I have to. I get paid in copies, not cash. And I do it under a pseudonym because I want to keep my job. Burke-Hart Publishing—and the *Chronicle* in particular—has strict rules governing how employees are allowed to communicate with outside media.

I also write my column because Fergus and I have less in common than we did fifteen years ago. If it wasn't for our shared history and current proximity, I'm not sure we'd still be in touch with each other. And that scares me sometimes. Before Christopher Finchley came along, I used to imagine the day when our thoughts would diverge for the final time. We'd sit in silence, occasionally filling our cups of tea, having exhausted all of our shared memories and run out of mutually relevant topics through which our minds might reconnect.

"So how's your next article coming along?" says Fergus at last.

"It's coming," I lie. "I'm thinking about Unicorns."

"I've got a unicorn," Beryl says absentmindedly.

"She loves them," says Fergus.

I smile, playing for time. "I don't really want to talk about it till it's perfect. It's a new take on how companies go about finding the leaders in their organization, how they're fixated on building an A-team, on finding Unicorns among the Horses."

"Sounds good," says Fergus. "Just don't miss your deadline again."

"I'll get it to you by tomorrow night," I promise.

We're silent for another little while. The tower Beryl is creating is already taller than she is.

"I want to write it from the Horse's point of view," I muse. "The kind of Horse who asks, 'Why am I supposed to follow this idiotic creature? Just because of that dopey horn stuck on its head?'" I take a bite of a stale, damp cookie. "I had lunch with Henry yesterday. In the same restaurant as Larry Ghosh."

"Ah. The evil Larry Ghosh." Fergus despises Ghosh as much for the cultural impact of the Ghosh Corporation as for the hundreds of back-office jobs the company has sent to India. In the years between the grocery cart scandal and the Burke-Hart acquisition, Ghosh Films became famous for its low-budget "sick-flick" horror franchises, and the Ghosh Radio Network became home to a slew of trash-talking right-wing radio hosts. On the big screen, torture became entertainment. On the airwaves, the treatment of prisoners at Abu Ghraib was applauded as a necessary deterrent.

"How do you work for a guy like that?" asks Fergus.

"I don't," I say. "I work for the *Daily Business Chronicle*. I work for Henry. Henry works for Jack. Jack works for Connie. She's the only one who actually talks to Larry Ghosh."

"And you just follow orders?"

"I like to think I'm fighting the good fight from within."

We pause. We're getting into dangerous territory. I try and steer us back into the DMZ.

"Maybe you're right," I concede. "Maybe I should get out. Things have been crazy since Ghosh bought us. Everybody's freaking out. We've been cutting costs so long it seems like that's become our only strategy. The internet is killing us. But nobody has a plan to do anything about it."

Beryl's tower falls and she squeals delightedly. She looks to Angus for further instructions. He commands her to start building again, which she does.

"And now you have Larry Ghosh to deal with. The man who manages to poison everything he touches."

"You're right," I say. "Except he doesn't even have to touch us. Whatever it is, it travels through the air. And then it mutates like a crazy, unethical bird flu. Larry Ghosh is the only one infected with the original strain. When Connie Darwin catches it from him, it changes. It combines with her own ruthless, unpredictable, self-aggrandizing DNA. Then it mutates again through each of her direct reports. By the time Jack Tennant passes it on to Henry, it's got a piece of Jack's political savvy attached. But when that combines with Henry's alcoholic paranoia, it creates a highly toxic strain—one that could kill us all."

"Not the fire truck," says Fergus sternly. He gets up and takes the metal toy from Beryl's hand before she puts it on top of her Angus-designed tower. "Why not put your new monkey on top?" he says, handing her the stuffed animal Sam brought. "Doesn't that look great? It's King Kong. *Raaaaarrrrr!!!* How about some juice?" He tickles Beryl's belly, then picks her up and heads to the kitchen. He holds Beryl sideways against him, still tickling her as she giggles and struggles.

"The Donald," he says. "You want some too?"

"Sure," says Angus, following his dad to the fridge.

"We call him The Donald," Fergus informs me, pouring juice into two glasses. "He likes building things."

Fergus sits back down and bunches his thick, rusty eyebrows, accentuating the deep crease on his forehead.

"With everything you tell me," he says, "I don't understand why you just don't get out. Don't you want to do something you feel passionate about?"

"Ha! Do you think I could deal with the frustrations, the politics, the backstabbing and the ineptitude if I was working toward something I really cared about? Banging my head against the wall trying to make the world a better place? That would be too heartbreaking. As long as I get paid well, I prefer to be good at something that has absolutely no value in the real world. We're all going to die anyway. I can't stop wars or global warming. I can't stop AIDS in Africa or bring about peace in the Middle East."

"Who knows what you could do? Doesn't the individual still have the power to change the world?" The DVD that's been playing ends. Fergus reaches for the remote control and starts the movie again.

"And what about you?" I ask. "How are you going to change the world if you keep turning down jobs at bigger magazines?"

"Maybe I just haven't had the right offer yet," he says.

Suddenly Beryl's crying. Her tower has fallen again. Her juice has spilled. Angus is denying his alleged involvement in either incident.

Julie appears with a sponge and some paper towels, reassuring Beryl that everything will be OK.

"She needs her nap," says Julie.

Fergus ruffles Beryl's hair. "If Angus is being a pain, why don't you go and hang out with Mommy and Auntie Sam?"

I update Fergus on my lunch at Fabrice, Henry's latest schemes and my fears that Henry, no matter what ideas he comes up with, no matter how well he fights each battle, can no longer win. He'll never be seen as the kind of next-generation leader the company now needs.

I tell him that more layoffs are coming. That Henry is ready to abandon his allegiance to Jack, the guy who's taken care of him all these years. He's pinning all his hopes, I say, on a new consultant who's starting Monday, for whom I have to provide top-secret support.

"Fuck-rying out loud," says Fergus, trying not to swear in front of the kids. "Why don't you just get out now?"

"And miss all the fun?"

"I thought the good times were over for newspapers."

"You're right," I say. "Something changed between the time Google went public and Craigslist ate all the classified ads."

My big fear, I want to tell Fergus, is that Larry Ghosh realizes the *Chronicle* is not really in the newspaper business. It's in the information business. He knows there's no future being the number four newspaper in a market that can at best sustain three titles. If he were to shut the newspaper down and take the whole business online, he could give the *Chronicle* at least a fighting chance to become a profitable Web-based, multimedia brand. He'd have to replace Mark Sand, the idiot who runs our online group. But after that, things would be relatively easy. With the radio and TV resources of Ghosh Media behind it, and none of the newsprint, distribution and subscriber-acquisition costs, the *Daily Business Chronicle* might even regain its relevance and secure its future.

"Listen up," says Julie. She has just emerged from the bathroom holding Beryl by the hand. She waits till she is sure of our attention. She has an announcement to make.

"Guess who did number twos in the grown-up toilet?"

Fergus, Julie, Angus, Sam and I all gather round to inspect one at a time the rodent-size pellets at the bottom of the toilet bowl.

"Wow," says Fergus, sounding genuinely impressed.

"What a big girl," says Julie.

"Great job," says Sam.

"Is she getting enough fiber?" I ask.

Julie lifts Beryl up to have her flush the toilet. And as we watch the water swirl and Beryl's poo-poo disappear, Fergus yells "Hooray!" and bursts into proud applause.

Beryl seems rejuvenated, but only briefly. After a little more running and shrieking, she starts getting grumpy. Meanwhile Angus, hungry now, insists on being allowed to microwave himself some macaroni and cheese for dinner. I call a car service to take Sam and me home.

In the car, Sam leans against her window, looking out at the brownstones going by. Neighborhood families and friends are sitting out in the late afternoon sun, chatting on their stoops.

One time, years ago, when Sam and I were first living together, we were driving back home from a party in a car just like this. We were both tipsy. Sam lay down suddenly on her back with her head in my lap, took my hand and guided it inside her panties. Before my hesitant fingers even had time to react, Sam was moaning loudly, as if she were putting on a show for the driver.

Today she seems more interested in the world beyond the backseat of our car.

"They seem so happy," she says at last. "Julie wants another one, but Fergus isn't sure they can afford it."

"Having kids is tough on just one salary," I say.

On Sundays, Mondays and Wednesdays, Sam works from noon to six at Artyfacts, Park Slope's "first-class, secondhand" store.

The store's run by her friend Shila Hawthorne. Sam makes fourteen bucks an hour, or $252 a week. That's enough, theoretically, to allow her to cover her day-to-day expenses and even shop for some occasional groceries. In practice, though, she gets paid in merchandise. She's unable to withstand the temptation to convert her salary into lightly used and slightly worn items from the store, taking advantage of the substantial employee discount Shila offers.

Sam's schedule allows me to devote Sundays to researching and writing my Christopher Finchley columns. I make a pot of coffee. My home office is set up at a small desk in the corner of the living room. I get out my Leadership, Management-by-Magazine and Unicorn files. I skim some articles I've already read and highlighted, then lay them out in a semicircle on the floor behind my chair. I open a new Word document. While I'm thinking of a great opening line, I log on to eMusic to select this month's tunes. Some great independent stuff that, even as it's downloading, I know I'll never listen to. I take a quick look at YouTube and start clicking on all kinds of two-minute videos, each of which seems ninety seconds too long. After that, I skim the news, quickly getting entangled in the lives of the latest batch of celebutantes, tracking their drunken antics, nipple slips, anorexia denials and embarrassing emails all the way from TMZ to Defamer to Go Fug Yourself and back again. Suddenly I'm nauseous. Like a teenager drained by too much porn, I can't look at this stuff anymore.

It's already three fifteen. I need to get my day back on track. Fast.

I reach into the back of my file drawer for my AntiCrastination Workbook.

Last summer, Henry decided that his whole team was not getting things done fast enough. He made us sit through a half-day seminar on AntiCrastination. Boiled down, the training consisted of three steps to ensure we would never drag our feet, goof off, or make Henry look bad ever again.

THE SECRETS OF ANTICRASTINATION

1. *List your Works in Progress (WIPs).* Now prioritize them!!
2. *Complete your WIPs.* Set yourself a deadline and don't start new projects till your current WIPs are finished!!
3. *Reward yourself.* Do something fun to celebrate the completion of each project before moving on to the next!!

Not everyone found the seminar worthwhile. "Do you realize," said Susan Trevor, "how much progress I could have been making instead of sitting through that shit?"

Maybe Susan was right at the time. But today, this shit is the best I've got. I've accomplished nothing today. I'm still wearing the clothes I slept in. I need to start AntiCrastinating…*immediately!!*

I list my WIPs. I circle my top priorities. I give myself a deadline for each.

THIS AFTERNOON: Finish new Christopher Finchley column… *Email to Fergus!!*

BY WEDNESDAY NIGHT: Seduce Sam… *Code Red Status: 27 days and counting!!*

BY NOON ON FRIDAY: Livingston Kidd… *Deliver finished presentation to Henry!!*

That was productive. I've finished my WIP list. To reward myself, I click on my Netflix bookmark and spend the next fifteen minutes rearranging the movies in my queue. As soon as I'm sure I've listed all my Ingmar Bergman movies in order of their original release date—safely in the mid-300s, with no chance they'll ever rise to the top—I feel ready to attack my first project with gusto.

By five thirty I email a draft to Fergus.

"Is this a joke?" he says.

"Not at all," I say. "Don't you like it?"

"What happened to the Unicorns?"

"I need more time for that. This came out better."

"'Look at My Poopie!'" Fergus reads aloud. "'Tracing the Origins of Workplace Competitiveness to Your Early Childhood Years.'"

"What can I tell you? Beryl inspired me."

"OK. I'll read it and call you back."

I reread the article myself. A thousand words on our childish need to please our workplace mommies and daddies. How some of us never get beyond the need to be overly praised for every symbolic bowel movement we produce. How the most needy among us rush to our bosses once, twice, three times a day looking to be acknowledged for the unimpressive brown pellets we're cupping in our trembling hands.

"This is great," says Fergus, calling me back.

"You like it?"

"Yes, Russell. You did good poopie."

I hang up the phone. For my reward, I crank up the volume on my iPod speakers and do a funny little dance to a couple of Rilo Kiley tunes.

I stop when the neighbors below start banging on their ceiling. I take a shower before Sam gets home, then put on real clothes for the first time today. A clean T-shirt and my favorite relaxed-fit khakis. I plan to work on my next priority when Sam gets home.

"What the hell happened here?" she says.

"I was working. I had a creative burst. Wrote a whole new article today."

"So when where you planning on picking this shit up?"

"No problem. I thought maybe I would ravish your sexy young body first."

"Don't start with that the moment I walk through the door. I'm not in the mood."

"I'm just excited to see you."

"This isn't your office, Russell. If you can't file all this away tonight, it's going in the basement tomorrow."

CHAPTER SIX

Before I walk into Henry's nine a.m. staff meeting, I already know the three main obstacles Judd Walker has to overcome on his first day of his new assignment:

1. *He's a consultant.* Years ago I claimed an old book from my dad's collection called *Up the Organization.* It's packed with handy advice for navigating the corporate world, including a warning about consultants: They will borrow your watch just to tell you the time. Then they are likely to walk off with it too.
2. *He's arriving at a bad time.* Henry's already tipped me off that more layoffs and budget cuts are coming soon. When the rest of his team hears what's going on, any shred of motivation they may have to help Judd will evaporate.
3. *It's my twenty-eighth day without sex.* And I'm not in the best of moods.

At least I thought those were going to be Judd's main obstacles. But when I walk into the small conference room on the twenty-sixth floor, I immediately see three more:

1. *He's sitting at Henry's right hand.* Henry's in the dad seat at the head of the conference table. But Judd's right next to him. In my usual spot.
2. *He's wearing suspenders.* Not a good fashion choice. Not on the first day. Not when you're the youngest person in the room. It makes people suspicious, even before you open your mouth.
3. *He's planning to present.* The projector is set up in the middle of the table. Connected to a laptop PC. Just waiting to be powered up.

I nod in Henry's direction and walk around the table to sit on Henry's left, opposite Judd. Dave Douglas and Susan Trevor are already entering. Susan sits next to Judd, with Dave on her right. None of us speak. Henry only wants to go through the formalities once. Hank Sullivan arrives, then Ben Shapiro hurries in, apologizing for being late.

"Let's wait a minute to see if Martin gets here," says Henry. We sit in silence for thirty-five seconds more.

Susan makes a fuss of dunking her teabag several times in her milky tea before getting up to deposit the bag in the wastebasket.

"I told Jeanie to skip this meeting. She's got a lot to prepare for the budget review this afternoon," says Henry. A few moments later he leans close to Judd and whispers something that makes Judd nod in a serious manner. Judd is wearing cufflinks, I notice. I score that as another point against him.

Twelve more seconds tick by.

"OK," says Henry. "Let's get started."

He introduces Judd. Gives a glowing overview of his academic and business credentials. Then he suggests we go around the room and each tell Judd our name and our role at the *Chronicle.* I start the ball rolling. As I speak, Judd draws an oblong shape on his notepad. It represents the table we're sitting at. He writes my name near a corner of his oblong to indicate where I'm sitting.

The baton passes quickly. By now, we all have our thirty-second intros down pat. We reach Susan, who sighs and says simply, "Susan Trevor. Director of ad services."

"Great," says Henry. He explains that he has brought Judd in to assist him in developing a new strategic plan for the *Chronicle.* Judd will likely have questions for each of us, and Henry expects us to give Judd all the help he needs.

As Henry is talking, Judd goes through a discreet warm-up routine, adjusting his cuffs, clearing his throat softly, sipping from his premium-brand bottled water. I glance around the table. Hank and Dave are professionally blank, waiting to see what happens. Ben raises his eyebrows and purses his lips at me. Susan is staring at Judd with open hostility.

Henry tells us that Judd has recently completed an analysis of the newspaper industry. A white paper, if you will. It outlines the challenges facing our whole industry.

Martin enters quietly and takes his seat. Henry continues speaking, choosing to downplay the interruption.

"I thought it would be useful if Judd were to summarize his analysis and add a few initial thoughts on the specific obstacles facing the *Daily Business Chronicle,*" says Henry. "Judd?"

Judd takes another sip of water, says, "Thank you, Henry," then reaches over to power up the projector while telling us how much he's looking forward to working with us all. Even though the room is small, he stands to present.

His title slide appears:

MACRO TRENDS IN THE NEWSPAPER INDUSTRY:
THE FUTURE OF PULP IN A PIXEL-BASED WORLD

Susan groans aloud.

I walk down the corridor with Dave, Martin and Susan.

"Asswipe," says Dave.

"Dickwad," says Martin.

"Fuckheel," says Susan.

I sense ears pricking up within a six-cubicle radius.

"Fuckheel?" I say. "He wasn't that bad."

We reach the doors to the elevator bank. Dave punches the security panel with the side of his fist, pushes hard on the door so it bounces back off the wall.

"Business school bullshit," he says.

"Don't let him get to you," I say. "He's just some upstart consultant. He's here on a project. He'll be gone as soon as he files his report."

"Don't be so sure," says Susan, who sees the downside to everything. "This is how Henry operates."

"Do we even know how long he's officially here?" says Martin. "Or did I miss that part?" Martin prides himself on his constant curiosity. But he's never quite curious enough to get to Henry's nine o'clock meetings on time.

"You didn't miss much," says Susan. "Henry played up the new boy's credentials. Told us he first met Judd when he was still in diapers."

Martin looks at me for clarification.

"He started out in packaged goods," I tell him. "Not just diapers. Detergents and air fresheners too. Then Harvard for his MBA."

"Major Bloody Attitude," says Susan.

"Fucking Harvard fucking MBAs," says Dave.

"Couldn't he get a real job?" says Martin.

Dave's up elevator arrives, but he lets it go, waits for the next one. He's still mumbling to himself as Martin, Susan and I get on our elevator down to twenty-five.

The phone in my office is ringing.

"What the hell was all that about?" says Ben Shapiro. Ben runs our events department. Hank Sullivan pulled him aside after Henry's meeting to discuss plans for his next big client boondoggle. "I thought Dave was going to throttle the cute new consultant. And Henry just—"

"Hold on, Ben," I say. "That's my other line."

"Can you believe that?" says Hank Sullivan, our sales director. "How does Henry let a kid walk in off the street and talk to Dave like that? I mean, we all know Dave *is* inflexible and arrogant, but you can't just come out and say it."

"Don't worry," I tell Hank. "Dave will be all right. Henry will take care of it. He can't afford to piss Dave and the production people off. He'll take the kid aside, smooth out his rough edges. We won't be seeing any performances like that again. But hey, let's catch up later, can we? I've got another call holding."

I click back to Ben and tell him the same thing—including the part about having another call, even though it's no longer true. I hang up the phone and stare out my window for a second or two.

"I hear I missed a good meeting," says Jeanie Tusa, our finance director. I swivel in my chair to see her leaning against my doorframe. Jeanie doesn't enter my office unless she really has to. I've heard through the grapevine that she thinks I should "clean my room."

"Hi, Jeanie," I say. "You didn't miss much. Just the usual horse hockey."

"That's not what I heard," she says. "I heard Dave Douglas is really pissed at Henry's new consultant." Jeanie's dirty blonde hair is curly in the way it gets when she doesn't have time to blow it dry. She smiles, lips closed, her whole face scrunched up. It's not her best look.

"Judd?" I say. "I guess he did ruffle a couple of feathers." I immediately regret saying even that much. It's a violation of one of my cardinal rules: never tell anyone from finance anything. People from finance have the power to fuck you over. And Jeanie is no exception, even if she devotes large chunks of time to acting like a pal to me, Susan, Ben and Martin. She'll always be the person who meets with Henry behind closed doors each week, reviewing spreadsheets, catching up on office gossip and deciding when and how to cut our staff or our budgets.

"Who came up with 'Diaper Boy'? I love it." She smiles again to indicate how much fun this gossipy stuff can be.

I don't take the bait this time.

"So how's the budget reforecast shaping up?"

"Good news!" says Jeanie. "I was just coming to tell you. I found an extra hundred and twenty-nine thousand. I've put it into your trade advertising budget."

"You just found it?"

"Not so loud." She perches herself on my guest chair, puts an elbow onto the papers on my desk and leans toward me.

She's wearing a long-sleeved top with horizontal blue and white stripes. Most of the mothers in our office wouldn't even attempt such a look. But Jeanie works out so much she can almost pull it off. "Let's just keep this between us. There's no need to tell Henry."

I'm not sure what surprises me more these days—the amount of trust Henry still places in Jeanie, or the number of little secrets she manages to keep from him.

"OK," I say. "But what if he notices we're running a lot more ads?"

"Don't book the ads yet. We may have some budget cuts coming."

"So how much of the one-twenty-nine will I be giving back?"

Jeanie sucks air through her teeth. "We'll probably ask you for three hundred."

"So instead of being plus one-twenty-nine, I'm actually minus one-seventy-one?"

She looks confused. As if she didn't know math was something you could do in your head. "Something like that. But it's better than being minus three hundred, right?"

"I guess so," I tell her. "Well, listen, thanks for bringing me the good news."

Instead of leaving, Jeanie leans even further across my desk. "So," she says, "did you hear about Ben's bathrobes?"

"Bathrobes?" I'm trying to sound noncommittal. I know exactly what she's talking about. I have one hanging in my closet at home.

"Did you know those bathrobes he ordered for Georgina's spa day cost three hundred and forty dollars each?"

"Wow. They must be pretty good quality."

"You don't think that's a little extravagant?"

Ben's title is special events director. Before he joined us, the position was just called "events director." But Ben won't produce any event unless it's special. Which means we're hosting more lavish, more talked-about, more well-attended events than ever before. Jeanie spends so much time going after Ben it makes me wonder if she's under secret instructions from Henry to build a file on him. It has nothing to do with Ben's homosexuality, of course. Henry is a highly evolved executive and a tolerant individual. He would never be seen to discriminate against anybody based on his own personal phobias.

"Didn't Georgina have a budget?" I ask. "I thought that her spa day was for twenty-five of our best clients. I heard it was a big success."

"Well, it's hard for us to judge how successful it was. We weren't there."

I sit back and clasp my chin in my hand, thinking how I might change the subject. Because now's not the time to tell Jeanie that I was the person Georgina Bird called when a client canceled on her at the last minute. That I took a break from the stress of my day to enjoy a one-hour hot-stone massage, followed by a European facial, capped off with a hydrating body wrap. It was one of those company-paid thank-yous sales managers try to give their friends in marketing whenever they can. Taking home an imported designer robe in my gift bag seemed like the perfect end to my very special day.

"How's Justin doing?" I ask, feigning concern for Jeanie's obnoxious second child. "Did he get over that infection OK?"

After Jeanie leaves, I send Ben an instant message telling him to call me. I want to explain to him how important it is to keep Jeanie sweet, how she should always get a leftover robe if he has one, or even be added to the guest list for a special event once in a while.

I bump into Henry on my way to the kitchen area. He looks approvingly at the company-issued mug I'm holding, emblazoned with the purple and yellow Ghosh Media logo.

"What did you think of this morning's meeting?" he says, following me into the kitchen area. He seems a little jazzed up.

I study the buttons on the machine and make my selections cautiously. Coffee. Caffeinated. Medium strength. Full cup. The machine whirrs into action. The display panel reads: PLEASE WAIT.

"Well, I think it was terrific," says Henry. "A great exchange of ideas. I was really impressed with the way Judd articulated his thinking." Henry seems a bit like his old self again. As if he believes having Judd around will actually help him get things back on track.

I try my best to smile and adopt a positive air while wondering if Henry has any hope of ever rejuvenating his career under the current regime. He's still under forty-five, but his thick head of gray hair makes most people assume he's older. The gray adds an air of maturity to his boyish features, his almost artificial blue eyes. I've seen photos from Henry's first management training course. Back then, he was virtually indistinguishable from the other handsome Ivy Leaguers who used to dominate the company. If he hadn't gone gray—people once suspected him of using some kind of reverse-Grecian formula—it would have been easy to dismiss him as just another pretty-boy lightweight. These days, no one questions the authenticity of Henry's hair color. At work, he's lived through three mergers. At home, he's fathered three kids he still has to put through college.

"He certainly made a strong impression," I say.

"Exactly," says Henry. "He's sharp. He's confident. He's aggressive."

I put my mug on the counter and open the fridge to look for some milk. The only thing inside is a homemade sandwich with a note stuck on top that reads: DO NOT TOUCH. I'm baffled. There were about seven unopened quarts of milk in here on Friday. Someone must be taking it home. I close the fridge and turn back to Henry.

I sip from my steaming coffee mug. I've never liked black coffee. Since I gave up sugar, it tastes more bitter than ever.

"Like I said Friday, I'm counting on you to look after him," says Henry. "Take him around. Show him the ropes. Make sure he gets everything he needs to complete his project."

"What exactly is the project?"

"Just some data gathering to start. Some analysis. Let's see what he puts together before we decide where it leads us." Henry pats me on the shoulder and walks away. He pauses at the kitchen door. "I'm counting on you," he says then disappears.

I stare for a moment at the dark brew I'm holding, then pour it into the sink, wash and dry my mug, and head outside to treat myself to a triple-shot extra-foam latte.

CHAPTER SEVEN

I'm on the phone with Sam when Judd arrives at my office. He walks right in, clutching a manila file folder, oblivious to the fact that I'm engaged in a conversation and fazed only for a split second by the clutter that surrounds me, the piles of folders that litter the floor, the layouts and printouts and spiral-bound presentations that cover every available surface. He takes the one clear path to my guest chair, sits, then holds his body tensely in a way that conveys his urgency and purpose. I hold up a finger to let him know I'll be just a minute.

"Tell me again why we should do this," I say into the phone. On the other end of the line, Sam repeats to me all the reasons why the patterned rug Shila has just brought into her store will work perfectly in the corridor between our bathroom and bedroom.

I sit back and size Judd up some more. For his first day at his new consulting assignment, along with his suspenders and cufflinks, he is wearing a bold, blue-and-white-striped shirt and a red tie with small blue dots. His curly brown hair is cropped short, and he wears thick-rimmed, fashionable-nerd glasses.

I try to imagine Judd 1.0, how he might have been in the days before he went to Harvard and earned his MBA. The picture I'm getting is of a shy wage slave failing to make a significant impression in the world of packaged goods, unsuccessfully trying to line up dates on Match.com. Judd 2.0 is someone completely different. Like a convict who's spent two years working out obsessively in the prison yard, he has used his time at business school to re-create himself. In his case, the workouts have targeted the ego, arrogance and condescension muscles, which ripple impressively beneath his corporate attire.

"What kind of budget are we talking about?" I say to Sam, swiveling in my chair so I can gaze thoughtfully out the window.

"What do you mean?" she says. "I told you it was only two hundred dollars. I'm going to buy it."

"It's definitely an interesting concept. How soon do you need an approval?"

"What are you talking about? Is someone there?"

Judd is fidgeting in his seat, holding his folder toward me and tapping it lightly on my desk. He's printed a label that reads D-SAW PROJECT and stuck it neatly on the tab of his folder. I have no idea how to print labels like that and no time to figure it out. It must be something they teach you at Harvard.

"Affirmative," I tell Sam. "But I don't think we need to rush into anything." Even though I'm starting to grow curious about what Judd wants, there's a principle involved here. He walked right into my office while I was on the phone. There's a minimum time that must elapse before I can give him my focused attention.

"I'll talk to you later," says Sam.

"Just hold on," I say.

I'm silent for several seconds, holding the receiver to my ear, avoiding Judd's expectant gaze, instead looking thoughtfully at a corner of his folder. He's a few years younger than me, but because of his MBA he projects a lot more self-importance. What he doesn't realize is that while he went off to Beantown, he lost out on two years of real-world experience. He's showing up at the *Chronicle* with an outdated knowledge of how to sell baby care and personal hygiene products and no real clue about how a newspaper operates.

"Stop playing your stupid games," says Sam. "I'm hanging up now."

"OK. Can we talk about this later? I have someone in my office."

"Whatever," says Sam and hangs up.

"Sorry about that," I say to Judd.

He sits down, opens his manila folder, pulls out a sheet of paper and lays it on my desk. He starts describing the project Henry wants him to work on. He's excited. It's a launch opportunity—a brand extension that could herald a new era of growth for our stagnating division.

"Stage one is information gathering," he says, pointing with a nail-bitten finger to the first column on the page.

"This is a nice looking table," I say. "Did you do all this in Excel?"

Judd looks at me for a second and then carries on with his explanation. He tells me that Henry wants him to schedule one-on-one interviews with me, Susan, Martin and Dave. He doesn't mention Ben, but I assume that's an oversight.

Next, he pulls out a stapled black-and-white document I recognize immediately. I realize why Henry doesn't want his full-time team working on this. We've all seen this project before. It's a harebrained scheme that we've each been asked to work on at one time or another. If this is the best Henry can come up with, we're in worse shape than I thought.

I sit back and listen as Judd describes the project in as much detail as he feels comfortable sharing, detailing the marketplace analytics, the key revenue drivers and the performance metrics he'll be building into his model. I pretend all this is new to me, paraphrasing back what he says so he knows I'm not intimidated by his B-school jabber.

"Maybe we can take some time now," says Judd. "Get started. I'd love to pick your brain. Jack speaks very highly of you. Henry tells me you're the smartest person in the building."

I look at my watch to camouflage any reaction to the news that Judd has already had face time with Jack. I haven't talked to Jack since he moved up to the thirty-fourth floor.

"You know, I'd love to," I say. "Trouble is I'm cranking on a Livingston Kidd proposal for Henry. I've got a lunch I really can't get out of. Then we've got that big budget meeting this afternoon. Maybe I can swing by at the end of the day. If not, call Barbara and have her slot you into my schedule."

I stand up to let him know the meeting is over.

"It's great to have you here," I tell him. "I'm really looking forward to working with you. Whatever you need, I'm here to help. My department is at your disposal."

I don't tell him that he's wasting his time, that the project he's been asked to work on was ludicrous when I started at the company four years ago. Today, unless someone somewhere comes up with a whole new approach, it's even more certain to fail. Knowing Henry as I do, I'm not optimistic. So far, the only thing I can see different is the code name he's dreamed up for the project.

The day I started at the company, Henry Moss met me at the elevator.

"Welcome aboard, Russell," he said. "We're excited to have you on the team." He walked me to a small interior room, which I thought at first was a supply closet.

"This is not your office," he said, switching on the overhead light. "But I think you'll find it has everything you need." He left and closed the door behind him.

I walked around the desk, looked at the computer, the telephone, the tape dispenser and the stapler. The room was small, the walls undecorated. There was a swivel chair behind the desk and a straight-backed chair with fraying upholstery on the other side. Two vertical filing cabinets stood against the wall. Beneath the desk were a short, circular wastepaper basket and a tall blue trash can with a recycling symbol on its side.

I sat at the desk and swiveled in the chair, noticing the pinholes and pockmarks on the beige colored walls.

I picked up the phone. There was no dial tone.

I switched on the computer and waited for it to boot up. A window appeared asking for my name and password.

I pulled off a strip of scotch tape and dabbed for lint on my blue suit jacket.

I rolled the tape into a tiny ball and flicked it toward the wastepaper basket.

I bent down to pick up the tape from where it landed on the floor and placed it into the basket.

I checked my watch.

I stood up from my chair and looked inside the filing cabinets. Each drawer was empty, save for one or two paper clips and the dust and human hair that had gathered in the corners.

I sat back down and pressed the button to adjust the height of my seat. The chair made a whooshing sound and I sank gently toward the floor.

Henry walked back into the office and closed the door behind him. He placed a stack of files on my desk and sat down opposite me. In those days Henry was the director of sales development. His hair was thick and brown, with flecks of gray just starting at his temples. He was the boss of my new boss, Ann Stark.

"Listen," he said, "I hate to do this to you on your first day, but I'm heading out to brief our Chicago, Detroit, Dallas, Atlanta, LA and San Francisco offices on a new product launch we're planning for the third quarter. It's top secret and I don't have time to tell you about it. The details are in these files. Everything's completely hush-hush. We won't even announce it internally till the twenty-ninth, so you can't mention this to anybody. But we need to have a PowerPoint on every salesperson's laptop by the first of next month. I'll be back in two weeks. Can you have it written by then?"

While he said all this, I was fumbling with the button on the chair, trying to get myself back to a normal sitting position. So I wasn't really focused on what Henry was saying.

"No problem," I said. "Everything I need is right here?"

"Everything," he said. "But if you need anything else, call my assistant Ellen. She's the only other person on the floor who knows about this project. Even when you speak to her about it you must use the code name."

I glanced down at the label on the top file.

"Is the code name 'Focus Two'?" I asked.

"Of course not," he said. "The code name is WICTY."

"Interesting. What does that mean?"

"Wish I could tell you," said Henry.

"OK. I guess it doesn't matter."

"No," said Henry. "WICTY is an acronym for 'wish I could tell you.' I came up with it myself."

"Got it," I said.

"Questions?" said Henry.

"Who do I talk to about my phone?"

"Ellen."

"Access to the network?"

"Ellen."

Henry stood up and hesitated at the door. "By the way," he said. "When I said the WICTY project was top secret, that includes even Ann Stark. I know you report to her, but don't under any circumstances give her any idea what you're working on."

"Got it."

"I'm trusting you with this."

"Got it," I said. "Should I talk to Ellen about my ID card?"

"Of course not. Call building services." He opened the door. "See you in two weeks," he said, and disappeared.

The files Henry left behind contained transcripts from several focus groups conducted in different cities to gauge consumer reaction to our new product. According to the summary report, this product was a daily tabloid newspaper from the editors of the *Chronicle* designed to appeal especially to younger readers and urban commuters. Apparently this meant that most of the articles would be replaced by colorful photographs and graphics. I scanned the report and the transcripts, trying in vain to find a more detailed description. But all I could find was the name: the *Daily Edge*. After twenty minutes I had read all the material, and avoiding Ann Stark's office, I walked the long way round to Ellen's cubicle and asked her to make arrangements for my phone and computer.

As soon as my phone was working, I called building services and scheduled my ID card appointment.

I sat in the office that wasn't my office studying the files Henry had given me.

I tried to avoid Ann Stark, who worked in a two-windowed office down the hall.

Several of my new colleagues in the marketing department and even a few salespeople introduced themselves and showed an interest in what I was doing.

A typical conversation would go something like this:

"So, you're the new guy."

"That's right."

"What's your name?"

"Russell," I said. "Russell Wiley."

"It's great to meet you, Russell. What do you do?"

I told them what I did.

"That's great. Where do you come from?"

I gave the name of my former company.

"So. What do they have you working on?"

"Just a project Henry asked me to look at."

"Really. Which one?"

"Wish I could tell you."

I quickly gained a reputation for being arrogant and aloof.

Each day I ate lunch alone in the corner of the staff cafeteria.

Each night I worked till nine or ten o'clock, trying to write a presentation for a product I knew little about. To make matters worse, the people in the focus groups were all regular readers of the text-heavy, broadsheet *Chronicle*. They had nothing good to say about the eye-popping tabloid they were being shown.

One night the phone rang at nine thirty. It was Henry from Atlanta. I told him I was having trouble articulating the new sales proposition. He told me he hadn't expected to find me in the office and just wanted to leave a voicemail.

"Shall I hang up?"

"Of course not. Didn't I give you the file marked YANA?"

"I didn't see it."

"That's right. I'm not allowed to show it to you."

"Why not?"

"You are not authorized."

"That's what YANA means?"

"Yes, but forget I mentioned it. Just use what's in the files I gave you."

"OK. But I'm not sure it's the most compelling stuff."

"Be creative," he said. "I'm relying on you."

He hung up the phone.

Over the next few days and nights, I took Henry's advice and developed some creative ways to use the quotes in my focus group files.

When a lady in Philadelphia said, "I hate what you've done. It's like you've taken an old friend and made him unrecognizable," I simply selected the words, "It's like…an old friend."

And when a war veteran from Minneapolis said, "I've never seen such a piece of shit. I want to read the *Chronicle*, not a comic book. Why couldn't you leave a good thing alone?" I was able to spin the slightly more positive, "I've never seen such…a good thing."

I put these quotes under the heading, "Everybody needs an *Edge*!"

After two weeks, I had assembled a forty-page presentation packed with benefit-oriented bullet points and enthusiastic quotes. I still had no idea what the *Daily Edge* actually looked like.

Then Henry returned and told me the WICTY project was canceled and that Ann Stark had been fired.

He walked me round the sales and marketing departments and introduced me to everyone. He joked with people that they may have seen someone who looked like me hanging around for the past two weeks, but that guy was an imposter and the real me was now officially starting.

When the memo came out explaining that Ann Stark had left the company for personal reasons, Henry's popularity soared and people viewed me with new respect.

Henry grew more popular because, I discovered, the entire marketing staff had hated Ann Stark. They had given her the nickname S.R.M., which stood for Stark Raving Mad. Her departure meant they would no longer have to endure her instructing them to "let their creativity flow" with every assignment, only to insist later they change all the typefaces to her specifications and add a green border to everything.

I gained respect because my new colleagues thought I had somehow played a role in getting Ann Stark fired. And if that were the case, it meant I possessed a power they might have cause to fear.

I moved into my new office. Unlike the temporary one where Henry had left me, this one had a single window. Ellen showed me a catalog and invited me to select a potted plant. She informed me that I would not be allowed to water it because that task had been outsourced to a specialist company. I filed my work on the WICTY project into my new filing cabinets.

Ann Stark was replaced by Colin Desmond, who lasted only seven weeks before being fired. Then came Barney Barnes, who was promoted to a more senior position reporting to Jack within six months. Then came Paula Davies, who lasted almost a year. After Paula was asked to leave, Henry did something surprising. He stopped looking outside for his next candidate. He promoted me.

Last year, when we shuffled the deck chairs one more time, Jack Tennant became president of the Burke-Hart Business Group and publisher of the *Chronicle*, Henry outmaneuvered Hank Sullivan to become vice president of sales and marketing, and I was promoted into Henry's old job as sales development director.

Late in the morning, the day's interruptions seem to have slowed and I somehow get absorbed in my work. I stick at it through the lunch hour, with an excuse at the ready in case Judd reappears. Suddenly, close to two o'clock, my hunger hits. I run down to our cafeteria to grab a cheeseburger and fries to go, then head upstairs with my hot food and plastic cutlery.

I'm squeezing two packets of ketchup onto my burger when Roger Jones wheezes into my office, angles himself through the turns of my office obstacle course, perches unhappily on my guest chair and places a large plastic cup of soda on my desk.

Roger is the smartest and fattest guy I know. If there were a contest to find the employee with the highest weight-plus-IQ total, Roger would win hands down. I brought him over from my former company as soon as Henry promoted me to director. Between my old company and this one, Roger and I have worked together for more than seven years.

"Hey," I say. I put the top half of my bun back on the burger, mushing it down to soak up some ketchup. But I don't pick it up.

"Well," he says, "I'm finally fucking doing it."

"I heard," I say. "When the fuck were you going to tell me?"

"I wanted to make sure it was a hundred percent. I called the surgeon's office this morning. They can take me two weeks on Wednesday."

"That soon?"

"I've been sitting on a pre-approval for weeks. I don't think I can wait any longer. Who knows what's going on around here? Henry's brought in a new fucking consultant. Everyone's shit-scared there are more layoffs coming. I've got to do this while I still have the coverage."

"How long will you be out?"

"Six weeks max. Four if the doctor says I can come back sooner."

"Jeez," I say. "This is hardly the best time."

"There's never a best time. So you didn't deny it. I guess there are going to be layoffs."

I look into Roger's intelligent eyes long enough to confirm his suspicion without saying anything. If he survives his operation, I'll do all I can to protect his job. I'm sure he's researched this gastric bypass procedure as thoroughly as anyone can. In one recent study, two percent of people were dead within a month of the surgery.

"You don't have anything to worry about," I say.

"That's reassuring."

"Can you at least get that Tiffany proposal out before you go?" I say. "I don't want you to leave that for Cindy."

"Fucking Cindy," he says with a snort. "Will you make sure she's the first to go? Anyway, don't worry. She didn't go near Tiffany's. The whole thing's done. I emailed it to Georgina and Randy yesterday. I'm just waiting for comments."

"OK. Well, fuck. Good luck, man." I stand up.

"No fucking hugs."

"OK." I sit back down.

Roger stands, waves his soda cup at me. "This was diet, by the way."

"I didn't say anything." I take a second to select a french fry and pop it into my mouth.

"You know what? I'm just sick of all the fucking looks I get."

"I keep telling you. The mustache doesn't help."

"Well maybe I'll fucking lose that too."

I chew and swallow my fry as he wades to the door.

"Roger," I say, and he turns back to me, still scowling. "I'm giving you a mental hug right now."

"Whatever," he says and walks off down the hall.

CHAPTER EIGHT

At three o'clock Susan, Martin, Ben and I gather again in the small conference room. Judd's not here. But Jeanie is now sitting on Henry's right.

I glance around the room again, wondering if the others were also given advance word that budget cuts were coming. Henry and Jeanie often confide these things to each of us individually to cut down on the possibility of surprise or dissent being shown in group meetings.

Henry never likes to deliver bad news directly. As soon as we're all seated, he suggests we "get right into it" and hands off to Jeanie.

"Given the revenue picture, corporate finance is asking everyone to reduce controllable expenses," says Jeanie, staring straight at Henry as she speaks. "They asked us to cut as deep as possible. But Henry and I really pushed back. We told them we could only squeeze out another three million."

"How are we expected to find that?" says Susan. "The third quarter's done. All of my projects are already committed."

"We'll be looking everywhere," says Henry. "For example, as of today, there's an immediate freeze on nonessential travel." He glances at Jeanie, from whom the idea obviously originated.

"We've had that in place for six months," says Susan.

"OK," says Henry. "We'll freeze all travel."

"Even essential travel?" asks Ben. "I'm supposed to be in DC next week for the dinner Hank's hosting for ExxonMobil. Stan Lyford's speaking," he adds, dropping the name of our deputy managing editor.

"OK," says Henry. "Communicate to your staffs that the freeze on nonessential travel now includes all travel, with the exception of essential travel."

"So should I go to DC?" says Ben.

"If it's essential," says Henry.

"What about Erika?" says Ben. "She was supposed to be coming with me."

"Let's not get too granular," says Henry. "The purpose of today's meeting is to discuss broad strokes."

"Precisely," says Jeanie, immediately getting granular and handing out some spreadsheets. "I've tried to make this as painless as possible." She wiggles her shoulders to convey how much fun this might be. "I've isolated a dozen projects where we are underspent. The first question is how many of these we can cut completely and how many we can defer till next year."

We look down the list of projects Jeanie wants to cut. Five in Ben's group; four in Susan's; two in Martin's; only one in mine. Jeanie gives me a little wink. As I always do when Jeanie hands out a spreadsheet, I eyeball the numbers to look for obvious mistakes. It looks like the total in her year-to-date column is off by about two million, but I file that for later. Maybe the cuts we need won't actually be that bad.

"What the hell is this?" says Susan.

Henry stands up, walks away from Susan to the far end of the conference table, then turns to face us.

"Look," he says. "We're all grown-ups here. This is serious stuff. The fact is, Susan, that Jack wants our primary focus to be on generating revenue, and we just don't see that kind of immediate return on most of what you do."

"What I do supports the entire business," says Susan.

"Don't think we don't respect that."

"You and Jack don't even have a clue what I do, do you?"

Henry doesn't respond well to confrontation. Sometimes he doesn't respond at all. In the silence, Ben pipes up: "You've cut the budget for Hank's holiday party by fifty percent?" He's looking at Jeanie.

"I think we could be creative and find ways to economize," she says, throwing a glance at Henry.

"Who's going to tell Hank?"

"Listen," says Henry. "We don't have much time. Jeanie and I need to get back to corporate by Wednesday. Take this list. Use it as your starting point. If you don't agree with the specific cuts we've identified, you'll need to come up with alternative savings by end of day. I'll review the details with Jeanie tomorrow."

"That's it?" says Susan.

"Not quite," says Henry. "There's one more thing we need to discuss." He pauses to let the gravity of what he's about to say sink in.

"Jesus," says Susan.

"What is it?" says Martin.

Henry sighs meaningfully and says, "We've been asked to implement another twenty-five percent reduction in force before year-end."

We sit quietly for a minute, translating Henry's words and doing the math in our heads: Reduction in force means firing people. Twenty-five percent means six of our people will have to go.

Based on the size of our respective departments, Martin and Ben will each have to cut one person, and Susan and I will need to fire two.

"Why isn't Hank here?" says Susan. "Do these layoffs apply to sales too?"

Jeanie looks at Henry, making it clear that she's not going to answer that one. Eventually, Henry says, "There are no plans for layoffs in the sales department. We need to keep as many feet on the street as possible right now."

"Well, the salespeople are already complaining that they're not getting all the support they need," says Ben.

"What can I tell you?" says Henry. "We'll just have to keep our eye on the ball, work smarter, maintain our intensity and keep our heads down."

"If our heads are down, what balls are we supposed to be looking at?" says Ben.

"Christ," says Susan. "I can't take this place anymore."

I'm curious to see what kind of temporary work quarters Henry has asked Ellen to set up for Judd. But I wait until five fifteen before heading up to twenty-six to check out his digs. On a slow first day, there's a good chance he cut out at five, in which case I'll leave him a note to prove I didn't blow him off completely. I look into a couple of vacant cubicles but see no sign of recent activity.

Further down the hall, just three doors down from Henry, is the only spare office on the floor. It's a two-windowed space Hank Sullivan has been trying to move Randy Baker, his star sales manager, into for quite a while.

As I approach, I hear Judd's voice and realize that: a) Henry has given him this office, which means: b) even if it is only temporary, Judd is working in a director-size space as big as mine.

He's on the phone when I arrive, looking very much at home. "Hey, buddy," he says into the receiver as he waves me in. "Gotta go. I'm meeting right now with one of the majordomos here."

I glance around the freshly painted office. It looks like Henry took some extra steps to ensure Judd's comfort right from day one. He even authorized one of the new executive chairs recommended by our ergonomic consultants. I guess Henry wants to send a message to Hank and doesn't care how much this pisses off Randy Baker.

"Definitely. We'll do that," says Judd. "Call me when you get into town."

I sit in his guest chair as he hangs up the phone. The upright cover of his laptop is facing me, the screen hidden from view. It's not a company-issued machine. Interesting. It shows that Judd lacks the confidence to start his new assignment from scratch. He's not comfortable working with a PC whose hard drive has been wiped clean. Judd needs his pretested, B-school approved templates. He wants the ability to reduce, reuse and recycle all the ideas and presentation formats he's been taught elsewhere. It doesn't matter whether or not his prepackaged ways of thinking offer the best solutions to our specific challenges. He'll tailor his recommendations to whatever he thinks Henry wants to hear. And because Judd's tired language will sound new to Henry's ears, he'll value Judd's work even more highly.

"Russell," he says, looking at me over his computer, "thanks for stopping by. Just let me save this." He taps a few buttons on his keyboard, then closes the screen and pushes the laptop aside. He leans forward. "Jesus. I spent all afternoon reading some more of the historical files. I saw your name on a WICTY project memo. You should have told me you were already a big player last time around."

I shrug. "I came in at the back end. Put a few slides together. Then they pulled the plug."

Judd looks at me closely. "So tell me, Russell. I guess we might as well be frank. What the hell have I gotten myself into? Am I doing the right thing taking this on? Or should I just quit now and cut my losses?"

I search for the kind of language Judd might understand. "Well," I tell him, "we do need new ways to monetize our value proposition."

"Let me come right out with it. I don't like to spin my wheels. There are other things I could be doing. Sure, I'm interested in broadening my base of industry knowledge. But we both know the real action for branded content is in cross-platform integration. Without the online and mobile plays, the newspaper story just doesn't excite advertisers. Am I missing something? I don't want to take on a project that's doomed to fail."

"You said it yourself this morning. Our existing business models are broken. We need a new way to leverage our strategic assets. If we can't change our corporate structure, all we can focus on is the daily newspaper business. And if our editors don't start attracting younger readers soon, we're all dead. Everything's riding on the D-SAW project. Of course, we do have a major hurdle in that our own readers hated the concept last time around. But that's why you're here. Henry and Jack have a lot riding on this."

"OK, Russell," says Judd, pushing back in his chair and putting his hands behind his head. I notice sweat stains in his armpits and I'm reminded of an old antiperspirant commercial. This is the moment when the word UNSURE would have been slapped across the screen. "Let's just say you had a new prototype to work with. Let's say you had three million to throw at the problem. What would you do? More focus groups? Online research? What would you spend more on: product development or creative testing?"

Despite myself, I'm tempted to tell him that more focus groups would be a waste of time. We know our customers. We know what they want. More important, we know what they don't want. As for the younger readers we need to attract, it's hard to imagine that gathering them in a room, disconnecting them from their iPods and cell phones, getting them hopped up on M&Ms and soda, and cross-examining them for two hours about a concept as alien to them as a newspaper will yield any useful information.

I make a special effort and resist the urge to tell Judd what I'm thinking. "Wow," I say instead. "Three million? Completely discretionary? That's unheard of around here. Do me a favor. Let me think about it."

And here's what I think:

Three million. Sounds familiar. That's exactly how much Henry and Jeanie have just pulled from me and my colleagues—the team they are relying on to keep the current business on track. And they've given it all, no questions asked, to a thirty-five-year-old newspaper neophyte who doesn't have a clue what to do with it.

Three million, I'd like to tell Jeanie, could buy us a hell of a lot of bathrobes.

CHAPTER NINE

One of the funny things about my work life is how I spend all day being as nice as humanly possible to people I wouldn't otherwise choose to socialize with. By the time I get home, my cheerful battery has run down. My kindness settings have been changed. "Pleasant" is no longer my default option.

That's why, when I arrive home to find my wife wiping a strange brown lump in the middle of the living room floor, I don't say, "Hi, Sam. You look great. You can't imagine how much I missed you today." Instead I say, "Jesus. What the hell is that?"

"Isn't it amazing?" Sam stands up, smiling excitedly, a bottle of all-purpose cleaner in one hand, a darkly stained cloth in the other. She loves this stuff in a way I don't quite understand.

The fact is, she does look—she always looks—great. Wearing just a sweatshirt and some flannel shorts. Hair pulled back in a rubber band. Her legs and feet are bare. Maybe I should go out and come in again. But it's too late for that.

"I thought you were buying a rug."

"I'm still thinking about the rug. When I saw this piece, I told Shila I just had to have it."

"This piece? What is it?" I ask again. "It looks like an elephant turd."

Sam rolls with that one. "It's a footstool, I think. We could use it lots of different ways."

"Do we need another footstool? How much was it?"

"Shila let me have it for forty bucks."

"What did she pay for it?"

The last remnant of Sam's smile fades. "She had it on sale for one-twenty."

"Wow. That's like getting an eighty-dollar bonus. Except for the fact you're out forty dollars."

"That's so like you."

I sit on the couch, throw my suit jacket on the cushion next to me.

"Can I put my feet on it at least?"

"No. I just cleaned it." Her mouth is set in a firm line.

"Maybe we should just lie down for a while. We don't have to do anything."

"I'm not having sex with you. I don't want to get all sweaty."

"Come on," I say. "If you start using the No Sweat Clause, we'll never have sex ever again."

"What do you mean, the No Sweat Clause?"

"It's that catch-22 you always use. You don't want sex when you're already sweaty. And you especially don't want sex if you're *not* sweaty, in case it makes you sweaty."

"What are you talking about? Where do you come up with this stuff?"

"I don't make it up. These are your rules. If you're worried about perspiration, we could try it with a sheet between us."

"I just washed the sheets."

"I'll turn on the air conditioner."

"Then you'll want me to cook you dinner."

"I don't care about food. We'll order Chinese."

"I don't want Chinese. I don't want to hear you complain we're spending too much money ordering in."

"It's OK," I say. "If times get tough, we'll sell the footstool."

"Maybe you were right. I don't think I want to have sex with you ever again."

"OK. What shall we have for dinner?"

"I have half a sandwich in the fridge. That's all I need."

"So what shall I do?"

"Whatever you want."

"OK. Hand me the remote."

Sam throws the remote at me, walks to the kitchen with her cleaning products. I kick off my shoes, turn on the TV.

A few seconds later, Sam comes out of the kitchen and heads down the uncarpeted hall toward our bedroom. At first I think she's ignoring me completely, but she stops, retraces her steps and snaps, "Get your fucking feet off that thing."

Day twenty-nine of my reclaimed virginity. I wake before the alarm. Get dressed in the dark. Head out to work half an hour earlier than usual.

Sam and I somehow got through the rest of last night, mainly by avoiding each other. I watched TV. Sam went to the bedroom for about forty-five minutes, called someone on the phone. Her mother, I think. I used my cell phone to order a pizza, half with broccoli and extra cheese, the way she likes it. She emerged from the bedroom, and in a silent gesture of détente, I handed her the remote. I brought two trays from the kitchen and we ate together on the couch, using paper plates from the pizzeria. She forgot about her half sandwich and made me sit through a marathon of British TV on BBC America. I went to bed midway through the third back-to-back episode of her favorite gardening show. I was asleep by the time she joined me.

On my way to the subway, I flip open my cell phone and dial Fergus's office number. He won't be there. Even on a normal day, it's way too early for him. And I know he closed the new issue of *Vicious Circle* last night.

I leave a message inviting him to lunch then snap the phone shut and try to organize the important, early-morning questions I have banging around in my head. I'd love to sit down with Fergus and ask him: Are you actually happy with how your life has turned out, or is your contented family guy persona some kind of act? Did you plan all this responsibility, or did it just happen that way? Where have you deposited all your huge, naïve, premarital ambitions, your dreams of potential greatness? Do you and Julie still fuck on a regular basis? If yes, how regular? Who initiates? By the way, what do you think of me these days? Truthfully. Does it annoy you that I make so much money helping sell ads to the kinds of corporations whose pathological pursuit of profits you find obscene? Do you think I'm a sellout? Do you think it's OK that Sam doesn't want a career anymore? What if I told you that she doesn't want to sleep with me either? Does that change your answer? Do I have a right to demand more sex? On what basis? Because she loves me, or because I pay for everything? Or should I be the one who accommodates her? Should I accept her lack of desire and live without sex just because I love her? And if I did accept that, shouldn't I still insist she get a proper job?

I swipe my MetroCard and head down into the swarm of irritable, Manhattan-bound workers on my Brooklyn subway platform.

My plan is to eat breakfast at my desk and get focused on the Livingston Kidd proposal that's at the top of my WIP list. I stop in at the second-floor cafeteria. Coffee. Juice. Scrambled egg wrap. The spicy kind. All loaded onto a disposal cardboard tray.

It's eight fifteen. Most of the early crowd does what I'm doing. They get breakfast to go. But after paying there's only one way out: you have to walk through the nearly deserted cafeteria. I scan the large room. There are only a few tables occupied by solo *Chronicle* readers or small groups from the lifestyle group talking about the return of taupe. Over at a table by the window, Ben Shapiro and Erika Fallon are hard to miss. And even harder to ignore.

"Yoo-hoo," calls Ben, waving a little more than he needs to to get my attention. He's wearing a turquoise shirt, open at the neck. I wander over, trying to be discreet in the glances I throw in Erika's direction. I stop a little short of their table.

"Hi, guys," I say. "What are you doing here?"

"You know me," says Ben. "I'm up when the cock crows."

Erika shakes her head. Her hair, I notice, is especially lustrous in the morning light. "We're just catching up on a few projects. Why don't you join us, Russell Wiley?"

"Project number one," says Ben. "We need to decide about Mr. Judd Walker. Is he a suitable candidate for the irresistible but impossibly hard-to-please Erika?"

I chuckle and give Erika my most rueful, wide-eyed look. "I don't think I can go there. Plus, I came in early because I have an urgent—"

"Shush, shush, shush," says Ben. "This is urgent. Sit. We need the straight man's perspective."

"OK, I'll sit. But don't expect me to get drawn into any inappropriate conversation. Anyway," I say absentmindedly, "isn't Judd gay?"

"Negatory, my friend. He scores a zero on my homometer. And in case you didn't know, little Miss Erika's milkshake has already brought him out to the yard."

"Ben!"

"Really?" I say, biting into my sandwich, trying to appear only moderately interested.

"We had one conversation," says Erika. "He seems cute."

"Hmmm. I thought the cute ones were usually gay."

"Gay or married," says Erika.

"Or both," says Ben. "But let's not go there. Anyway, a little birdie apparently told Mr. Judd about our DC event next week. Suddenly he's planning his own trip down there, telling Erika he'd love to join us if the dates line up."

"Really?" I say again. "He's a fast worker."

"He sure is," says Ben. "But is he worth breaking the rules for?"

"Rules?"

I sip some juice through my straw and watch Erika's expression as Ben explains. "Apparently young Erika has imposed some highly restrictive rules on her love life. No wonder she's going through such a dry spell."

"Maybe Erika Fallon just intimidates people," I say.

"Thank you, Russell Wiley."

I tip my coffee cup to her in reply.

"Maybe so," says Ben. "But when you rule out two-thirds of the male population, you make getting laid way too difficult."

"Ben!" says Erika again.

"I'll be your witness," I tell her, "when you report him to HR."

"That won't be necessary," says Ben, who proceeds to articulate and offer commentary on Erika's three rules for dating:

1. No married men.
2. No coworkers.
3. Never, ever with your boss.

"Imagine if I tried to live like that," says Ben.

"I'll tell Henry to stop leading you on," I say.

Erika laughs.

"Puh-lease," says Ben. "The question is, does Judd qualify as a coworker if he's actually a consultant, not a member of staff?"

I think for a moment, trying to come up with a counter-argument that doesn't make me sound too petty or jealous. "Well, that sounds like a technicality," I say. "He *has* been given an office. And he *will* be coming in every day like a regular employee."

"Phhhww," says Ben.

"Plus," I say before he can go on, "isn't it a slippery slope? If Erika Fallon breaks the rule for Judd, won't every other single man in the office feel they have the right to ask her out in the future?"

"Why not!" says Ben. "Let's open the floodgates instead of bolting all the doors."

I sip my coffee and say, "My advice to you, Erika Fallon, is to wait a while. Maybe when you get to know Judd better you won't think he's so cute after all. Why break the rule now when you can always break it later?"

"That's a good idea," says Erika.

"That's a terrible idea," says Ben. "You need to flirt with him like crazy and make sure he gets his butt down to that hotel in Washington next week."

"I can do that," says Erika. "Flirting's easy. Especially when you know someone's off limits. You can relax with them. Isn't that right, Russell Wiley?" She fixes me with her warm brown eyes and waits for me to come right back at her with something witty and profound.

"Er, I guess so," I say.

"Russell," says Jeremy Stent, bursting eagerly into my office. "I have this fantastic idea I want to run by you."

It's 9:01. I'm still not fully recovered from my breakfast experience. My spicy egg wrap isn't sitting well in my stomach. And the sight of Jeremy isn't helping.

Jeremy's a smart misfit who hasn't managed to gel with his colleagues or understand why the work he produces, which makes perfect sense to him, is completely unusable based on the way we like to do things around here. The best thing about Jeremy is that he's only been with us three months. Which will make him easiest to fire when the layoffs come.

"What does Pete think?" I ask, knowing already that Pete Hughes, Jeremy's nominal boss, has not yet been zapped by Jeremy's latest brain wave.

Jeremy's eagerness to come up with new ideas would be endearing if he could just stop his ego from showing. In his junior role he needs to be respectful and supportive to his immediate supervisor. And not barge into my office and attempt to dazzle me with ideas that, while new to him, I've invariably seen before.

"I wanted to bring it to you first," he says in a tone that manages to sound both obsequious and patronizing.

I should just tell him to get back to work. To do what he's told. To stop trying to come up with ideas we haven't asked him for. I need him producing the work that will justify his meager salary and his inflated self-opinion.

But I indulge Jeremy and listen to him as best I can. He thinks he has devised another great money-saving idea for the company that would also be astonishingly easy to execute. There's only one problem with it: Jeremy's idea would require Burke-Hart's business and lifestyle groups to work together with a spirit of selfless cross-divisional partnership. In Jeremy's utopian worldview, he imagines somehow that both sides would be willing to put the overall good of the company ahead of their individual priorities.

As soon as that level of impossibility is established, I start to lose interest. My mind wanders. It becomes harder and harder for me to concentrate on the exact details of what Jeremy's saying.

I try to quantify the sources of my distraction.

Five percent is pure nostalgia. Jeremy's reminding me of my own idealistic youth. When I thought it was possible to make a meaningful contribution to the corporate world. That my ideas would be listened to and my memos read. There was a god we worshipped then. A powerful god called Synergy. He was a god who promised us a bright, harmonious future. But that god was the devil in disguise. He's dead now. We are no longer allowed to mention his name.

Twenty percent is the fact I haven't had sex in twenty-nine days. It's causing something to build up inside me. And not just physically. There's a resentment taking hold, a sense that I'm being taken advantage of in ways I never consciously agreed to. Something has changed between Sam and me. What used to be a dance now feels more like hand-to-hand combat.

Thirty percent is the residual impact of spending twenty minutes this morning in the company of Erika Fallon. Her bottom teeth are slightly crooked, I noticed. But crooked in the most delightful way.

The remaining forty-five percent of my distraction revolves around Judd and the thought of him flexing his MBA muscles for Erika. I shouldn't care. I'm a married man. It's not as if Erika Fallon and I could ever be together. But if she is going to be with somebody, she needs to choose someone other than Judd. Lucky Cat understands. I had a quiet conversation with him this morning. I told him I didn't want to become the kind of bitter, tormented person who can't stand to see other people having fun. But still, I pointed out, I have to draw the line somewhere. Lucky smiled at me wisely. I think he could really empathize with what I was feeling.

Jeremy is recapping his idea to make sure I fully understand it. I nod to give the impression I do. It's a shame because his idea isn't bad, and our operating methods could certainly use improving. But Jeremy still hasn't grasped the basic truth: we can't accept any of his ideas until we accept him. New employees are like organ transplants: if you're not compatible, the body rejects you.

"Look, Jeremy, I can't argue with you about your idea. We could be way more profitable if we could combine our resources in the way you describe. There's only one problem: it's way too logical."

"Too logical?" I watch the excitement drain from his cheeks.

"Have you ever heard of the writer Christopher Finchley?" I ask. I open the drawer of my filing cabinet and bend down, skimming through the handwritten tabs of the manila folders haphazardly arranged inside.

"Finchley?"

"He's actually very good. You might find him worth studying. He writes a column each month in *Vicious Circle.* It's a magazine not many people have heard of, but it's very well read in opinion leader circles. Ahh. Here it is." I sit back up and lay a folder on the desk. "When I read this particular article, I thought I should make some copies. It was almost as if Finchley were speaking directly to me, talking specifically about our company."

"'History versus Logic,'" reads Jeremy. "'Why Some Businesses Prefer to Repeat Their Past Mistakes Rather Than Risk Making New Ones.'"

"It's a great article," I say. "Take a copy. The basic gist of it is that all old economy companies like to talk about doing things differently. They yearn to stretch themselves in new directions. But when push comes to shove, they snap back into their old habits. They can't quite combine their desire to create 'a new paradigm' with their corporate need to do things 'a certain way'—i.e., the way they've always done those things before."

"But that's not how it is here, is it?" says Jeremy. "Everyone's always talking about the need for reinvention and new ideas."

"Talking and doing are two different things. Finchley points out that history and logic can be combined in only three ways." I pick up one of the photocopied sheets and read aloud: "'One: historical and logical. Two: historical and illogical. And three: logical and nonhistorical.'"

"But what I'm suggesting would be so easy to implement," Jeremy protests.

"Hold on," I say, scanning the article. "Here's the part you need to understand: 'Ninety-five percent of all corporate activity involves repeating historical mistakes that have become clearly illogical in the current business climate. Historical-illogical business practices represent a classic form of time- and money-wasting madness: doing the same thing over and over again and expecting a different result.'" I pause to make sure Jeremy's paying attention and because the cell phone in my bag is ringing. I wait for it to stop. "Interesting, no? Here's the last part. 'Logical and nonhistorical.' That's how I would describe your idea. 'Logical and nonhistorical approaches might be called commonsense in the real world but are likely to be labeled as radical and unworkable in the corporate sphere. New, more logical approaches to problems result in resources being applied where they can deliver the greatest return even if it means abandoning habitual yet obsolete procedures. At most companies, management has identified 'resistance to change' as one of the major problems holding their organization back.

These companies often request bold new ideas to be presented that show them how they might overcome this resistance and reinvent themselves, reinvigorate their processes, and refocus their people. These proposals are usually rejected as impossible to implement by the same management teams who commission them. Why? Because they are a direct repudiation of the company's existing culture and approach to business.'" I put the article down. "Pretty interesting, huh?"

"Is that meant to be serious?" says Jeremy.

"I hate to say it. But you can't make this stuff up."

Jeremy looks crestfallen. He means well, I realize. If only he were willing to suck it up and concentrate on the work we actually need him to do, he could really go places.

"Listen," I say. "It's a great idea. Thanks for bringing it forward. I'll put it in my file."

CHAPTER TEN

The message on my cell phone is from Fergus: "Russki, got your message. Lunch would be good. Julie packed me a sandwich if you want to sit outside. Of course, I could save it till tomorrow if your capitalist masters are paying."

I call my favorite sushi restaurant to snag a reservation then call him back and connect with his voicemail: "Ferg, refrigerate your sandwich. We're on for sushi. Twelve thirty. Usual place."

Three hours later we're munching edamame, throwing the husks into an elegantly handcrafted, multihued ceramic bowl. Fergus has just finished telling me how his publisher has negotiated the necessary financing to keep *Vicious Çircle* afloat for another two years.

"We're hoping that once we make it to 2008, with all the excitement of the Olympics and the presidential election, there will be more than enough advertising money sloshing around for us to reach break-even," he says. "After that, smooth sailing."

"That sounds like a really well-thought-out plan," I say. "But I still think you'd be better off at *Forbes*. Things can only get better now that Bono's invested."

I watch Fergus think while he chews. He has strange, curly hair the color of dark rust. His skin, as always, is extremely pale.

"You know what?" he says. "I like where I am. We have all the usual bullshit. But at least we stand for something."

"What? Financial insecurity?"

He makes a sound that's part laugh, part snort. "That's for sure. But we're true to ourselves too. Just because our ideas aren't in favor right now doesn't mean we should throw in the towel. Not everything's about money. Some things are still worth fighting for."

I glance around at the expensive surroundings, the power brokers at adjacent tables. Fergus never complains when I bring him here.

"Listen, Ferg, you know I admire what you're doing. I just don't know how you hold it all together." I sip my green tea.

"What do you mean?" he asks, biting into an edamame pod and pulling it through his teeth so the peas pop into his mouth.

"The whole thing," I say. "One job. Two kids. Four mouths to feed. And all the shit you have to look forward to. Guns in schools. Playground kidnappers. Child molesters. Paying for college."

"Ha ha," he says. "When you put it like that."

"You know what I mean."

"You're looking at it from the outside. From the inside it's not like that. You construct it differently in your head."

"What do you mean?"

"You have to make decisions in life," Fergus continues. "If you make the wrong choices, you're trapped. If you make the right choices, you're liberated."

"And you're liberated?"

"I love my wife, Russell. She loves me. We want to be together for the rest of our lives. We wanted a family. So we had one. We love our kids. We'll do anything we can to care for them, keep them safe, give them a good education. It would destroy us if anything ever happened to them. But we can't live in fear. The world may end tomorrow. Julie was pregnant with Angus when 9/11 happened, for God's sake. You have to make the life you want and live it today."

I chew on that silently.

"You know what?" says Fergus. "I am liberated. I'm free of torment. I'm committed to the path I've taken. When you're single, you can do whatever the fuck you want. When you're in a couple, you have to ask yourself, 'Is this person, is this situation really right for me?' You can still turn back. When you become a parent, that's it. You can't change it. There's no fucking around anymore. And I mean that in more ways than one."

"I don't get it. How can you feel liberated? You need money. You've got a whole family to feed. Aren't you trapped by that reality?"

"Hey, man," says Fergus, "reality is where it's at. You can only be trapped by unreality."

"What does that mean?"

"I like who I am. You may think I'm a poor, fat fuck. But I wear the same clothes to work that I wear on the weekend. My wife puts love notes in my sandwiches each morning. My kids wrap themselves around me when I get home," he says.

"I'm fat and happy, Russell. That's what I call reality. You don't need to feel sorry for me. You're the one who has to wear a corporate uniform. You're the one with the secret identity. Does anyone get to see the real Russell Wiley anymore?"

Two miso soups are set in front of us.

"*Arigato*," I say to the waitress, who doesn't reply.

Fergus slurps some soup from the bowl-like spoon. "And how are you and Sam doing? Everything OK with you two?"

"I don't know," I say. "What's OK?"

"OK is one level down from good."

"Did Julie mention something? What did Sam say to her?" I pick the wedge of lime from the rim of my glass, squeeze it, then drop it into my sparkling water.

"Not much."

I drink some water, wait him out.

"I guess she implied you guys were having problems. That you're on her case about money and stuff."

"Not everything's about money," I remind him.

While we work our way through a selection of eel, salmon, and tuna rolls, I bring Fergus up to date with the mishmash that constitutes my current state of mind. I feel uncomfortable sitting in a crowded restaurant and cataloguing my dissatisfactions. And talking about my sex life or lack of it doesn't come naturally to me. But Fergus is a good listener. He lets me ramble. He seems to understand what I'm saying even when I'm at my most disjointed. The questions I had this morning—about what exactly I should expect Sam to contribute to our marriage—are now wrapped in with the burning issues of management incompetence, budget cuts and the arrival of Judd Walker. "This new consultant is a complete jerk," I find myself saying. "But, of course, you'd think Henry had seen the Second Coming." I remind him of the "huge, secret project" Henry assigned to me when I joined the company. "It's exactly the same project he has this new guy doing. Only this time around the code name is D-SAW: don't say a word."

Once we've worked our way through our lunch specials, we order a few extra pieces of sushi. Fergus isn't the best when it comes to marriage counseling. But at least he's always sympathetic to stories of corporate stupidity and the way workers like me get exploited by management. Either that, or expensive raw fish increases his tolerance for my work-related whining.

I eye my tamago—the egg custard sushi I've saved till last. It's a glistening yellow slab, flecked with white.

"Have you ever cheated on Julie?" I ask him.

"Whoa," he says. "Where's that coming from? You know I haven't."

"Would you, if the chance arose?"

Fergus laughs. The waitress comes to refresh our green teas, and I tell her we'll take the check.

"First off, I resent the implication that a husky guy like me hasn't had his fair share of chances. Second, the question I always ask myself in those situations is 'What would J.C. do?'"

"Jesus Christ?"

"Jimmy Carter," he says. "The best president you and I have ever seen. Just like him, I know what it feels like to have lust in my heart. But that's as far as it goes."

I hand my corporate credit card to the waitress as she brings the check.

"Whoever she is," says Fergus, "don't do it. Sam deserves better than that."

I'm late back from the accepted two o'clock lunch hour cutoff. Just late enough that I'd be embarrassed if I were spotted by my boss. At the elevator bank, I bump into Cindy Lang. She's wearing a short, expensive-looking raincoat and carrying a recyclable cardboard tray from our cafeteria. A small gym bag is slung over her shoulder. Unlike the rest of us, she doesn't let her heavy workload distract her from these more important commitments.

"Hi," she says, without a trace of shame.

"Busy?" I say.

"Crazy," she says. "But we're teaming things. I'm trying to get a lot done before Roger deserts us."

I can't think of anything else to say to Cindy. She's a dead weight holding my department down. But her politicking makes her loom larger in the eyes of management. Even more so since she persuaded Henry to add her to the team that won our company's annual Gold Anvil Award last month. The judges didn't even notice that she inherited this success—the winning program was executed months before she got here. Henry even sat her at Jack's table at the awards luncheon. Now both Henry and Jack think she's a star performer. It's as if her predecessor, Alison Mead, who actually worked on the project and is now at home taking care of her newborn twins, never existed.

We ride the elevator in silence. Getting rid of Cindy won't be easy. It's something I'll need to think about.

I walk down the hallway to my office.

One of the mailroom guys is leaning over the wall of Angela's cubicle. I hear her laugh at something he says.

Barbara is busy uploading photos of various relatives onto Flickr.com. She doesn't even notice me as I pass by.

I close the door of my office. Lucky Cat tries to cheer me up, but the mess that surrounds me is starting to feel oppressive.

I check my email. Ellen, Henry's assistant, informs me the Livingston Kidd people have reconfirmed our partnership review meeting next week. Also, Judd's sent a meeting request: he wants me to commit to a ten o'clock brainstorming session tomorrow.

I don't see how I can put him off any longer. I click accept, then lay my head on the desk the way we used to do in grade school during nap time.

When I get home, the big brown lump of furniture Sam brought home on Monday is sitting like a huge turd beside the coffee table.

"I'm in the bedroom," she calls out, so I go right in without even taking off my jacket.

She's bending over, face down, palms flat on the floor, her ass presented toward me. She's been doing yoga for three weeks now, learning the positions from the *Yoga for Beginners* DVD that's playing on our bedroom TV. She wants to feel a minimal level of competence before performing in front of other people.

"What pose is that?" I ask. She's wearing the company T-shirt I brought back from the last sales meeting in Florida, tucked into a pair of running shorts. Her feet are bare. The nail polish on her toes is chipped in places.

"Salutation to the sun," she says.

"Can I take a picture?" I study her tilted head, the curve of her buttocks, her taut leg muscles.

"Shut up."

"Relax," I say. "Breathe."

"Leave me alone."

I hang my jacket and tie, then head to the living room. I sit on the turd-stool, sink into it, and reach for the remote. I flick through the TV channels, half-recognizing certain shows, celebrities and characters. People at work still talk about this stuff sometimes. But none of it grabs me. I guess you really have to watch every week to truly feel connected.

By the time Sam sticks her head around the door, I've turned off the TV and I'm skimming through one of her home design magazines.

"I'm taking a shower."

"Want me to join you?"

"No thanks."

"I could help you with those hard-to-reach places."

"Don't pester me tonight. I'm trying to de-stress. I have to shave my legs."

While Sam showers, I experiment with ways to incorporate the turd-stool into some stretching exercises and faux-yoga positions—arching my back over it, then lying on my stomach, arms and legs stretched out in midair. After a couple of minutes, I roll off and sit on the floor. I lean back against the stool and close my eyes, waiting for the sound of running water to come to an end.

CHAPTER ELEVEN

There's a screen in my office elevator displaying the date and time alongside the latest headlines. I try to ignore the breaking news alert that says, "RUSSELL WILEY ENTERS THIRTIETH DAY WITHOUT SEX."

The seconds tick by, confirming that this morning's subway delays have left me running five minutes late. Not bad for a normal day. But this is a day when Henry's called me into a meeting. Not a real meeting—an informal one.

The kind that gets scheduled late in the afternoon when Henry pokes his head around your office door—just far enough for you to see he already has his coat on—and says, "Come see me when you get in tomorrow. We should catch up."

And you say, "Sure thing, Henry."

And Henry pauses for an extra half second, just to let you know he's holding something back, and says, "Great. Lots to talk about."

And then he disappears, leaving you to wonder what exactly the meeting is about.

I step out of the elevator and turn right, dipping my body slightly to wave the ID card that dangles round my neck in front of the black security panel bolted to the wall. The panel's red light turns green, and I pull open the door. Christine Lynch, the human resources director who oversees our division, steps through.

"Thanks," she says and walks swiftly to the elevators. She stabs the call button with her index finger and steps back to wait, clutching a black leather folder at her side.

In my office I hang my jacket behind my door, drop my messenger bag by the side of my desk, and search among my papers and project folders till I find a reasonably fresh legal notepad. There are no pens in sight, so I hunt around in the assorted junk of my top-right desk drawer before finding a slightly mangled yellow pencil. There are teeth marks up and down its surface that gross me out—I don't think they're mine—and the stubby pink eraser that the pencil came with has long since disappeared, but it's the best I can do.

Seeing Christine Lynch on the floor is never a good sign. I rub Lucky's paw and make a nonspecific wish that things will be OK. Then I'm out the door.

I'm heading back to the elevators when my fingers remind my brain of something: lately, every time I've looked in my bag for a lost item of any kind, the only things I've found are pens.

I hurry back to the office, grab seventeen assorted ballpoints from my bag, spread them across my desk, and choose the most expensive-looking one. As he waves me off for a second time, something in Lucky's smile suggests he's trying to take credit for helping me find the pens.

I'm on twenty-six outside Henry's office by ten after nine, which is close enough to nine o'clock that I don't feel too bad, but Henry's door is closed. Ellen shakes her head in an almost imperceptible way that somehow communicates in the clearest possible fashion that NOW IS NOT A GOOD TIME TO GO IN THERE.

Then I hear a raised female voice and I know exactly why. Susan Trevor is inside, reacting to some new corporate injustice. When she's finished shouting, I hear an indistinct yet reassuring mumble that can only belong to Henry. After that, Susan starts shouting again.

"I'll call you when Henry's ready," Ellen says.

I decide to go back down to my office while I wait. It's the best way to avoid running into Judd. Stepping off the elevator, I head to the kitchen to grab a sugar-free hot chocolate. As I pass through the creative department, all is quiet. No one's around, but that doesn't surprise me. Except for Mondays, when Henry holds his nine a.m. meeting, Martin rarely shows up before nine thirty. His timekeeping sets the tone for the rest of his department. They usually drift in around nine twenty-five.

Ben's office is on the other side of Martin's. As I glance over, I see that both of Ben's event managers—Erika Fallon and Sally Yun—are standing in front of his desk, focusing intently on what Ben, out of my line of sight, is telling them. Sally unfolds her arms so she can raise a hand to her mouth. Erika Fallon keeps her hands on her hips. But sensing my eyes upon her, she turns to shoot me a blank, impersonal look.

I duck into the kitchen and hunt in the cupboards for the box that contains our single-serving packets of hot chocolate. I rip open a packet and pour the powder into a disposable cup. I press the hot water button on our vending machine, then hunt around for a spoon or a stirrer as the water spurts out. I find a discarded spoon in the sink, rinse it quickly, then shake it dry.

I head back to my office. The hot chocolate tastes good. I should drink it more often. I need to remember it's a year-round option—it's not just for winter anymore.

I keep talking to myself like this to keep any thoughts of Erika Fallon from creeping back into my head. Though I do wonder why she looked so angry. With Erika Fallon, there's always something new to obsess over. One day last week I got a jolt when I saw her walking half a block ahead of me down Forty-seventh Street. It wasn't till she turned onto Broadway that I realized it wasn't even her.

My phone is ringing when I get back to my office. Ellen says Henry can see me now.

Carrying my hot chocolate, I take a necessary detour on my way to the elevators. I need to retrieve the notepad and pen I left on the kitchen counter.

I'm moving quickly, but the sight of Erika Fallon standing by the water cooler makes me stop abruptly. She's wearing a mauve top and gray checked pants. She's already poured water into a waxed paper cup, but now she's just standing, staring at the wall.

I move past her in slow motion and pull my notepad toward me, trying to roll the pen into the crook of my thumb so I can grab both without putting down my mug of chocolate. The pen clatters to the floor and rolls toward the water cooler, coming to rest by the point of Erika Fallon's right shoe.

I put my mug down, and keeping my eyes on the floor, I bend and scoop in a single motion. By the time my fingers touch the pen, my body is already moving away from her mannequin-like presence. The whole action takes only a second, but in that time I can't help noticing the toe cleavage that's being revealed by Erika Fallon's dangerously fashionable shoes. Her toes look delicate and slightly mangled. Three of them are sporting small, skin-toned adhesive bandages.

She makes a sniffing sound as I grab my mug, but I don't look back. I'm almost through the door when she says, "I guess you know already."

I turn slowly. "Know what?"

"About Ben."

I look into Erika Fallon's luminous, watery eyes. Her lips are trembling.

"What about Ben?" I'm scared now. Maybe he's sick. Erika Fallon says something back to me. But I can't focus on that. I'm fighting an urge to hold her in my arms and comfort her.

"I'm sorry," I say. "I'm late for a meeting with Henry."

I turn and flee.

I walk into Henry's office clutching my pen and notepad in one hand and my hot chocolate in the other.

Henry looks up from behind his mahogany desk and smiles when he sees it's me.

"Russell," he says. "Come on in."

Henry always wears expensive white shirts with wide-spread collars and French cuffs. Today his tie is predominantly pink, a softer color than he usually prefers.

"Good morning, Henry."

"Sit down. Close the door."

I'm distracted by my still-fresh experience with Erika Fallon. I take two steps towards Henry's studded leather couch before realizing I should reverse his instructions and close the door first.

I sit, place my cup on one of the marble coasters on Henry's coffee table, and wait while Henry files a manila folder in his desk's cabinet drawer.

Just being in Henry's space helps shift my focus away from my water cooler encounter. I sip my hot chocolate, reflect on its attributes as a beverage, and try to concentrate on living in the moment. Henry's office is unlike any other in our department: its nine-windowed corner location offers southern views that overlook the bustling energy and illumination of Times Square, plus a western vista which, although partially obstructed, carries across the Hudson to the most sought-after apartment buildings in New Jersey. The décor is predominantly dark wood, creating a comfortable, lived-in feel. Henry researched and ordered all the pieces himself, shunning the generic furniture options that are recycled and mismatched throughout the rest of our offices and cubicles.

He locks the filing cabinet and tosses the key in his top desk drawer. He sighs, stands up, walks over to where I'm sitting, and eases into his usual spot—the matching leather armchair that sits catty-corner to the couch—so that our knees are almost touching.

"How's everything?" he says.

"Great," I say.

"You helping Judd settle in OK?"

"I sat down with him Monday end of day."

"Good meeting?"

"Highly productive."

"Judd's a great guy."

"Extraordinary."

"I think he's going to be a huge asset."

I flirt mentally with the word *Titanic* but change tack just in time.

"Major," I say.

"Excellent," says Henry. "And everything OK with you?"

"Everything's great." It's hardly true, but just being in Henry's office has already perked me up a little.

"Now..." Henry pauses to prepare me for a change of topic. "I guess you've heard about Ben."

"No, I haven't heard anything."

Henry pauses and bites his lip to simulate concern. "We let Ben go this morning," he says.

"Oh," I say, finally understanding why Erika Fallon was so upset.

"These things are never easy."

"No." I sip my hot chocolate and try to stay focused on the conversation.

"But he took it well, all things considered."

"When's he leaving?" I ask, resting the warm base of my cup in my left palm.

"We're trying to do this the right way," says Henry. "I've asked him to move out of his office today, just to make it easier for everyone."

I raise my cup slowly and take a longer gulp. I realize that when Henry says "easier for everyone," he means everyone other than the talented and hardworking Ben, who has just been fired.

"You know how these things work," says Henry. "This has nothing to do with Ben. He was doing a great job. We're giving him a spot on forty-one through the end of the year."

"That's good," I say. The forty-first floor is where many fired executives sit, making and receiving calls, pretending they still have a job while they search for another.

"We're going to help him out if we can. There's a strong possibility he'll find something in the lifestyle group."

"That's good," I say again. After he's established them as rejects, Henry doesn't mind when people from our division go to work for Yolanda and Barney.

"I've already heard it from Susan Trevor," says Henry. "Jesus. Don't repeat this, but she needs to know she's skating on thin ice."

"I won't say anything." When we're alone, bonding like this, Henry often makes negative remarks about someone in the company. Stuff that I never repeat outside his office. On the rare occasions he singles out someone on his own staff for criticism, it's usually Susan Trevor.

"I don't care what you tell her. Just make sure she knows I'm sick of her bad attitude. But don't say you heard it from me."

Henry sits back and squeezes the arms of his chair as if they were stress balls. In the brief silence, I look over to the large antique mirror that hangs on the north wall of his office. From where I'm sitting, I see a reflection of the building across the street and a sliver of sky. When Henry is sitting behind his desk, he only has to look up to see an image of himself with the lights of Times Square behind.

"Why is Ben leaving?" I ask, remembering to phrase the question in a way that sounds most empowering to Ben.

"It's a strategic decision," says Henry. "Jack wants our primary focus to be on generating revenue."

"OK," I say, even though this answer tells me nothing new. Every time our company starts firing people, we call it a strategic decision so the people who are let go don't take it personally. And every time Jack Tennant talks to our department, he tells us that our primary focus needs to be on generating revenue.

"Don't events drive revenue?" I ask.

"That may be true," says Henry. "But events are tactical. We're de-emphasizing them from a strategic standpoint. Which means we no longer need a dedicated events department."

"We're not doing events anymore?" I'm concerned about what will happen to Erika Fallon. And Sally too.

"I didn't say that."

"The salespeople love them."

"We'll still be doing events. We'll just be looking at them differently."

"From a tactical basis?"

"And from a cost-containment perspective. Which is where Ben let us down."

"The big show in Miami?"

"We're still doing Miami."

"And San Diego in February?"

"We're still doing San Diego."

"What about Hank Sullivan's holiday party?"

"We're not canceling Hank's party."

"How can we do it all without an events department?"

Henry leans forward and locks me in the beam of his almost-artificial blue eyes. He smiles without parting his lips and raises and lowers his eyebrows a couple of times. This is his way of signaling he's about to tell me the best part.

"How long have we worked together, Russell?" It's a question he asks me at least three times a month. Usually when he wants something.

"Four years, two months, five days."

"Really? That long?"

"Uh-huh."

"We're a good team, aren't we?"

"Oh yes." I add a series of small, rapid nods to emphasize the point.

"You trust me to make decisions that are good for you?"

"Sure," I say. But I stop with the nodding. I've seen enough movies to know you can never really trust the person who says trust me.

Henry sits back again. This time, instead of squeezing the arms of his chair, he runs his hands slowly along them, from front to back and back to front, savoring the feel of the well-worn leather. The sleeves of his shirt are so wrinkled they look ruffled, while his cuffs are starched white slabs, held in place by brown, cigar-like cufflinks wrapped in the middle with a thin gold band. "Do you remember the conversation we had about you taking on some additional responsibility?" he says.

"Not exactly," I say. I'm not sure what he's thinking, but I know this is not a good turn in the conversation. When Henry talks about "additional responsibility," it usually involves the dumping of a crippling workload on an unsuspecting schmuck like me.

"I remember these things," says Henry. "I even said it to Jack: 'We've got a good man in Russell Wiley,' I said. 'We need to treat him right. Make sure he's challenged. Keep him motivated.' Those were my exact words." Henry has a way of looking at you when he says something meaningful. It's an imitation of sincerity so convincing it can easily catch you off guard.

"I'm already extremely challenged," I say. "And motivated."

"This will be good for you," says Henry. "Your empire is expanding."

"My empire?"

"You'll have two extra people to manage. A lot more visibility with sales."

"Two more people? Are you saying what I think you're saying?"

"That's right. I'm putting you in charge of events and moving Erika and Sally into your group."

"Henry. I don't think that's a good idea."

"Why not?"

"I'm not sure I can handle it."

"Russell, I know you can handle it. Jack knows you can handle it. You just need to trust yourself a little more."

"Henry, it's not that I don't appreciate being considered for an opportunity like this. But I'm already swamped. Roger is going out on medical leave any day now. This will be a major distraction."

"Russell, I know it's extra work. And Jack and I really appreciate it."

"Henry, it's not just the work. There are other factors involved."

"Russell, just trust me on the money thing. You know how tight things are with the budget right now. Do a good job. We can get to the money later."

"Can I at least think about it? There may be another way we could do this."

"It's effective immediately. Check your email. The memo's already gone out."

Henry stands up. The meeting's over. He's holding out his hand. I give him mine. Despite the lack of negotiation, it's a done deal.

"Congratulations, Russell. This will be good for you." When Henry smiles, a web of tiny wrinkles appears under his eyes.

As we get to the door, I turn and am surprised to see how close to me he is standing. He places a hand on my shoulder and squeezes. It's a simple paternal gesture that feels awkward and overly familiar. My body tightens, but Henry's hand lingers for a couple of seconds before it drops back to his side.

"Russell," he says, "you're the best."

CHAPTER TWELVE

I'm in my office. Door closed. I don't want any interruptions. I've printed Henry's memo, and I'm reading it through for a second time.

Ben's out.

I shouldn't be surprised, even though I didn't see it coming. Ben's dismissal is one of those shocking, random things that happen all the time. I've gotten used to the ax falling on other people. I try not to get caught up in the sadness or guilt, focusing instead on the dread that such a thing could one day happen to me. This dread is what sustains me. Today it's mingling with a new kind of apprehension: a stomach-constricting anxiety that accompanies my new management challenge. I'm Erika Fallon's new boss. Somehow I have to integrate her into my team and treat her as if she were not just a regular employee, but also a normal human being.

I call Ben's number and leave him a message, tell him the usual stuff about how sorry I am, how I'll help him any way I can, how I'm here if he wants to talk. Then I pick up my pen and start doodling in the margins of Henry's memo. I start with a shape that looks like a penis, but I decide that it's really a nose. I add two round eyes that float above it and slightly parted lips below. I draw more faces—a series of squiggly, surprised-looking caricatures with alternately drooping or pointy noses, gaping mouths, big ears and wrinkled foreheads.

"Knock knock," says Susan Trevor. Without waiting for an answer, she steps into my office, closes the door behind her, and marches to my guest chair. I crumple the paper containing Henry's words and my scribbles and toss it casually into my wastebasket.

"So what do you think?" she says. "Has Henry finally lost it?"

I shrug but don't say anything. I'm not in the mood to get into it with Susan, nor to share any of Henry's comments about her attitude and the fragile ice on which she's skating.

"This is such bullshit," she says. "Everyone knows that Ben is the best events director in the company. So what does Henry do? He fires him. Meanwhile, I've got that fucking know-nothing Judd knocking on my door every five minutes expecting me to tell him everything I know. Do you know what I'm saying?"

I grunt sympathetically.

"This never would have happened five years ago," she says, and she's right. But what's her point? Five years ago we lived in a different world. Everything has changed. If Ben's abrupt firing signals a new way of doing business, so what? Maybe Henry's trying to prove that he's changed his DNA. That his corporate blood transfusion is complete. In the old days, Henry might have been the kind of boss who preferred to ease people out—telling them privately when he thought they should be looking for something new, eventually alerting colleagues to the employee's plans to move on, and only when absolutely necessary, if the targeted employee was seriously dragging his feet, putting an end to the situation by announcing a mutually agreed upon departure date at a respectable point in the future.

I could interrupt Susan to inform her that Old Henry is dead. New Henry has taken his place. New Henry is ruthless. He's not afraid to fire good people like Ben purely to send a signal. New Henry is confident. He thinks big, seizes opportunities and brings in new talent like Judd.

But that wouldn't be exactly true. Old Henry would have eliminated Ben in exactly the same way: cuts needed to be made. Ben wasn't Henry's kind of guy. And Jeanie certainly fed him enough bogus data to justify the decision.

I don't interrupt Susan because there's really no point in doing so. She's not looking for a dialogue, just a sympathetic ear. All she wants from me is an occasional grunt or supportive word to create the semblance of two-way communication. I indulge her for a few minutes because her presence and agitation is reassuringly familiar.

"Don't get me wrong, Russell," Susan is saying. "You may be great at what you do, but you know jack shit about events. You know what I'm saying?"

It occurs to me that everything Susan is saying is absolutely correct. She is a woman of extraordinary intelligence, vivacity, insight, experience, loyalty and commitment. Unfortunately for her, the company places absolutely no value on these attributes. It's too late for me to help Susan. But if I'm not careful, I will become her in another ten years.

I make a clucking sound. It's hard to disagree with Susan's conclusion that everything Henry's doing—hiring Judd, firing Ben, killing so many of Susan's projects—is utterly ridiculous. She gave Henry a piece of her mind this morning. But as usual, Henry didn't listen.

"Let them fire me next," she says. "I'll take the severance package. You know what I'm saying?"

I reach across the desk and put my hand on hers.

"Yes," I say. "I know exactly what you're saying." Her hand is round and warm, like a trapped mouse. Her wedding ring scratches against my fingers as she jerks it away.

"I've got to go," she says and hurries from my office.

In the aftermath of a director-level firing like Ben's, it's foolish of me to even attempt to get any actual work done. This is a time when my peers need to gossip and my existing staff needs to hear from me. Most of all, Ben's people, the new members of my team, need me to reach out and reassure them that we will find the right way to navigate this transition.

But my instinct is to hide. After Susan leaves, I tell Barbara to cancel my weekly staff meeting and reschedule my ten o'clock brainstorm with Judd. Livingston Kidd has to be my number one priority, I tell myself. Everything's at stake. Randy Baker's freaking out. Losing this business will ruin his year. He's clinging to the hope that he and Henry can still turn things around. Which means it's time for me to kick it into gear. I should have delivered a draft of the presentation to the art department yesterday. Now, there's no time to lose.

I take a deep breath, turn to my computer, open a new document and start tapping out an outline for the presentation.

This is when I do my best work. Things just flow. I'm in the zone.

"Do you need to get that?" says Martin. I haven't noticed him come in or the fact that my phone is ringing. I look at Martin, at the phone, at the screensaver that indicates at least five minutes of inactivity. The ringing stops. At some point, I realize, I veered out of the zone and started thinking about Erika Fallon. The image of her crushed and wounded toes had stayed in my mind. In my new role as her boss, I began to wonder how I might help relieve her suffering by removing her shoes and peeling off, one by one, the tiny round bandages. In homage to Ben, I imagined a tasteful, spa-like treatment room. As the scene began, Erika Fallon was seated in her pedicure chair, wearing a plush, $340 bathrobe. I gave a cameo role in my fantasy to Natalie Portman, looking especially fierce with her close-cropped, *V for Vendetta* haircut. Dressed in an esthetician's uniform, she stepped forward with the bowl of hot, scented water into which I gently guided Erika Fallon's feet. The hands on the clock sped up to indicate the passage of time, and when they slowed down again, Sienna Miller appeared to hand me a thick, fluffy spa towel with which to wrap Erika Fallon's rejuvenated feet. And then suddenly I was alone with Erika Fallon, squirting a healing massage lotion into my hands. "That tickles," she said, giggling and pulling away. But then she relaxed, leaned back in her loosely tied cotton robe, and stretched her foot toward me again. I grasped it more confidently and she murmured her appreciation as my fingers massaged her toes and my thumbs started kneading the soles of her feet. I was tracing my fingers around her ankles, moving slowly up her calves when Martin entered my office.

"So," he says, standing at my window, fiddling with the cords of my venetian blinds. "Ben is the latest sacrifice."

Martin swings the cord so it taps against the window, and says without turning to look at me, "What do you make of all this, Russell?"

"I don't know," I say. My hands feel sticky. "Things are weird around here lately."

"Do you know how old Ben is?" asks Martin.

"No," I say. I don't usually ask older guys at my level to reveal their age. It's the younger ones who concern me. "Forty-one, forty-two?"

"Ben's forty-five," he says meaningfully.

"Wow," I say. "He looks good for his age."

"I finally got the call from Barney Barnes," says Martin, picking up Lucky Cat and shaking him a little. "He wants to create a new position. Executive creative director in the lifestyle group. Overseeing new launches and development projects."

"Jeez. Are you going for it?"

"I don't know," says Martin. "You know the history. If I quit to go over there, there's no coming back."

"Fuck," I say. "What can I tell you?"

Martin moves toward my desk and slides into the chair still warmed by Susan's tirade.

"I know people are going to say I know shit about fashion. But that's not why they want me. They have enough twenty-five-year-olds already. Barney says he needs a grown-up, someone in their late-thirties who can train people and talk to him about strategy."

"Well, it sounds like a great opportunity."

"It's a big step up," says Martin.

"You've got to grab these things before you turn forty."

That one floats right by Martin.

"And who's to say I even have a future if I stick with what I'm doing?" he says. "Look what happened to Ben. You know as well as I do that Henry doesn't stand up for his people. He could throw any one of us to the wolves tomorrow."

"I can't argue with you on that."

"People are going to say I'm just a pussy-hound. But that's not what this is about."

"I'm with you," I say. "The lifestyle group's the only part of the company that's growing right now. It's the best career move you could make. You have to think about yourself and your future. Plus, all those hot young chicks in their tight little outfits definitely need someone who can provide some discipline."

"That's exactly the kind of shit I don't want."

"Why do you care? You'll be like the cool college professor. Just don't abuse your position when your students start developing crushes."

I'm bullshitting again. But Martin smiles at the prospect. He talks more about the great opportunity he's being offered. He needs to hear himself say it out loud a couple more times to feel fully comfortable with the idea. I'm already wondering what this news will mean for the rest of us. If Henry promotes from within—I'm sure Liz Cooke could do the job—he'll have one less person to fire.

As he leaves, I ask Martin to close the door behind him. Chitchat time is over. I have to shut out all distractions. Saving the Livingston Kidd business is going to be a near-impossible task. I need to get to work. But even as Martin is closing the door, Jeanie Tusa slips under his arm and rushes to my desk. Martin rolls his eyes at me, then closes the door anyway.

"Congratulations!" says Jeanie, smiling broadly to display her overly bleached teeth. She's wearing one of those clingy tops I thought were sold only in young people's stores. I suspect she's still high on endorphins from her early-morning workout with Luis, her Peruvian personal trainer.

"For what exactly?"

"Henry's put you in charge of events! Isn't that cool?"

"I'm not sure I'm there yet. I'm still kind of adjusting to the news about Ben."

"Well, I've got lots of ideas. I'd love to help."

Before I can object, Jeanie is sitting in my guest chair, throwing off ideas for extravagant parties she thinks we should be creating for customers. When Jeanie's not selling us out to Henry, she spends a large part of her workweek trying to ingratiate herself into the team. In this role, she wants us to perceive her as Jeanie, the creative, fun-loving accountant, not afraid to cut loose and challenge those nerdy, green-eye-shade stereotypes. It's obvious she's unaware what a lousy job she's doing with our department's finances if she thinks she has time on her hands for frivolous stuff like this.

Jeanie is saying the *Chronicle* needs to throw more celebrity-packed events, the kind that get covered on the local TV news and written up in the gossip columns. Her vivacious side has taken over. Sometimes I wish she had an inner number cruncher she could get back in touch with.

"Jeanie, these are great concepts. Ben would have loved to do events like these. I always thought it was a question of budget."

At the mention of Ben, Jeanie stops waving her arms in the air and parks her hands in her lap.

"Did you know that Ben was over budget at fourteen different events in the past twelve months?" says Jeanie. "That he gave approval for a dozen bottles of Cristal to be served after the bar had closed down at Hank's Christmas party last year?"

Suddenly, Jeanie's vindictiveness shines through a little too clearly. She knows Henry and Hank were both there to authorize the champagne.

I sit back, grasping the arms of my chair. "You know what, Jeanie?" I say. "I'm probably going to need your help with more than ideas. Do you think you could start auditing more of our events? I mean personally checking them out. Hank's party especially. And any others you could possibly spare the time for. I hate to impose. But unless you're there to keep an eye, it's going to be hard to know if we're spending our money wisely."

"I could do that," says Jeanie. "You know me. I'll do anything for the team." And she's smiling and bubbly and back in full nose-scrunching mode.

Before she leaves she turns at the door and stage-whispers, "Don't tell Henry. But I've put an extra twenty thousand in your T&E for next year."

Jeanie disappears, and I open my printer tray and grab a stack of paper. I can't take any more of these interruptions. I'm going to the cafeteria so I can get some work done.

CHAPTER THIRTEEN

The back corner table of our staff cafeteria is one of the first hiding places I discovered when I joined the company. Out of sight of the cashiers. Far away from the minimal midmorning traffic. I have about an hour before the early lunch crowd will start drifting in to break up my concentration.

Sometimes I work better by abandoning my computer and literally putting pen to paper. I scribble quickly, shuffling pages around, watching the presentation I'm writing take shape in front of me. The change of location has helped. I'm in a groove. My head's down. Things are finally starting to flow. And just when I think absolutely nothing can distract me, Erika Fallon giggles in my head. My pen hand freezes in midair. The giggling stops, but I don't know whether I should spend the next few seconds questioning my sanity or struggling to recapture my interrupted thought.

Then Erika Fallon says, "Don't worry. You'll get used to it." I look up. The voice isn't inside my head. Erika Fallon is sitting several tables away. With Judd.

Judd waves at me, and Erika Fallon turns and says, "Oh hi, Russell Wiley."

"Hi guys," I say with a casual nod. I begin retracing some of the words on the sheet of paper closest to me.

Erika Fallon and Judd are having coffee. Two single colleagues taking a break together. In a quiet corner of the cafeteria. Nothing wrong with that. There's no reason anyone should jump to any conclusions.

"So what do you do for fun?" I hear him ask.

She leans into his space and speaks softly in reply.

"Jeez!" says Judd. He laughs. "How did you get into *that*?"

I guess I should be happy that Erika Fallon has gotten over her upset about Ben so quickly. Resilience is a good character trait. But the interruption has ruined my flow. I wait a minute, then gather all my papers into a single pile, not caring if they get out of order. I need to get back upstairs and start typing this up.

In the elevator it occurs me that Ben's T&E budget must have been way more than the twenty thousand dollars extra Jeanie's given me. She acted like she was doing me a favor. In reality I was getting stiffed.

Back at my desk, I have forty-five new emails, five new voicemails, a note on my chair from Judd asking me to call him, and another from Randy Baker asking for an update on the Livingston Kidd proposal. Nothing about my day is going right. I grab my jacket and head out to the street. Through Times Square and onto Forty-second Street. Past Madame Tussaud's and through the doors of the AMC 25 Theater. I pick the one movie I've heard nothing about. A 12:10 show. The title gives nothing away. I sit in the partial darkness with a large Coke and popcorn combo, waiting for the lights to go down. It's a Chinese movie. About a fisherman. Who's about to set off on a long, lonely journey.

"Hey there, Wiley Coyote."

"What's up, Hot Mama?" I say, without looking up. For the past five minutes I've been trying to assemble my handwritten Livingston Kidd notes into some kind of order. The paper piles and other assorted detritus on my desk make it difficult to spread things out in a logical sequence. Either that, or maybe my ideas weren't as well structured as I first thought.

The only person who calls me Wiley Coyote is Liz Cooke, one of the two senior designers in Martin's group. She started calling me that a few years ago when we used to hang out a lot. Confiding in each other about our respective relationships. All platonic, of course. But with enough of an undercurrent to keep us both amused.

Something changed about three years ago, when I made director. We stopped collaborating directly on projects. Shortly after that she got engaged to her longtime boyfriend, Toby.

Immediately, we both forgot all the personal things she'd ever told me about Toby. The small things that drove her crazy. The big things that made her question their future together. We also forgot the comment she made the last time we were alone on adjacent barstools. She'd been silent for a while, looking thoughtfully at the hand with which she was holding her glass. "What I really need, Russell," she said, her wrist tilted toward me, "is a man like you."

Within a year of her marriage, Liz gave birth to a girl called Macy. She and Toby moved from the East Village to Pelham, closer to his parents. But Liz refuses to be defined by her new suburban/maternal existence. She's thinner now than before she got married, with a new tattoo visible above her ankle and another that can be glimpsed occasionally on her lower back. She favors spaghetti-strapped tank tops with no bra beneath.

"There's something I need to run by you," she says, all businesslike.

"And I need to talk to you," I say in a serious voice. "Could you do me a favor and give our intern Angela some instruction on our corporate dress code?"

"Can't we just leave the kid alone? Listen. Have you heard anything about Martin leaving?" She looks at me intently. Her latest hairdo is short and spiky. She's either oblivious to the way her ears stick out from her head like jug handles, or she's choosing to accentuate the feature. After all, we live in an age when the new beauty icons are celebrated for their carefully crafted lack of perfection.

"Martin? Jesus. I haven't got over the news about Ben yet."

"So you don't know anything about him going to work for Barney Barnes? Some big new job? Executive director title?" Liz crosses her arms in a way that lets her caress and pinch her wiry biceps.

"You know how this place is with rumors," I say. "Martin probably started that one himself. Can you really see him over there? He knows shit about fashion."

"Do me a favor," says Liz. "If he is leaving, I want your support when I go for the job."

"You want it? I'm sure it'd be yours in a second."

Liz leans across the desk and says, "I just want to make sure that bitch Rachel doesn't get it."

I'm not the only one who hires people who piss off their coworkers. Nine months ago, Martin hired Rachel Felsenfeld after reading a Christopher Finchley article I'd given him on the topic of creative anarchy. Of course, he misunderstood some of the writer's key points. Martin thought Rachel was a hot-shit designer. He liked the fact that she had attitude. But instead of creative anarchy, she's delivered interpersonal disruption. Worse, her egotism and rudeness aren't matched by her work, which is too safe and conventional—too newspapery-looking at a time when we need to make advertisers look beyond the fact that we're an old-fashioned, ink-on-paper product. Rachel doesn't realize that twentysomething media planners couldn't care less about newspapers. They're being bombarded with glitzy multiplatform proposals from media companies far bigger than ours. We need to show them new ways to look at the *Chronicle*—and visualize our message with a style that's actually relevant to them.

"Look," I say. "Here's an article you may want to read. It's about creative anarchy. I hear the guy who wrote it is pretty good. And don't get too bent out of shape. Let's wait and see if this Martin thing actually happens before we worry about taking Rachel down."

After Liz leaves, I take my iPod out of my bag, put in my earbuds, and sit staring with unfocused eyes at the work spread across my desk.

This hasn't been a good day. Ben's been fired. That Chinese fisherman's son died of cancer. And I'm falling behind in my two most urgent projects.

On days like this, I'd like to think that people's basic goodness would shine through. We should be mourning Ben's departure. We should be bonding as a team. We should be pulling together. But it seems that everyone around me is thinking first and only about themselves. Meanwhile, Jarvis Cocker's not helping. He's singing in my ears that cunts are still running the world.

I turn off the music and lay my iPod down. I think about myself. I think about Sam. I think about Sam and me having sex. Then I tell myself to stop thinking about sex. Thinking about sex in the office is never a good thing.

I flick through an old Livingston Kidd presentation and apply sticky notes to some pages I may want to adapt for my new version. This is better. One project at a time. Stay focused.

I head down the hall to make some photocopies. I'm thinking only about work. No thoughts of sex will be allowed to enter my mind while I'm in the office ever again.

I walk into our copy room and find a young Asian woman kneeling on the floor.

It's Kiko. She's crouched by the side of the open copier, trying to remove a paper jam without touching any of the CAUTION, HOT SURFACE stickers inside the machine.

"So sorry," she says, gazing up at me with a sweet, smooth face and a look of fear and excitement in her eyes. She's wearing a red mesh tank over a sleeveless pink T. Her outfit is completed by a tartan miniskirt, tall white socks and black shoes with wedge-like heels. I'm not sure if this look is inspired by the street fashions of the East Village or Shinjuku, but the whole effect is doll-like, cartoonish.

"Not a problem," I tell her.

She turns back to the machine and fiddles with the large black roller inside. I study the Japanese brand name that appears in raised lettering on the side of the copier. I hear paper tearing.

"Let me help," I say.

Kiko stands up and backs away.

"So sorry," she says again, this time bowing slightly. Her skinny arms and legs look pliable, seemingly muscle-free. Kiko is here on a work visa arranged through our international department. She wants to find out if she's suited for a career in graphic design. She's here because her father is one of our Tokyo office's largest clients.

Despite her shy persona, rumor is that Kiko has been partying hard since she got to New York while making hundreds of new friends on MySpace. Her dad rented her a furnished apartment in a midtown doorman building, and apparently she likes to invite guys up to see more than the view.

"Shit," I say as my hand touches the hot metal inside the copier. I suck my finger, perform a visual check to make sure the skin's still there, then make a halfhearted attempt to clear the jam for a minute more. I make sure not to look at the band of skin between the top of Kiko's socks and the hem of her miniskirt, bouncing my glance off the wall as I stand up.

"You better try on the other side," I tell her. "I'll ask Barbara to put in a service call."

I hurry back to my desk. Sometimes I wish I kept a flask of whiskey in the bottom desk drawer. But that's not the solution to my problem. My problem is waiting for me at home. And it's time for me to do something about it.

I already have my bag on my shoulder when Judd appears. He thinks we have a four o'clock meeting. Barbara confirmed it, he says. I look on my calendar. There's nothing there.

I'm sorry, I tell him. I don't have time. We'll have to reschedule. I'm dealing with a crisis situation. An urgent project that truly cannot wait.

CHAPTER FOURTEEN

I cut out of the office at 4:05. My plan is to beat the rush, get a seat on the F train for the ride home, and arrive at the apartment ahead of Sam. I still have one foolproof seduction routine I reserve only for true crises. I call it the Emergency Cleaning Method. It's a technique that demands obsessive attention to humdrum household chores, whether they need doing or not. Because only when I lavish attention on grease, mildew and shower scum does Sam return the favor and lavish attention on me.

I haven't left the office this early in a while, but as soon as I approach the subway station I realize I am part of a pre-rush-hour frenzy every bit as crazed as the charge of the five o'clock brigade. As the doors close, I jam myself between an exceptionally tall woman in a floral dress and a Chinese man with several bags containing small boxes of toys that dig into my legs. I am still twisting myself to limit the bruising to my calves when the train stops in a tunnel and the lights go out.

Someone says, "Move your hand," and another passenger says, "Sorry." The lights come back on and the conductor announces we will be delayed due to a police action at Thirty-fourth Street. Everyone tries to remain polite. With my arms pinned to my side, I have plenty of time to study the prominent Adam's apple of the increasingly masculine-seeming, big-handed woman at my side.

When Sam gets home from Artyfacts, I'm on my hands and knees scrubbing the kitchen floor. I've changed into a T-shirt and khaki shorts. The oven is preheating to 350 degrees.

"Hi," she says to my ass.

"Hi," I say, not turning round.

"You're home early," she says.

"Do we have any more fabric softener?" I ask. "I have to run down to the laundry room to put stuff in the dryer once I've finished this floor."

"What are these?" she says from the living room. I bought a cheap bouquet from the Korean deli where I usually shop, which is across the street from the one Sam favors.

"I thought they'd brighten the place up," I say.

"They're lovely," she says. "Look in the cupboard next to the cupboard under the sink."

I take my bucket of dirty water to pour down the toilet. I take off my rubber gloves, wipe my brow with the back of my forearm, and wash my hands.

"Kiss," says Sam.

"Stop it," I say and rush back to the kitchen.

I put my tuna casserole in the oven, find the fabric softener, throw it into our laundry basket, and head down to the laundry room. When I get back upstairs, Sam is on the couch, flicking through the pages of a home decorating magazine. I get out the vacuum cleaner.

"Something smells good," she says.

"Lift your legs," I say as I zip around the area rug.

"Sit with me," she says when I put the vacuum away.

"Hush," I say. I go to the kitchen to stir my casserole, mix the breadcrumbs into some margarine, and sprinkle them on top. I put the casserole back in the oven, set the timer, then rush into the bathroom to scrub the toilet.

Ten minutes later I'm uncorking some wine, lighting a candle, and inviting Sam to join me at the small glass-topped café table in the corner of the kitchen. It's a table Sam bought from Shila six months ago in exchange for three weeks' salary.

"So how was your day?" I ask. Now that my housework is complete, I'm able to focus on my wife.

Sam tells me about a large new consignment Shila has acquired following the death of an elderly woman in the neighborhood. She's wearing a purple lipstick I haven't noticed before.

"You wouldn't believe the treasures she had," says Sam. There have been times lately when Sam's nose and chin have been set so hard they seemed pointed. But at moments like this, when she's relaxed and smiling, her features seem much softer. "She'd lived in that house for, like, sixty years."

Sam is wearing a dark blue V-necked top that exposes the smooth triangle of skin above her cleavage and a thin necklace adorned with antique black glass beads. I focus on the principles of the attentive listening seminar I attended four months ago. I nod continually and say "uh-huh" or "go on" during pauses in Sam's anecdotes. At the end of each story, I paraphrase it back to her to show I'm really taking it in.

"Wow. So she lived there sixty years. You guys must have a lot of stuff to sort through."

Sam has seventeen exquisite freckles on her nose and cheeks. She explains that the surviving family members take the really good stuff first—the jewelry, the silver, all the heirlooms they want to keep—and then they sell the rest off as a job lot.

"Wow. So after the family takes all the obviously valuable stuff, you get what's left."

Sam explains that a lot of the leftover stuff, which might have been considered junk just a few years ago, can be fixed up, polished and re-sold for quite a decent markup, especially to young people just buying an apartment or house for the first time. Sam thinks her seventeen facial freckles are the only ones she has. In a short while, I plan to inspect her naked body for verification.

"Wow. That's really fascinating," I say. "I guess it's cheaper than buying new stuff and has a little bit more personality too?"

Sam tells me I'm exactly right. Of course, you can buy some new things cheap, but they are all mass-produced and lack the character of an older piece that has sat in someone's house for a few decades.

"This is so interesting," I say, pouring a little more wine. I'd love to point out the miracle that allows her to have just enough skin to cover her entire body. Instead I say, "What kind of customers did you have today?"

She tells me about her customers, and I repeat back key snippets.

"So you thought she was trying to steal the hat until you remembered she bought it from you two weeks ago? That's hilarious!"

I insist on doing the dishes. Sam hugs me from behind, presses her body against me.

"Thanks for a great meal," she says. She leans her cheek against my back. I'm scrubbing at the casserole dish with a wire pad.

"No biggie," I say.

She touches me through my shorts.

"I'm not so sure about that," she says.

"You're distracting me," I say.

"Why not leave the rest?"

I take off my rubber gloves, and she leads me by the hand to our bedroom. I pad along after her, trying not to display any signs of eagerness.

Sam pulls the curtains. She usually prefers darkness. But she doesn't complain as I switch on the light.

She stands me at the foot of the bed, unbuttons and unzips my shorts. I'm already hard. I raise my arms as she pulls my T-shirt over my head. I'm conscious of the smell of dried sweat, but she pretends not to notice. I let my arms fall back to my side.

She pulls down my shorts and underwear. I lift my feet one by one as she takes them off. I'm breathing heavily through my nose. My heart is beating fast.

Sam kisses the insides of my thighs, nuzzles my balls, licks the shaft of my cock. This is highly unexpected. Not that I'm keeping count, but Sam hasn't given me a blowjob this calendar year. Tonight, however, she seems intent on performing the act. I can't let that happen. If she puts me in her mouth, this party might be over before it's even started.

Plus, there's something else I need to do.

I reach down and pull her up from under her arms. I kiss her hard on the mouth, then pull away.

"I have to pee," I say.

"Hurry," she says.

Back in the bedroom, Sam is under the covers. She's turned off the overhead light and switched on the vintage basket-shade lamp on her side of the bed. Her clothes are in a pile on the floor. I've missed watching her undress, but I pretend I don't mind. I pull back the comforter and look at her naked body. She curls herself on the bed and raises her eyebrows mischievously. The lamplight gives her skin a warm glow.

I jump onto the bed and press my body against her. I run my hand up her leg as I bend my head to suck at her nipple. She parts her thighs, and I feel her wetness. I rub my fingers against her in a circular motion. She raises her hips to respond to my touch. I watch myself slide one, then two fingers inside her.

She pulls my face to hers and kisses me with parted lips, her tongue plunging—soft, warm, forceful—into my mouth.

I climb on top, and she guides me inside her. I raise myself up on my arms. Like a mountaineer who has reached a new summit, I concentrate on savoring every aspect of the view. I move slowly at first. Sam looks at me intently. Her small breasts are flat against her ribcage. She's pushing herself against me, matching my undulating motion.

Then we're kissing again, this time more urgently. I'm thrusting deeper and harder, trying to pace myself, listening for the change in breathing that signals her approaching orgasm. Suddenly she wraps her legs around me, a move almost calculated to push me over the edge. I stop moving.

"Let's go slow a minute," I say.

"God, I was so close."

Sam unwraps her legs and we lie still a while. I curse myself inwardly. I know from experience that it will be difficult for Sam to build back to her crescendo if she thinks I'm going to come any second.

I close my eyes, start reciting to myself as much of Marc Antony's speech to the Romans as I can remember. When I start rocking against her, Sam doesn't respond immediately. I take my time. I want to make this last. Gradually my rhythm grows less tentative. I feel her moving with me again. I kiss her neck, caress the side of her legs, her torso.

Suddenly, it seems, we have regained our connection. We're moving together in a way that's intuitive, animalistic, spiritual, electrifying.

I feel powerful, completely in control. I'm waiting for her now. Ready to let myself go as soon as her orgasm erupts through her body. This is the way it should always be, I tell myself.

Sam's breathing shortens, and I can sense her starting to come. I thrust harder, faster, finally letting myself go, pulsing fiercely inside her. My orgasm lasts longer than usual. I feel my body sag, but I continue moving, slower now, enjoying the afterglow.

I open my eyes and smile down at Sam, who is staring at the wall.

"Jesus," she says. "Couldn't you have held it just a few seconds longer?"

"What? You didn't come? I thought you were coming."

"This happens every time."

"No it doesn't."

"Yes it does."

"Let's keep going. I can go again."

We stare at each other for a few seconds while my penis shrinks inside her.

"Forget it," she says. "Just get off me."

CHAPTER FIFTEEN

Thursday is a new day. I wake refreshed, ready to drink heartily from the half-full glass of life. All my socks and underwear are freshly laundered. The apartment is clean. And the history books will show I had sex with my wife last night. Maybe it wasn't pretty. But as with any finished project, I should honor its completion. I'm determined to head out into the world with a new spring in my step. A renewed sense of purpose. An unwavering confidence in my decision-making abilities.

"Is this tie OK with this shirt?" I ask, holding the curtain back, standing in a shaft of morning light.

Sam props her head on her hand and squints at me. "I prefer the other one."

"I'm already late."

"Then why did you ask?"

"I guess I was just seeking some kind of validation. I wanted to make sure I don't look like a total dweeb."

Sam yawns, stretches, snakes a bare leg out from under the comforter. "Do you even need a tie anyway?" she asks.

"I just want to look good. I have to leave now."

"So why ask for my advice if you don't want to take it?"

"When I say now I really mean five minutes ago."

"So you're going to go like that?"

"That was my plan. Pending your approval."

"Go then."

"Is it that bad?"

"No. It's OK, I guess."

"What's the matter? Is the tie too much?"

"No. The tie's OK."

"I need to change my shirt?"

"No. The shirt's fine."

"So what's the matter?"

"I don't like the belt."

"What are you grinning at?" I say to Lucky as I push my office door shut and hang my jacket behind it. He smiles but says nothing. I smile back. "Yeah, I guess it does take one lucky cat to know another," I say. "What's that? Thanks. I like this tie too. And the belt's cool, right?"

I grip his hard plastic paw, trying to draw an extra burst of superpower energy to get me through the day ahead.

"Strength," I say, as my wish for the day.

I sit at my desk with only one thought in mind: I need to get the Livingston Kidd proposal in to the art department. I can't avoid it any longer.

But first, I call Meg Wilson and ask her to stop by. After steering clear of everybody yesterday, I have to catch up with people and find out what's been going on without me. Meg is my most senior manager. She's been at the company fourteen years. She knows where the bodies are buried and how to get things done. She serves as my unofficial deputy, occasional career coach and most reliable bullshit detector.

"So how's the mood out there?" I ask.

"You really want to know?"

"Maybe."

"Well, everyone's sad about Ben, yada yada. And rumors are flying that he's only the first. That we're going to have another round of layoffs. Erika and Sally seem pretty shaken up. But the boys are excited to have the new girls on the team. Roger is counting the days till his extreme makeover. He's got a thing for Sally, it seems."

"Really? That's interesting."

"Apparently, she reminds him of Drew Barrymore."

"Uncanny. Must be the black hair and the fact that she's Chinese."

Meg shakes her head. She's one of the few women at the company who does nothing to conceal the gray in her hair. "Did you know this was coming?"

"I was as surprised as anyone. If Henry had asked me, I would have told him Ben was irreplaceable."

"That's for sure. As long as you know what you're getting yourself into. Events are a ton of work."

"That's the other thing," I say. I look away from Meg, gazing thoughtfully toward the window. Lucky smiles his assent toward my jacket on the door. "I'm so overwhelmed with other stuff, I was thinking of having Erika Fallon report in to you."

"No thanks."

"Come on. It makes perfect sense. You and Kelly have more experience with events than anyone."

"Kelly and I already have more work than we can handle. I used to have two people reporting to me, remember?"

Meg is resisting. But I'm not ready to give up. What would Henry do? I ask myself. And then the words start flowing.

"I was talking to Henry about this yesterday. I told him you were the best person I've got. That we needed to keep you challenged. To make sure you stay motivated. How perfect would this be? It's a chance to expand your empire. You'll have two extra people to manage. A lot more visibility with sales."

"Why would I want any more visibility with sales?"

"Events are fun," I say. "Aren't they?"

"Let me think about it," says Meg. "I'm assuming there's a title to go with it. And of course more money."

"You know how tough things are with the budget right now," I say. "And Henry can be funny about titles. Let's meet with Erika and Sally first. See how things shape up. We can keep it informal. I'll have Barbara schedule a meeting before lunch."

"Don't worry," says Meg. "I'll set it up."

When Randy Baker shows up at my office, the pages of my Livingston Kidd proposal are once again spread around my desk, in no particular order. I've been putting Randy off for days. He's expecting me to place in his hands a finished proposal, clearly articulated and beautifully designed, filled with never-before-seen-but-already-proven-successful ideas that will convince his client to keep spending with the *Chronicle*. But I'm not quite there yet. And today I'm having trouble concentrating.

I look up, all set to apologize and play for more time. But something in his expression makes me hold my tongue.

"Hey, Russell," he says. "Just got a call from the assistant over at Livingston. Meeting's canceled. They're only interested in big, integrated programs right now. They want to hear what Time Warner and Viacom can put on the table before they start talking to individual titles."

"Typical," I say. "We'll be fighting for scraps again."

"Tell me about it. They wouldn't even commit to a new date. We probably won't hear back for two or three more weeks."

"Shit, I wish I'd known sooner. I pushed everything else to one side for this."

"Sorry, Russell. I know you've been working flat out."

"Don't worry. Not your fault. I've got plenty of other stuff I can get to."

For once, I'm grateful for the way our clients choose to jerk us around.

Once Randy leaves, I close my door and do the robotic version of my funny little dance.

I walk down to the conference room at a minute past eleven. Erika and Sally are already inside. I sit opposite Erika. She's wearing a tight-fitting green turtleneck with ruffles at the collar. It's the kind of thing she might have worn in high school to conceal a hickey. I realize how much I would have hated a guy like Judd 2.0 in high school. Meg arrives, sits next to me.

I look over at Sally, who seems to be holding back a mischievous Drew Barrymore–like smile. Somewhere along the way, I have a vague recollection that Drew dyed her hair black for a while.

Meg coughs, and I turn to her. She is looking at me with wide, expectant eyes.

"Let's get started," I say. "I've asked Meg to join us so we could all, um…catch up, plan our next steps." I realize I'm staring at the conference table. I raise my head, glance at Sally, then fix Erika with the self-assured yet humble look of leadership that befits my new role as her boss.

"First, I want to acknowledge that…" I sigh heavily. "Ben's gone. It's upsetting for all of us. It's not going to be the same without him." Erika and Sally nod but don't speak. I realize there's another side effect of Ben's departure: I will no longer be invited to participate in inappropriate discussions of Erika's love life.

"But we can't let Ben's departure throw us off course. We've got a lot we still need to accomplish." I adjust the knot of my Italian silk tie and smile knowingly. All morning long I've been reminding myself that I'm a vigorous married man who still gets laid on school nights by his eager wife.

Before I lose my vigor, I explain that I've asked Meg to work directly with the two of them over the next few months to ensure we keep everything—from budgets to planning to execution—on track. "Meg will be your contact," I say. "To make sure you get all the approvals you need from senior management and any help you need from the marketing and creative departments."

"Great," says Erika. "I brought the project list you asked for." She hands us each a copy. I study the list.

"Excellent," I say. "Very organized."

I sit back and let Meg take charge. She asks Erika to run through the status of each project, discuss all the issues of timing and expenses and travel and invitations and signage and product samples and goody bags. Details are noted. Procedures are clarified.

I lose track of some of the finer points, but I'm impressed with the professionalism that radiates from Erika, the inexplicable fun that Sally seems to find in every aspect of her job, and the competence with which Meg steers the meeting.

"You'll let me know," I say as the meeting winds down, "if you need me to attend any of the major out-of-town events."

"Sure thing," says Sally.

I look at the project list again. "What's next? DC? Wasn't Ben planning on being there? Do you need me?"

Erika Fallon looks at the list and thinks a second. "I think we've got that one covered. It might be good if you came down to Miami for the conference we're sponsoring next month."

"OK," I say. "If anything changes, let me know."

"That was great," I say as Meg and I walk back down the hall together. "I knew you could handle it."

"Just remember, you owe me," says Meg. "Big time."

Judd is loitering outside my office when I get back, clutching a large, blue, three-ring binder.

"Have a minute?" he asks. "I know you're busy, but it's been tough to get on your calendar."

I pause in my doorway, look at my watch, and count two elephants in my head.

"It'll have to be quick. I've got to get a Livingston Kidd proposal over to the art department. Liz Cooke is waiting for me. We have to get something to Randy Baker by end of day." This isn't exactly true anymore. But I'm guessing Judd doesn't know that.

"I'll be quick." He follows me into my office. Beneath the transparent plastic pocket on his binder's spine he has inserted a small typed card that reads:

D-SAW
Confidential

I realize immediately that Judd has mastered the two basic requirements of being a consultant: 1) Packaging existing data into a new physical format designed to impress management; and 2) Demonstrating the lost art of printing something out on a small piece of card.

Judd opens the binder. He's arranged it into four sections, each with a typed label on the tab. I read the tabs quickly:

Focus 1
Focus 2
WICTY Presentation
YANA

"These are the key documents from the last go-round," he says. He turns the binder toward me and flips it open at the WICTY Presentation tab. "I think we can use them to take away some key learnings to inform our process this time."

"OK. What exactly did we learn back then?" I ask. I flick through the pages quickly, moving toward the tab marked YANA. I shouldn't let it bug me that Judd's already seen Henry's mystery file. I'm just curious to see what it contains.

When I get to the end of my old WICTY presentation, I turn the blue divider page as any casual reader would, revealing the document beneath.

"Tell me what you think of this," says Judd, resting his hand flat on the page before I have a chance to start reading. "I'm going to propose we take the updated prototype out to a whole new series of focus groups. A lot has changed in the last four years. I think we could get some great new perspectives."

"Sounds like a plan."

"Henry thought so. He said you could help with the presentation once the transcripts come in."

"Just tell me what you need. I'll make sure it gets done."

"Thanks, Russell." He snaps the binder shut and hands it to me. "I've only made three copies of this binder. One for you. One for me. One for Henry."

"OK. I'll guard it with my life."

Judd gets up, walks to the door, and turns. "Hey, fancy grabbing a drink after work tonight?"

"Sounds great," I say with enthusiasm as I struggle to invent a plausible excuse.

"Five thirty good?"

"Oh shoot. I'll have to take a rain check. Sam and I have yoga tonight." I stretch out my arms and swivel slightly in my seat. "Have you tried it? It's a great workout and really helps your flexibility."

Judd hesitates a moment. Maybe it's just the idea of me doing yoga. But I realize he knows nothing personal about me—and that the name "Sam" could be taken either way. I'm not about to help him out on that one.

"That's cool," he says. "Some other time."

"What about next week?" I ask. "I'm here all week. How does Thursday sound?"

"That's good," he says. "Oh shit. I'm heading to DC next Thursday. Meeting with a research company."

"No problem," I say. "We'll figure something out."

I turn my attention to the mysteries of the YANA file.

CHAPTER SIXTEEN

It's a warm October evening. Sam and I are taking a walk around the neighborhood. Other couples are out too, strolling arm in arm. Families are gathering out on their stoops. The restaurants on Seventh Avenue are filling up.

My hands are in my pockets. Sam is holding a brown box with metal-edged corners—an empty musical instrument case she found discarded on Union Street. Our conversation stalled a block or two after she picked it up. We left off somewhere on the road from Garbage Picking to the Value of Objects to the Difference Between Hobbies and Real Jobs without quite getting our heads around the question Why Is It When I Say the Word Passion You Immediately Want to Talk About Sex?

Waiting for the light on the corner of Ninth Street, I study the profile of her face, trying to detect evidence of those gradual changes that are impossible to spot while they're actually happening.

"All couples fight about sex and money," she says at last.

"How do you know?"

"My friends tell me. I read magazines."

"So you tell your friends we fight about sex and money?"

"Only the sex. The money stuff bores them."

"It must be a brief conversation then."

"Ha ha. Tell me about it."

"I didn't mean it that way."

We're quiet again. I sense the box she's carrying is getting heavy in her arms, but she doesn't ask me to help and I don't offer.

Sam and I met in a pub in London called the Goose and Gherkin. It was two years after my dad died. I'd convinced my mom to fund a semester abroad. I told her all kinds of academic and cultural reasons why it made sense. But really I was on a mission to meet English girls. I was immediately drawn to Sam—her style, her bravado, and of course, her accent.

Her dark brown hair was short and spiky.

She wore a faded "The Queen Is Dead" T-shirt, camouflage pants and black Doc Martens.

The pub was loud, and a lot of people were jabbering. But I could feel we had an instant connection.

"That's mega," she said when I told her it was my first night in town, that it had taken me most of the previous day and night to fly from Columbus, Ohio, via Chicago to get here.

"Cheers," she said when I bought her a drink.

"A small pickled cucumber," she said when I asked her what a gherkin was anyway.

"Brilliant," she said when I told her the group I'd come with were heading to a nightclub in Camden Town. When we left the club at three in the morning, we kissed and parted in separate cabs. Back at my dorm, alcohol and jet lag kicked in. I slept for ten hours. When I woke, I called the number Sam had given me. She answered on the second ring, inviting me to join her for a "fry up" at her favorite café and for a tour of Portobello Road Market.

"Trust me," she said, ordering us each a plateful of fried eggs, fried sausages, fried bacon, fried tomatoes and fried bread. "This is how we do it here."

"I think I'm going to barf."

"You'll be fine. Just bite, chew, swallow, and wash it down with a mouthful of tea."

We walked from stall to stall as the grease congealed in my stomach. Sam was trying on a secondhand coat, a nubby, red woolen item that hung shapelessly on her, when I asked her what part of England she was from.

She spun around like a red cone. "I ain't from England, mate," she said in her best Cockney accent. "I grew up in Massachusetts. So, what do you think? Is this worth seventy-five quid?"

I converted the amount to dollars and said, "You could get a new one for that."

She bought it anyway, haggling with the girl who was working at the stall until she got her down to sixty pounds.

"It would have been a bargain at half the price," she said as we walked away.

She hadn't meant to fool me with the accent, she said. She couldn't help it. It was medically proven that some people pick up accents quickly. In reality she was an American student like me, in London for the full year. She'd arrived a semester earlier and was sharing a third-floor flat in a house in Bayswater with two fellow students, Shelley and Jennifer. When we stopped by to drop off her new purchase, I was expecting to meet them. But even though the devastating chaos of their existence was immediately visible, the place was quiet.

"Well, my good chap," she said, leaning against the just-closed front door. "It just so happens they're in Paris till Monday. So we have the run of the entire estate."

Sam dropped the blue-and-white striped plastic bag containing her new red coat on the floor. Then she hung my jacket on a crowded coatrack and wrapped her tan raincoat around it.

She walked through the living room, picked up a discarded bra from the back of an armchair, and tossed it onto a hill of clothes inside one of the bedrooms. She closed that door and headed into the kitchen.

"In England, you will quickly discover one thing," she said, turning on the cold tap and letting it run for a few seconds. "It's that no important decisions should ever be made without first putting the kettle on."

She filled the kettle, took a match from a large box with a picture of a ship on it, and lit one of the gas rings on her stove. As the water was heating, she opened a cupboard and placed two mugs on the counter. One of them had a picture of a red London bus on the side. She pulled two spoons from a drawer and let them clatter inside the mugs. She was wearing a man's white shirt, a pleated gray skirt, white ankle socks and chunky black shoes—a slightly ridiculous, quasi-schoolgirl look that somehow seemed the height of fashion among the crowds around Portobello Road.

She opened the fridge, studied the contents, then closed it again without taking anything out.

"Well, there's no milk, but you still have one choice you need to make." She shuffled among the tins and cartons on the counter. She turned to me, gesturing first with a jar of Nescafé in one hand and then with a box of Typhoo tea bags in the other. "Coffee, tea…or me?"

I pretended to act cool, as if seriously considering the different options. Sam's sleeves were rolled halfway up her forearms. The spiky hair from the previous night had been reconfigured into two ponytails, held together with rubber bands that stuck out from the side of her head. She was wearing black eyeliner and a dark red lipstick. It was the sexiest look I had ever seen.

I turned off the gas and lifted her onto the kitchen counter, kissing her hard as she wrapped her legs around me.

"Do you want me to take that?" I ask her now as we turn onto Eighth Avenue, still six blocks from home.

"I thought you said it was garbage."

"I said it was junk," I tell her. "But I meant it in the nicest possible way."

She hands me the wooden box.

"Did I tell you Greg's coming to town next week?" she says a minute later.

"Greg?"

"Greg Witchel. You've seen his picture."

I've seen several. Greg was Sam's boyfriend for two years in high school. Her first big love. His image appears in many of the family photos displayed on the walls of Sam's parents' house. A shaggy mop of blond hair, a goofy grin and a body built for the MTV beach house.

"He's coming for some big direct marketing conference," she says. "His company's paying for two nights in a hotel."

"That's nice."

"After that, I told him he could crash with us for a night."

"Oh, really."

"You have a problem with that?"

"Me?"

"Don't give me that look," she says. "He wanted to get together. What's your problem? He wants to meet you. I haven't seen him for twenty years."

"No problem," I say. "I always love to meet your friends."

On Friday morning, I decide it's important for me to make up the weekly staff meeting I canceled when Ben got fired on Wednesday.

I normally have the meeting at eleven thirty on Wednesdays. Eleven thirty's a good time for it. It motivates everyone to get through the topics we're discussing within an hour. That way we can all take a full ninety minutes for lunch. And Wednesday's usually a good day for it. It avoids conflicts with other weekly meetings. Plus, because it's in the middle of the week, it gives us time to correct the mistakes of the first half of the week and get things back on track by Friday. This timing doesn't allow us to correct the mistakes of the second half of the previous week. But those mistakes have often been forgotten or superseded by others long before the next Wednesday meeting rolls around.

If ever I cancel the meeting, I usually let things slide till the following Wednesday. But this hasn't been a normal week. My team needs to see me steering our departmental ship with confidence. Rumors are flying. They need me to confirm that management knows what it's doing and has a clear vision for the future. They need me to reassure them that their work is valued and their livelihoods are secure.

I can't do any of that. But the meeting may help me crystallize my thinking on how my team might function with two less people—and which two names I will give to HR next month so that severance packages can be prepared.

The first step will be to decide whom I *need* to keep. And then whom I *want* to keep. I will put on paper my optimal mix of people—a mix that will ensure I have a fully functioning, appropriately motivated team. After that, I will adjust as necessary for factors beyond my control, like Henry's misplaced love for Cindy.

Being on time for the meeting, I'm the first one seated in the small conference room. The rest of my team shuffles in over the next few minutes.

Barbara Ward is the first to arrive. Which makes sense. As the departmental assistant, she's the least busy. In theory, Barbara's job is to help ensure that my whole department runs smoothly. In reality, she is one of those old-timers at the company for whom any job description became superfluous many years ago. But I turn a blind eye to her photo-sharing and eBay addictions because Barbara does have one talent that makes her indispensable. Her capacity for endurance gossiping is unparalleled. She spends hours each week plugged in to a network of executive assistants throughout the company, which means she is always first with the scoop on upcoming hirings, firings, staff promotions and product launches.

"What's new?" I ask as she takes her seat two places down the table. And then, in case she feels the need to update me on her grandchildren's lives, I specify: "I hear they're staffing up in Yolanda Pew's division."

"How do you know?" she says. "It's all meant to be top secret." I suspect Barbara has a paranoid streak, that she thinks her internal calls are being recorded.

"I've talked to Barney Barnes," I say. She doesn't need to know that the last time I talked to him was a year ago at the cafeteria salad bar.

Barbara leans toward me and says in a loud whisper, "Can you believe it? Everyone else is getting laid off, and he's hiring eight new people. He's even talking to Martin."

Like I said, Barbara is indispensable.

The door opens and Angela Campos walks in with the notebook and pen she likes to carry. Today, Angela is in a tightly buttoned blouse with a cutout pattern down each arm. She walks around to sit opposite Barbara. Even though she's two seats down from me, she's close enough that I smell the flowers of her perfume.

"Hi, Mr. Wiley," she says.

Barbara makes a huffing sound.

"Russell," I say and clear my throat. We sit in silence for a while. I notice that Angela has drawn a series of interconnected swirls on the inside cover of her notebook.

Erika Fallon and Sally Yun arrive together. This is their first meeting as part of my team. They sit together at the far end of the table.

We all sit in silence for a while as I practice looking at Erika with the same expression of professional detachment I use on the rest of my team.

Kelly Gardner and Jeremy Stent, our two marketing coordinators, arrive. They're deep into a discussion of the cookies now being served in the staff cafeteria, where a new food service company has just taken over the contract.

Pete Hughes follows. He's one of the four managers who report to me. Pete's a short guy, mostly bald, who moves with his head down. He used to wrestle in college, but that was twenty years ago. He looks up briefly to check who's here, then sits in a chair close to the door. As usual, his top button is undone and his tie is loose at his collar. His sleeves are rolled up to reveal hairy arms. When forced to sit down at any kind of internal meeting, Pete can never shake the air of impatience that hangs over him. I sympathize. I know what it feels like to have a ton of work piled up on your desk, all with pressing deadlines, only to have to sit through another bullshit session that doesn't accomplish anything or help anyone move projects forward. But while I sympathize with Pete, he's starting to bug me too. As he waits for the meeting to begin, he makes conspicuous notes on his pad to remind us he has a lot on his mind and many better things to do.

I let the inconsequential chatter continue. I know it's important for a certain personality type to connect with people they work with on a more personal level. The discussion broadens from the specific (cookies) to the general (desserts). It's interesting to watch Kelly get passionate about carrot cake. She thinks it's "way too sweet" and "virtually inedible." Kelly is one of the invisible people, a quiet and hardworking employee who's too busy and too shy to worry about her profile with management.

Kelly's the first person Henry would want me to fire. He doesn't like the way she looks. He barely acknowledges her existence. He has no idea how much work she actually does.

The conversation ceases when Roger Jones arrives. It's an awkward silence. A line I once saw on a refrigerator magnet pops into my head: stressed is the opposite of desserts.

I start thinking about how I'm actually going to run my department with Roger out for six weeks and two others permanently gone. It won't be easy. My company is neither ruthless nor effective when it comes to firing people. We're not like those organizations that execute a rigid performance management plan—and eliminate the bottom ten percent of their workforce every year to make room for new hires. In those companies, everything's out in the open. People know if they are not measuring up. When the ax falls, the nonperformers get cut. There are really no surprises.

Burke-Hart is not like that. We like to promote collegiality. Our performance management system is directional, based on the personal, nonscientific observations of departmental managers. There's no penalty for poor performance built into our grading system. We don't have the annual cull of the lame, the weak and the unproductive. When business gets bad and layoffs come, we start to panic. We reduce headcount randomly. We're just as likely to eliminate star performers or reliable workers as we are to chop away the real dead wood.

Meg Wilson comes in and apologizes for being late. I'm mildly pissed, but at least she has a reason: she was held up at a client meeting.

Finally, Cindy Lang makes her entrance. Despite being almost fifteen minutes late, she's taken the time to stop in the kitchen and make a coffee. She sets her mug down at the head of the table opposite me.

"Are we all here?" she asks.

An outside observer might assume this was Cindy's meeting. That she was the boss we were here to serve. In fact, Cindy is the most junior of my four managers.

I look around the room, making eye contact with everyone but Cindy. "Right," I say, "let's get started."

We run through the items on my agenda. I welcome Erika Fallon and Sally Yun, announce formally that Roger will be taking a leave of absence starting in a week and a half, then update the team on revenue forecasts and details of the latest budget cuts. No one brings up the layoff rumors, so I glide right by that issue, asking each of my managers for their usual team update on current projects and issues. I allow the meeting to proceed and wind down at its normal pace. It looks like I'm taking occasional notes, but in reality I'm just writing down the names of the people in my department, putting each name into one of three columns. Halfway through the meeting, Angela picks up her pen and starts adding more swirls to the pattern she's creating on the inside cover of her notebook.

Erika Fallon pays attention to how Meg, Pete and Roger deliver their updates, then seamlessly takes her turn and delivers an efficient five-minute report.

Something about Erika Fallon's delivery reminds me of Sam. For two years after we got married, Sam threw herself into a career in public relations. She was passionate about her job, enthusiastic about her work, and eager to advance. Within a year, she became an account executive, working on a rotating client list, putting in long hours, bringing work home most nights. She was making good money. Just like Erika Fallon, she invested in a chic work wardrobe. She prided herself on being ultra-organized, always on top of things. Then something changed. Seemingly overnight, she became allergic to what she was doing. Nothing was right. She hated her clients. Her colleagues drove her crazy. The concept of spin—the basic mode of communication for the PR industry—disgusted her. I listened. I commiserated. After a while, I told her to look for another job. After that, I told her if she really couldn't stand it she should just quit. That was twelve years ago. Somewhere along the way, I realized that Sam and I were having a communication problem of our own. Maybe I should have taken into account the business she had worked in. When I said "quit," she spun it into "retire."

After Erika wraps up, Cindy speaks. In front of her peers, she's less of a showboat, hiding her true colors. Keeping one eye on the clock, she wraps up precisely at 12:29. Everyone starts closing their notebooks and acting as if the meeting's over.

"Oh," I say, "there's one more thing I should mention."

I remind them that Henry has hired a new consultant named Judd Walker to work on a special project. That he will be working on the twenty-sixth floor for the next couple of months. That he will likely need to speak to each of them individually.

"He's been round twice already," says Pete.

"What exactly is he working on?" asks Meg.

"Just some data gathering," I say. "Some analysis. Our job is to make sure he gets everything he needs to complete his project."

"What kind of data will he need?" asks Meg.

"We'll let him figure that out. Let's see what he asks for and help him any way we can."

"OK," says Meg.

"OK," says everyone else, starting to get out of their chairs.

"Just don't overburden him," I say. "I'm sure he'll be crunching a lot of numbers. Make sure not to give him anything he hasn't specifically requested."

"OK," says Meg.

"OK," says everyone else.

"How about this?" I say. "Anytime he asks you for anything, no matter how trivial it seems, please review the request with me before responding."

"OK," says Meg.

"OK," says everyone else.

"In the meantime," I say, "just try to ignore him. Pretend he's not here."

CHAPTER SEVENTEEN

I buy an egg salad sandwich and a diet iced tea and head to the concrete park around the corner from my office. It's a mini-refuge between the high-rises. I find a table being vacated by three Brazilian tourists near the trickling wall fountain. Within a minute, I allow the other two chairs to be dragged away. That suits me fine. No one will bother me now. And I need to think.

Henry's demanding a twenty-five percent staff reduction from my eight-person department. Excluding myself, I've got seven people to choose from, not including Erika and Sally, whose original department has already endured its trauma.

I unfold the sheet of paper on which I've written the names of the people in my department into three separate columns.

A	B	C
Meg Wilson	Kelly Gardner	Jeremy Stent
Roger Jones	Barbara Ward	Cindy Lang
Pete Hughes		

I take a bite of my sandwich and think about what to do next. I have a clear understanding of how to define my A players. Meg, Roger and Pete are the only ones I can rely on to take on and complete any assignment.

After that, we all rely on Kelly to help organize all the added-value extras we've promised to advertisers—such as cover wraps, special distributions and promotional mailings.

Beyond that, Barbara gets a free pass. She didn't take the voluntary early retirement package the Ghosh Corporation offered earlier this year. That means she wants to stay. After more than thirty years of loyal service, I simply can't fire her.

In my own head, it seems straightforward. Cindy and Jeremy have to go. There's only one snag. There's no way I'll convince Henry to agree with my assessment.

I break the problem into two.

I know I can sell Henry on the idea of firing Jeremy. He'll ask me to explain why I'm not firing Kelly instead. But my story's simple. Jeremy's not working out. He's still on probation. Besides, Henry will give me one of my picks. He may not like Kelly. But he doesn't even know Jeremy's name.

Cindy is the tough one. She recognized quickly that Henry shares a fatal flaw with many great salespeople. He not only loves to sell, he loves to be sold to. So that's how she spends her time. Fawning over him. Pushing herself forward. Maintaining the kind of unsullied workspace he admires. Taking credit whenever possible for other people's poopie. Convincing Henry that she, Cindy, is one of the company's future Unicorns.

My task won't be easy. But for the good of my team, it's important that I succeed.

I put my notepaper away and continue thinking.

There was a time in my youth—a brief, shining moment—when I thought I could take on the world. I would be unstoppable. I didn't know how I would do it, of course. But I was determined about one thing: I would refuse to be ordinary.

There was a time in my career when, through a combination of luck, circumstance and my own proven performance, things went really well. I was promoted fast. I changed companies a couple of times. My salary doubled in three years. Then doubled again in another five. When things started to slow, I jumped to the *Chronicle.* That was more than four years ago. I settled in. I got promoted, moved to a bigger office. And that's where I am today. On a slow train to obscurity. Stuck in the world of middle management. Navigating my way through a world defined by hiring freezes, reductions in force and faux-generous severance packages. Buried under an increasing workload. Getting calls from out-of-work former colleagues still looking for jobs—while the headhunters have all gone quiet.

I've dug myself into a hole. I assumed my performance would speak for itself. I had faith that management would recognize and reward good work. Then I sat back and watched as other people—aggressive, hard-charging, permanently networking types—charged ahead. I let it happen. Why? Because I was too busy digging my hole to do anything else. I didn't have time to deal with all the networking. I didn't realize the subtle difference between being labeled a high performer instead of a high potential. But that's all got to change. I can't sit back anymore. The company needs to see me as an investment in the future, not a cost it wants to contain. The company has to see a new side to Russell Wiley. There's only room for one Unicorn in my department. And that Unicorn has to be me.

I finish my iced tea, throw away an uneaten half sandwich, and head back to the office. I feel on the verge of a momentous decision. It won't be easy. But the time has come for me to step outside my comfort zone.

I run into Rachel Felsenfeld, Liz Cooke's nemesis, at the elevator bank in the lobby.

She looks at me out of the corner of a half-closed eye. Her hair is cropped short and plastered to her scalp with wet-look gel. She's wearing a designer ballet shirt, black tights and flat black shoes. The shirt is decorated with asymmetric orange and black stripes: horizontal on her right sleeve and across the front, vertical on her left sleeve. I realize the pattern isn't as anarchic as it looks. It's intended to represent something.

"Is that an elephant?" I ask.

She looks at me as if she hasn't quite understood. I'm not sure if she even knows my name.

"Your shirt. I figured it out." I lean forward and trace the pattern in the air, ignoring the fact that she takes half a step back. "Leg, body, leg, trunk."

Rachel's eyes are now fully open. Despite her anorexic frame and my clear height advantage, she looks ready to take me down if I move another inch closer.

I shrug and step back. "It looks like an elephant to me."

"Then I guess it is," she says.

We ride up to twenty-five in silence.

I realize that if Martin leaves, Rachel Felsenfeld will be Henry's first choice for the creative director position. Liz Cooke won't even be considered. Just as if I ever leave, the only internal candidate Henry will consider to lead my department is Cindy Lang.

I approach my office slowly. I've always defended my way of doing things. I tell people it's organized chaos. As long as the cleaning staff doesn't touch anything, I always know where everything is.

Today, I imagine the scene through Henry's eyes. Henry, who views his immaculate, virtually paper-free office as a reflection of both his well-ordered mind and the control he brings to every management challenge.

It's not pretty. Overstuffed folders stacked in precarious columns. Most of the carpet hidden, except for necessary pathways between chairs, window and door. More folders piled atop the desk, along with a seemingly random assortment of memos, clipped articles and half-filled spiral-bound notebooks.

To Henry, this office is a Horse's stable, not a Unicorn's lair.

"Barbara," I say, leaning over the wall of her cubicle and acting as if I don't notice the photograph of a porcelain farm boy figurine that dominates her computer screen. "I know you're busy. But how soon do you think you could get a dumpster delivered to my office?"

I come home from work to find Sam on the couch, reading a magazine. Her bare feet are on the coffee table, with cotton pads stuffed between her shiny red toes. Taking off my coat, I almost trip over the brown leather turd-stool she's moved close to the door.

"What's going on?" I ask.

"Just hanging out," she says innocently. "I'm testing a new nail polish. Which do you prefer? This one?" She tilts her left foot in my direction. "Or this?" She lifts her right foot off the table so I can see her toes better.

"I can't tell the difference."

"Come closer."

"Let me get changed first. What's this doing here?"

"I'm not really loving it anymore," she says. "I was thinking I'd take it back to the store tomorrow."

"You can't take it back," I say.

"Why not? Shila won't mind. And you hated it anyway."

"I've gotten used to it. It's comfortable. It's multipurpose. It's so much more than a stool, but still not quite a chair."

"It's ugly. It doesn't fit with the rest of our stuff."

"Nothing fits with the rest of our stuff," I say. "Anyway, you can't take it back. If you don't want it, I'll take it to my office. I might be able to use it."

"OK. Do that." She looks back at her toes and sighs. "Well, Rainy Day Red, I hate to break it to you like this, but it's over between us. I've fallen for Glistening Cherry."

"What's going on?" asks Cindy Lang.

"Just a little spring cleaning," I say. I wipe the first trace of sweat off my forehead with the back of my hand. I've been pitching files for about eight minutes, trying to ignore the slightly nauseous feeling in the pit of my stomach and focusing instead on the positive: I've already cleared two patches of carpet.

"I was looking for a copy of the IBM presentation," Cindy says.

"I'm busy now," I say.

"It's just that I have a meeting on it in ten minutes." She knows that's usually enough to make me drop what I'm doing.

"Which meeting is that?" I try and sound casual. I don't know of any meeting. I step past Cindy and drop the files I'm holding face-down in the dumpster.

"Ellen called," says Cindy. "She asked me to bring it to Henry."

"I thought Pete was handling IBM." I pick up some folders from the pile beneath the window and thread my way back to the door. Somewhere in the stack of papers I'm holding are the spare copies of the presentation she's asking for. We're standing close now. My armpits feel sticky, but I'm pretty sure any odor is being canceled out by her perfume. Cindy is looking at me with concern. My behavior doesn't compute, and she can't quite understand why.

"Excuse me," I say and tip the pile of documents upside-down into the dumpster. The papers slither against each other and fan out in a pattern I find quite pleasing.

It's been said that when two people of the opposite sex meet, they decide in less than four seconds whether or not they are in the presence of a potential marriage partner. And that the same thing happens in interviews, only faster. Within four seconds of meeting a potential recruit you have the chance to check for:

- A confident stride
- A firm handshake
- Appropriate eye contact

These are the initial warning signs. If present, you'll need to pay close attention to the candidate's verbal presentation, listening for:

- A thorough understanding of your company's current business challenges
- A clearly articulated rationale as to why the candidate's strengths will add value to your team

- An awareness of the potential career paths and roads to advancement your company offers

Once you have located a candidate with all these attributes, try to stay calm. It's your job to ensure he or she exits the building as quickly, but with as little disruption to your department, as possible. For appearances' sake, ask one or two more open-ended questions. These will allow the candidate an opportunity to bloviate as you assess the best way to escort him or her to the elevator bank. The key challenge is keeping the candidate away from even casual contact with a member of senior management. If necessary, ride with him or her to the ground floor in order to visually confirm that an exit from the building has taken place.

Looking back on the day I interviewed Cindy, I realize I should have followed my gut and shredded her résumé. If Henry wasn't breathing down my neck and telling me to fill the position quickly, I could have kept interviewing until I found a suitable, more modest, more demonstrably competent recruit.

The next time I see Pete Hughes he's heading down the hall, carrying a large, rolled-up sheet of paper—a layout from the art department.

"So, what's new?" I ask him.

"Not much. Same old shit."

I fall into step beside him.

"So, what are you working on these days?"

He runs through a list of projects he's trying to get completed. I interrupt him when he mentions Travelocity.

"What are you doing with that one?" I ask. "Shouldn't that be Cindy?" We cut through the hallway by the conference room.

"I'm helping her out," he says. "She said she was a little jammed up."

"Any new requests from Henry?"

"Nothing new," he says. "Ellen asked us to pull together some of our recent projects so Henry can see what we've been working on."

"Did you do that yet?" We're standing outside Rachel Felsenfeld's cubicle.

"I haven't had time yet. Didn't seem like a rush. Ellen said Henry needed them by the end of the week."

We stand in silence for a while.

"Anything else?" says Pete, tapping the rolled-up paper in his palm.

"No," I say. "That's all." He disappears into Rachel's cubicle, and I meander slowly back to my office.

CHAPTER EIGHTEEN

By Tuesday, the dumpster is gone and I'm embracing a new potential. It's reflected in the clutter-free work environment I've created. This morning I will rid myself of four piles of folders stacked beside my desk. After that, not a single piece of paper will be visible—not on the floor, not on the desk, not anywhere. Not even a sticky note on my computer screen.

My goal is to maintain my office as if it were a minimalist art installation. Central to my new artistic vision is the turd-stool now nestled, Zen-like, in the corner, surrounded by a vast expanse of freshly exposed gray carpet. I've also kept a few personal mementos on the credenza, spaced apart like props for a photo shoot. Lucky Cat now stands alone, waving bravely, on an otherwise pristine windowsill.

Cleaning out my office is only the first step. To fully achieve my new potential—to establish myself as the kind of Unicorn my company needs right now—I must also undergo an internal transformation. I must commit myself to a new philosophy of work. My job is no longer to spend energy. It is to release energy. My future success will not be based on my own hard work and sweat equity. It will be built, cartload by cartload, through the exertions of my team.

How will I measure success? When I know without a doubt I can enter my installation each day, move comfortably around within the environment, even invite others into the space for some focused discussions, and then, at five o'clock, simply leave. As the door closes behind me, the imprint of my ass on the just-vacated chair will disappear and not a single trace of my workday presence will be left behind.

The key to achieving this is simple: delegation.

One by one I call in my direct reports—Meg, Pete, Roger and Cindy. I have a brief discussion with each about the projects they're working on, future workflow and the need for them to take one hundred percent responsibility for each of their assignments.

I explain to each of them the concept of one hundred percent responsibility. It means that they can't blame anyone else if their work doesn't get done. None of that fifty-fifty crap where you can always blame the other person for not holding up their end of the deal.

"When you take one hundred percent responsibility, it doesn't matter if someone else lets you down, or gets struck by lightning, or simply doesn't give you what you need," I tell them. "If that happens, you find another solution, a new way to get it done, a workaround."

At the end of each meeting I pick up a stack of files, push it across my desk, and instruct the relevant person that I am now making them one hundred percent responsible for the projects these files contain. Also, I tell them that I will be amending their performance goals to reflect their responsibility for these assignments.

Once each member of my team assumes one hundred percent responsibility for the work I need them to do, I will, by definition, have zero percent responsibility for actually getting things done. My job will be to motivate, cajole, nurture, coach and encourage my team while saving time to polish the Unicorn horn growing out of my head. Beyond that, I will have ample time to communicate internally the great work that my team is producing and to position myself as someone with the 360-degree vision we need to move this company forward.

The conversations with my staff members start off well enough. I sprinkle each conversation with sporting metaphors. Pete reacts positively to this chance to step up to the plate. Meg tells me she is happy to swing for the fences. Even Roger, wheezing in at a biscuit under four hundred pounds, is looking forward to running with the ball when he gets back from medical leave.

Cindy Lang looks at me quizzically.

"I thought you told me I would be a manager."

"Absolutely," I say. "Managing is a key part of your role. But like I said, we're raising the bar, shooting from three-point range."

"You want me to do filing?"

"Cindy, I think you're missing the point here. It's not a question of filing, though of course I'll be more than happy to sign the requisition form if you need another filing cabinet. The important thing is that we need to put some more points on the board to show we're getting the job done."

"Isn't it already getting done?" She looks puzzled.

"Precisely," I say. "But we still need our A players to raise their game, be the ball, stay in the zone, block and tackle, hit it out of the park and slam-dunk with nothing but net. That's why I'm making you personally responsible for the Livingston Kidd proposal. It's super-urgent. We're expecting a call from the client any day. So it would be great if you can get something ready for Henry and Randy Baker within the next couple of days."

"This isn't what I signed on for," she says. She stares at me defiantly, and I realize she's afraid. If she takes these files, accepts these assignments, she will be committing herself to doing actual work of the kind she's never done before. There's a lot at stake. Her reputation. Her self-image. Her ability to sneak out for manicures in the middle of the afternoon.

"Listen, Cindy," I say. "This may not be exactly what you signed on for. But let me tell you something in confidence. You cannot breathe a word of this, but there are going to be some significant layoffs in this department in the very near future. I'm telling you this now because I don't want you to be concerned. You know how highly everyone thinks of you, so trust me, there's no need to worry about your job. Just understand, this is roll-up-your-sleeves time. We'll all have fewer resources to support us. We'll all be working harder than ever. And Henry and I will be relying on you. We've got a massive, monumental challenge ahead of us. It's not just about managing anymore. It's about digging deep, pitching in, soup to nuts, start to finish. But that can be fun too. You know how it is. Those long days when you're the last one in the office. You're trying to get the binding machine working normally with one hand, filling out the shipping label with the other.

The clock's ticking. You don't even know if you're going to make the deadline for overnight delivery. And when you do—always with just a minute to spare—it's the most exhilarating, satisfying feeling. It reminds you of what got us into this business."

Cindy looks at me with disgust.

"Thanks, Cindy, I knew you'd understand. Why not take these files just for starters. The Livingston Kidd proposal should really be in the art department already. If you could, make it your top priority. I'll be sure to let Henry know I've made you one hundred percent responsible for this."

I close my door and walk around my office, counting the number of steps it takes me to get from one side of the room to the other, from my desk to the door, from the door to the window. Apart from a few small stains, my carpet is a uniform gray. The large areas that were previously covered with files are no different in shade than the areas that have been exposed to sunlight every day. The turd-stool in the corner is somehow comforting and motivational. It reminds me to stay focused on getting more done by doing less.

I think of the work my team is producing in their offices and cubicles down the hall. I feel powerful and in control. Directing things the way a director should. I realize this is exactly how my days should be. Uncluttered. Unobstructed. A blank canvas filled with potential.

I stare out of my window for several minutes. In the building across the street, on the same floor as me, there's a guy about my age sitting in an office just like mine. His door is closed and he's shooting a small basketball into a hoop he has set up behind his door. When the ball bounces beyond his reach, he gets out of his seat to fetch it. When he makes a shot he's pleased with, he raises his arms triumphantly.

He answers the phone twice while I'm watching him. But the conversations are brief, and he quickly returns to his game. When he gets bored with one shot, he wheels his chair to a new position to change the angle.

My own phone doesn't ring. When I get bored watching basketball guy, I walk down the hall. I want my team to know I'm here for them. Maybe someone needs some input or feedback.

Meg, Pete and Roger are all in their offices, working on their computers or talking into the telephone headsets recommended by our company-funded ergonomics expert. Barbara is working in iPhoto, removing the red-eye in some pictures of her grandkids. Randy Baker is leaning over the wall of Angela's cubicle. Randy's one of those cheerful salesman types. He's a devoted family man, with a house in the suburbs and a small boat that offers him a weekend escape. His eldest daughter is just a couple of years younger than Angela.

I pass Kelly and Jeremy, working in their cubicles. It's hard to tell what anyone is doing, but I decide not to interrupt.

Cindy's is the only empty office.

I stride purposefully through Susan's department, keeping my eyes fixed straight ahead. I've got nothing to do and I'm headed nowhere in particular, but I still don't want to get accosted by Susan right now.

I pass through the creative department. Martin's office is empty. Rachel Felsenfeld is staring at a large image of what looks like wrinkled paper on the flat screen that dominates her cubicle. Liz Cooke is comparing some layouts with Kiko at the table in the middle of the art department.

I pause outside Ben's office. The furnishings haven't been touched, but all traces of Ben's personality and presence have been erased. I try to convince myself that I'm standing here to compare the space and the view. But there's no reason for me to covet Ben's office. It's smaller than mine, and the view's equally unspectacular.

"Hey, Russell Wiley."

Maybe that's the real reason I'm standing here. To say good-bye to "Erika Fallon." She not only works for me, she's also attracted the amorous attentions of Judd Walker. "Erika Fallon" and I had some good times together. But they don't really count because they were all in my head. Now it's time for our relationship to end.

I turn to her as if she were just an average coworker and say, "Hey, Erika. How's it going?"

She looks at me for a second. Just long enough for me to have a mental image of Judd creeping up behind her and nuzzling her neck.

"Everything's going great. Sally and I are all set. We're heading to Washington tomorrow. We just went over everything with Meg. Hank's happy. Eighty people have RSVP'd. We only expected sixty."

"That's great. So you're staying two nights?"

"Yeah, and Judd's coming too. He set up his research meeting for Thursday, so the timing worked out."

"That's great. Sounds like you guys have it all figured out."

"Yeah," she says. "It's all good." She looks at me in a way that lets me know that, in truth, it isn't all good. She knows that dating Judd will be a minor detour on the road to finding her one true everlasting love. She realizes that somewhere in an alternate universe—a universe where Russell Wiley wasn't married or her department head—things could have worked out different. We could have had a chance. She wouldn't have wasted time with a self-important, overconfident, high achiever like Judd.

"Great," I say. "Let me know how it all turns out."

We walk off in opposite directions.

"Hey, Erika."

She stops and turns. I notice she's wearing brown suede boots. They look soft, comfortable, soothing to her feet.

"Can you do me one favor?"

"Sure, Russell," she says, even though she looks decidedly unsure about what might come next.

"It's just the nametags. Hank has a thing about nametags. He gets crazy if the first guest arrives and the nametags aren't all laid out."

I head to the elevators, pleased at how well that worked out. At first I'm thinking I'll treat myself to a couple of the new chocolate cookies in the cafeteria. But somewhere along the way I convince myself that a fruit salad is the healthier choice.

Back in my office, I sit back and look at my orderly, well-filed office. Everything is in its place. But something doesn't feel right. I look over to the building opposite. Basketball guy is putting on his coat and heading out of his office. I check my watch. It's only four thirty.

For the first time in days, I have nothing to do. No urgent emails. No crazy deadlines. No WIPs to chain me. Amid all this inactivity, there's not even anyone bursting in to interrupt me.

I stab at the fruit with my plastic fork. It's mainly chunks of pale cantaloupe, anemic watermelon and flavorless honeydew, with a few sour-tasting strawberries, blueberries and grapes thrown in for color.

CHAPTER NINETEEN

I schedule a lunch with Barney Barnes. His assistant gives me a date three weeks in advance and then calls me back at 12:25 the same day and asks if I can meet Barney at Crime in five minutes. Barney's lunch date has canceled, and Barney, en route to the restaurant from another meeting, isn't answering his cell phone.

Crime is Fabrice de Monbrison's new midtown concept. It's one of those expensively chic places I would never think to go to. I'm aware it's had mixed reviews for its spartan décor, stripped-down menu and inefficient service. Some people say the only thing criminal about it is the prices. Nevertheless, it's one of *the* places to be seen right now, especially by younger media executives looking for a hipper alternative to the original Fabrice. When I walk in, I see prominent industry people at several tables—the kind of wannabe household names who strive to get written about in the trades and the tabloids as if they were bona fide celebs. Barney is sitting at a table in the corner, near the swinging doors to the kitchen.

Barney is Burke-Hart Publishing's version of a political animal. After failing to make the grade at Time Inc., Hearst and Condé Nast, he's parlayed all his assets—an impressive academic résumé, airtight connections dating back to prep school, plus constant networking inside our company—into a series of ever more substantial management positions. He's launched new products by shamelessly ripping off fashion and lifestyle concepts pioneered by his former companies. And he's done all this while demonstrating zero ability to relate to or understand the work of the people who report to him.

"Hey, Barney," I say and offer my hand.

Barney puts down his menu and smiles up at me. He's as round and hard as a potato—a former jock whose muscle somehow didn't turn to fat. I notice he's had his hair cut in the youthful style that many middle-aged businessmen are favoring this year—a short, close-cropped 'do that needs very little styling. It's the same 'do that swept through Hollywood a few months ago, and even though all the young male movie stars have already grown out of it, the look has found a new life on the East Coast.

His smile disappears when he realizes who I am.

"Russell," he says. "Great to see you. What are you doing here?" As he shakes my hand, he's looking over my shoulder to see if anyone else is coming.

To Barney's alarm, I sit at his table and grab a slice of focaccia from the bread basket, dipping it into the rosemary-seasoned olive oil.

"Hey, Russell. Don't get too cozy. I'm expecting someone."

"I'm subbing for your lunch date," I tell him. "Annika called me when she couldn't get hold of you." Annika is Barney's famously stunning Finnish assistant. She has striking blonde hair cropped around a perfectly shaped face and a fondness for wearing tight leather pants. Yolanda Pew's division is home to the majority of the company's most gorgeous women, but even so, Annika stands out.

"Annika's amazing," says Barney. "You wouldn't believe how organized and efficient that woman is."

"She's great on the phone too," I say.

Barney drinks a couple of glasses of wine with lunch while I nurse a nonalcoholic beer. We haven't spoken for a while. Recently divorced, he updates me on his new single life. He's back in the city in a furnished apartment, seeing his kid every other weekend. He implies that he's getting laid a lot, but I don't probe for details.

"How are things with you?" he asks.

"Things are cooking," I say. "Business is tough, but we're holding our own. I made a couple of great hires this year. My team's really firing on all cylinders."

"Who do you have working for you these days?" he asks.

"You know Meg Wilson? She's great. Pete Hughes? He's great. Just keeps chugging away. Gets it done. Roger Jones? He's a pain in the ass sometimes, but he's great too." Barney's eyes are glazing over. He's not interested in the reliable and dedicated members of my team. They're old news to him.

"So who are the new guys?" he says.

"I hired this kid Jeremy Stent back in June. He's great. Smart. Enthusiastic. One year out of school. He's like a one-man idea factory. And Cindy Lang? Have you met her? Jesus. She's phenomenal." I mention the school she went to and a couple of the leading companies where she used to pretend to work. "Henry loves Cindy. Just last week, we needed to pull together a two-million-dollar proposal for the Chicago office. Complete fire drill. They needed it overnight. But man, Cindy Lang. She made it look effortless." I don't mention that in Cindy's world, making something look effortless means leaving at five o'clock while Pete and Kelly stayed late to do the actual work. If there's one thing I've learned from Henry over the past four years, it's that it is entirely possible to tell the truth even when you want to mislead people.

"That's good to know," says Barney. "It's always tough to find talented people. We're looking for a couple of folks right now. You don't happen to know anyone who's looking?"

"Ha ha," I say. "Thanks, but I'm happy right now. And hey, don't come near my people. And Cindy Lang is *not* available. Henry would kill you."

Barney chuckles and picks up his butter knife. I sit quietly for several seconds, sending him telepathic signals to ensure the name Cindy Lang gets lodged deep into his brain.

Until Judd drops by my office around three o'clock, I thought my biggest challenge this afternoon was going to be digesting the fifty-four-dollar hamburger I made Barney pay for. It tastes the same as the sixty-dollar burger at Fabrice, but with ten percent less meat.

Judd's clutching his copy of the D-SAW binder he created, plus a manila folder containing his project notes. Like a good consultant, he's looking for more help on his project. What he doesn't know is that since we last spoke I've turned into a Unicorn. I have no intention of getting involved in the actual work his project requires. He looks around my office.

My two guest chairs are missing. Susan borrowed them this morning and hasn't brought them back yet.

"What's that?" he asks.

"Isn't it a fantastic piece? My wife picked it up at the store where she works. I told her it would look great in my office."

Judd turns away from the turd-stool. "I've already received two research proposals from companies here in New York," he says. "And I'm heading down to DC tomorrow morning to meet with one more group down there."

"Excellent," I say. "Will you get a chance to go to our event at the Intercontinental?"

"Yeah," he says. "That's where I'm staying. I told Erika I could help out."

"That's great. I'm glad you're not too busy to pitch in."

"I was just hoping that while I'm teaming that event, someone on your staff could keep this D-SAW work moving."

"Sure. What do you need? I'd be happy to do it myself, but I have a ton of other work here." I gesture at the uncluttered expanse of my desk.

Judd pushes his heavy glasses back up the bridge of his nose. "We still have a lot of analysis to get through and several deliverables," he says. "Perhaps we can parallel-process."

I lean back in my chair and look up at Judd as he stands across my desk. I consider what he actually means by "parallel-process." It's a phrase consultants use when they want to hoodwink you into thinking that there are two approximately equal tasks that need to be undertaken in order to complete a given project. What the phrase actually means is this: "Hey, you look like a strong carthorse, why don't we just load up all the heavy freight into these cars? Then why don't you pick up this rope and drag the whole train by yourself to yonder station? Don't worry about me. I'll ride in the first-class, air-conditioned Unicorn Express that's coming through on the next track over. We can meet up at the station when you get there."

I stand up and roll my executive chair around my desk, toward the brown lump of furniture I've placed by the window. I plant myself in my chair and gesture for Judd to do the same. "Sit down," I say. "Let's take a look. See what's going on."

"You want me to sit on this?"

"Try it. You'll be amazed."

Judd positions himself above the stool, hovering a second before sinking slowly into it. There's a gentle hissing sound as air is forced out. Judd stabilizes himself, feet set apart on the floor. His cuffed pants are riding up his legs, exposing his pale, almost hairless shins.

"It's not so bad, is it?" I tell him as he looks up at me. "Let's run through these and figure out some next steps."

I look at what Judd is expecting someone to do for him while he's out of town, starting with a complete analysis of the competitive landscape and followed by a review of our rivals' "best practices." This is exactly the kind of work Henry's hired Judd to produce as part of his exorbitant day rate. I read slowly while he squirms in his seat.

"Hold on." He gets up, drags the stool a couple of feet, and sits again, leaning his back against the wall. He still looks unsure about the situation, but he's going with it.

"Maybe we can work something out," I say. "Tell me your deadlines again."

Judd rattles off a few dates and the details of all the work he's expecting me to do over the next few days. As he talks, I glance over at the notepad and pen I've left on my desk and wonder if he was expecting me to be writing any of this down.

"Jeez," I say. "This timing's really working against us. I'm backed up on a couple of things for Henry. This Livingston Kidd proposal is really getting out of hand. Plus we've got Roger going out for his gastric bypass next week."

"Henry promised me the support I needed," Judd says, a little desperation creeping in. "I actually asked one or two of your guys already. They told me that I need to be a hundred percent responsible for my work just like they are for theirs."

"Well, they're all so swamped," I say. I pause to let him know I'm thinking of how best to work this. "Tell you what. You might be in luck. Cindy might have some time. I just reassigned several of her projects to Meg and Pete."

"Cindy?" says Judd. "Henry said I could work directly with you."

"Don't worry. Cindy's my best person. She works on all of Henry's top projects. She'll be a hundred percent responsible for getting at least fifty percent of this work done. If the two of you can't figure this out, I don't know who else can."

I stand up and offer my hand, pulling Judd out of the position he's sunken into.

Thursday's a quiet day. Erika, Sally and Judd are all in DC. Meg, Roger and Pete are hard at work on their projects. Cindy is still reeling from Judd's request for help. I decide to relocate before she comes to complain.

I call Fergus from my cell phone and invite him to meet me for coffee at the Starbucks that marks the halfway point between our offices.

While we're waiting for our nonfat lattes to be prepared, I tell him how I'm investing myself completely in the preparation for my next *Vicious Circle* column.

"I've become a Unicorn," I tell him. "It's amazing. Frees up so much of your time."

We sit with our drinks on the high stools by the window. It's midmorning, but there's a long line of people at the street vendor's coffee and donut cart outside. These are the consumers who still cling to the belief that coffee is a commodity product. I sip my latte, happy in the rationalization that I'm doing more than drinking coffee. I'm pampering myself. I'm not wasting money recklessly—I'm treating myself to a small but affordable luxury that, goddammit, I deserve.

Fergus updates me on the reaction to the latest issue of *Vicious Circle.* I convinced him a while back that he needed to count the total number of reader letters and emails the magazine receives each issue. If ever the number is impressive or shows signs of increasing, they could use it to show advertisers that at least some readers are engaging with the publication.

So far the numbers aren't creating much of a story.

"Forty-five this month," he tells me. "But six of those were people asking to cancel their subscriptions."

"Well, there's still time. You may get more. How many of those were in response to my poopie column?"

"You mean apart from the cancellations?"

"Ha."

"I guess a couple of people said they liked your poopie, Russell."

"Just knowing that makes it all worthwhile."

We sit quietly for a minute. I tell Fergus that I finally got to see the contents of the YANA file I'd been denied access to for so many years.

"Really? Any big revelations?"

"It was a confidential report from one of those companies specializing in brand marketing and research. Divided into two parts. The first part was all about why brands die, and other optimistic stuff."

"And the conclusion was that your brand is dying?"

"The conclusion was that our customers are dying. The *Chronicle* has huge strength with seniors, but we're not relevant to younger consumers. To them, we're a boring business newspaper filled with stuff they can always get free on the internet. We're not a brand that stands for something they care about." I sip my five-dollar latte. "Unless we transform that perception, we'll keep losing customers, along with our ability to charge a premium price to advertisers."

"And the second part?"

"That was the most important section. They called it 'brand permission' research. They looked at all the different ways we might expand our product into new markets or create new brand extensions that might allow us to succeed in the future. It was a pretty thorough analysis. Unfortunately, the conclusion was that our brand didn't have permission to do very much. People have a very fixed view of us. We're associated only with business. We would fail if we tried to compete in the major lifestyle segments. It's a vicious circle. You can appreciate that. If we do nothing, we'll be trapped in an unstoppable, accelerating decline. But anything we do will probably make things worse. This D-SAW project is our last chance to turn it around."

"How reliable is this company's research?"

"I don't know. I did a search on them. Seems like they went out of business two years ago."

"And what exactly is this D-SAW project?"

I tell him what it entails. How we'll be doubling down on a new newspaper product at a time when everyone else is moving rapidly online.

"That's *it*?"

I nod.

"Jesus. You guys are in worse shape than I thought." Fergus sips his coffee. I sip mine.

We're quiet for another minute. Then Fergus says, "So, we didn't even discuss the most important topic. Did you fuck that other chick or not?"

CHAPTER TWENTY

Erika, Sally and Judd travel back from Washington together. Erika reports the event was a success. Judd tells me the same thing. Neither of them gives any indication if their flirtation is blossoming into romance.

Meanwhile, I'm adapting to the Unicorn lifestyle. I've asked the managers on my team to start emailing me weekly reports so I can package these and deliver them to Henry.

It takes a few minutes to edit out all the duplication contained in Cindy's report. But even after I do that, I'm sure Henry will get the sense that a large volume of work is getting done.

Sometimes I walk the floor and peer over people's cubicle walls. Other times I sit and do nothing. When I'm really bored, I staple pieces of paper together, then take the staples back out with my staple remover.

I leave work at five each day. Which means I'm jammed in with other straphangers at the height of the rush hour. With frequent stops between stations, I have plenty of time to reflect on the carefree, subway-free, cubicle-free life my wife is leading. While I'm busy not working, she's finding new ways to spend all the money she's not earning.

"Do you notice anything different about me?" She's posing on the rug where our turd-stool used to be.

"Are those colored contacts?"

"Shut up. Be serious."

"I am being serious. Were your eyes always that color?"

"So you don't notice anything different?"

"Turn around at least."

She twirls slowly. She's had her hair cut and highlighted again. With tip the process runs about $260. I look beyond her at the thin, spiderweb cracks in the wall. We live in a prewar building. The painter told us this would happen.

"I don't know," I say. "Liposuction?"

Teaming Judd with Cindy proves to be an interesting experiment. I can only observe from a distance, but it is obvious that from a productivity standpoint their collaboration is a complete disaster. They hold regular meetings, outlining the scope of the project, discussing timelines and deliverables. But then—without access to anyone willing to do the actual work—they reconvene and discover no further progress has been made.

For the purpose of the experiment, I have instructed my staff not to accept any assignments directly from Judd or Cindy. And if any issues arise, they are to alert me immediately. One by one, my team members bring me the requests Judd leaves on their chairs while they are out at lunch or the assignment Cindy has tricked them into accepting by pretending the work is for a different project. One by one, I return these assignments to Cindy or Judd, with a note or a voicemail or an email reminder that we are all very busy and that I am confident that they, between them, can get this done.

Judd comes to my office to let me know he and Cindy have made tremendous progress in defining the scope of the project and the necessary next steps. He shows me a sheet he's formatted which describes the work required at each stage of the project. A second column shows the due date for each element. Next to that is a column of empty boxes under the heading "Owned By."

"Here's where I need your support," he says.

"The sheet looks great," I say. "I don't have any changes."

"I need your help building a team," he says. "We need people who are going to step up and take ownership."

"I'm not sure what you mean."

"Everything's set up. The whole thing is mapped out. All we need now are the resources."

"Judd," I say, "you and Cindy are the resources."

I visit Roger in his office to wish him all the best before his operation. He doesn't want any kind of send-off before he departs for his medical leave. During my empty workdays, I've had plenty of time to research the surgery he's having. It won't be fun. He's switching to a liquid diet tomorrow. Thankfully, his sister's coming to stay with him. He'll need her around for a few unpleasant days before the operation and for the uncomfortable first weeks of his recovery.

"Good luck," I tell him. "And seriously, think about the mustache too while you're gone."

The battle of wills between Judd and Cindy continues. Despite the importance of the D-SAW project, neither one of them is willing to break down and do any actual work.

Then Cindy disengages. She appears at my doorway, sheepish yet triumphant.

"Russell, can we talk?" she says.

I ask her to take a seat while I pretend to finish up an email. For once, I already know what's going down. She's here to tell me about the job she's accepted in Barney Barnes's group. The HR department alerted me yesterday that an offer was going to be made. The only surprising thing was that Cindy took a night to sleep on it.

"OK," I say. "Shoot."

"I don't know how to say this." She looks tired. There are lines around her mouth I haven't really noticed before.

I lean forward in my chair. "What's up?"

"Russell, I'm really torn about this. I haven't even been here six months, and I know it's not the done thing, but Barney Barnes approached me about a senior manager position and the offer was really too good to pass up. I'll be working on a more female-oriented product, which I think is a better fit for me when I think long-term, and I do want to stay at the company, and it seems like a really great group—not that this isn't, but I'll have four people reporting to me, and I'll manage my own advertising budget."

"Jeez," I say. "You're leaving us?"

"I'm sorry."

"I hope there's more money involved."

"It's not really about that, but yes."

"And a bigger office, I suppose?"

"One and a half windows."

"Wow. I don't know what to say. It sounds like a done deal."

"They've asked if I can start on the twelfth."

"Gosh," I say. "We'll miss you."

I break the news to Henry. "Cindy's leaving us. She's accepted a job with Barney Barnes."

I try to conceal my elation. I'm well aware that Henry takes it hard when an employee—especially one he considers a star—departs to work for another part of the company. When the person is leaving to join Barney's team, the blow is especially hard.

My job is to guide Henry carefully through his grieving process. There are five stages: Denial (of the Situation), Anger (at the Person Responsible), Panic (That This Might Reflect Badly on Him), Nostalgia (for the Lost Employee), and finally, Acceptance (Mixed with a Hearty Blend of False Optimism). With Henry, the whole process takes about sixty seconds.

"She can't leave us now," he says. "I absolutely won't allow it."

"It's a done deal, Henry."

"Shit. Didn't you have her working with Judd on the D-SAW project? And what about Livingston Kidd? What are we going to do?"

"You know how great Judd is. He can handle the D-SAW project. And I'll put Pete on Livingston Kidd. I think we'll be able to work through it."

"Thank God for Judd."

"He's a real pro."

"That fucking Barney."

"Barney's always had an eye for talent."

"What are people saying? Cindy's been here less than six months."

"We can spin it that you did her a favor. Managed her out. Gave her a nudge before the re-org."

"Will anyone buy it? We would never have won the ExxonMobil business without her."

"I hate to tell you, but Roger Jones did all the work on that one. Plus, everyone got that campaign, even *USA Today*."

"Roger worked on Exxon?" Henry's cheek twitches as he processes that information. "Anyway, she did a great job on Fidelity."

"Actually, I had to pull that one out of the fire myself. Don't you remember? Cindy had worked so hard in her first couple of months. You gave her a couple of extra personal days."

I worry that I'm pushing too hard. That Henry can't update his hard drive this quickly.

"I don't know," says Henry. "Can we afford to lose her?"

"It's a loss," I say. "But I think the rest of the team can step it up."

"I guess it saves someone else's job," he says.

I nod reflectively.

"You think we can do this?"

I nod sagely.

"We can do this!"

I nod eagerly.

"You and I did just fine before Cindy got here, didn't we?"

"Cindy?" I say, acting puzzled. "Cindy who?"

Henry slaps me on the back, squeezes my shoulder. He feels my body tighten, relaxes his grip slowly, then lets his hand drop back to his side.

Judd is hovering near my office when I get back from Henry's. He's wearing his casual Friday look—black turtleneck, black jeans—and looking slightly panicked. He follows me inside. I sit behind my desk and say, "What's new, Judd?"

"I just spoke to Cindy," he says. "She tells me she's accepted another position."

"It's a great move for her," I say. "Things are really happening over in Barney Barnes's group. It doesn't make it easy for us hold on to our stars."

"That's great," says Judd. "But frankly I'm concerned about D-SAW."

"You're worried she might say something to Barney?"

"No. I'm worried that Henry's expecting to see a presentation next Wednesday, and Cindy hasn't produced anything."

"That's surprises me," I say. "She's normally so reliable."

Judd starts pacing around my office. It's fun to watch. I wait to see how he tries to shift responsibility for the actionable items.

"How can I help you move this along?" he asks.

"That's up to you," I say. "It's your project."

He sits down opposite me. He takes out the document he created delineating the project timeline and takes me through the "actionable items" and "deliverables" he and Cindy had previously agreed on.

"Hen—" he says, his voice cracking slightly. "Henry said I could rely on you."

"You've put a lot of thought into the process," I observe. "What about the content?"

"I completed all my internal interviews," he says, as if that matters.

"That's no help now. Where are you with the P&Ls?"

"Jeanie's given me a first pass at the distribution, production and admin costs. I'm just waiting for Susan and Dave to sign off on their numbers," he says. "But Jeanie said Henry said I should get the marketing numbers directly from you."

Judd hands me a spreadsheet and looks at me expectantly. His blatant use of the double-name-drop technique is a clear sign of desperation. I study Jeanie's bogus numbers and understand why. Susan and Dave have been dragging their feet too. Someone who knows what they're doing is going to have to help him out soon.

"OK. Email this to me. Give me a copy of everything you gave Cindy. Come back on Monday. I'll take care of it."

"Thanks, Russell," Judd says. He smiles. The tension he's been holding releases visibly from his body. I realize there are two sides to Judd. There's the pain-in-the-ass, full-of-himself, unstoppable-force-of-nature side that we all know and dislike. But behind that mask there's also a helpless doofus—an innocent man-child who's just longing to be accepted into the grown-up world. It's a sensitive, vulnerable side that Judd doesn't show to many people. Probably because it's even more off-putting.

I work on the spreadsheet Judd sends me. He's one of those guys who really knows how to use the software. There are a lot of hidden formulas in his file. Every time I type in a new number, all the columns get recalculated. This is the kind of stuff that really impresses Henry. When the spreadsheet's this well formatted, it doesn't even matter that the underlying business assumptions are bogus. Every budget season guys like Judd produce sheets like this, altering numbers in little boxes to create the fictional view of our business that management wants to see. This fiction would be fun to read if it didn't create the kind of unrealistic expectations that are sure to make the lives of people like me slightly more miserable. Expectations that, when not met, will ultimately cost people their jobs.

I delete a number and something goes wrong with Judd's formula. A whole column of numbers gets replaced with the message "VALUE!!!!!###."

I give up and go home for the weekend.

CHAPTER TWENTY-ONE

It's already been more than three weeks since Sam and I last had sex. But I've decided to tough it out. If I'm a Unicorn at the office, I can be one at home too. It's her turn to take the lead, to demonstrate some interest. Of course, she hasn't cracked yet. Saturday comes and goes without any fireworks. On Sunday, in a burst of AntiCrastination, I finish a draft of my next Christopher Finchley column. I've titled it "Sometimes a Unicorn Points You in the Right Direction (and Sometimes He's Just Turning His Head)." I think it's good. But I don't send it to Fergus yet. I've still got another week to refine it based on additional workplace observations.

On Monday, I summon Angela into my office. I'm pleased to see she's wearing a sweater.

"Did you need me for something?" she says like an actress in a bad porn movie.

"Close the door," I say, vaguely aware that I am ignoring certain advice in the human resources manual.

Angela shuts the door and stands facing me across my desk. She is breathing deeply through her nose. I lean back in my chair and grip the armrests. I clear my throat and say, "Angela, do you know how to use Excel?"

"I think so," she says, swaying slightly from side to side. "Is that the spreadsheet one?"

"Great. Perhaps you have time to take on an additional project?" I say, opening a manila folder on my desk.

As I spread out my papers, Angela skips around the desk and stands next to my chair, so close I can smell her deodorant. I hand her a typed list of line item cost estimates and explain how and where I need these data points added into Judd's more complex spreadsheet. As Angela leans forward to study the numbers, her breast hovers inches from my face.

"You understand what I'm looking for?" I ask, not looking up from my desk.

"Oh yes," she says.

I rearrange the papers back into the folder.

"That will be all for now," I say. "Perhaps you can have that ready by lunchtime?"

"No problem," she says, picking up the folder. She walks slinkily to the door as if she expects I would be watching her.

"Angela," I say.

She turns and smiles again.

"If things ever get slow, please come and see me. I'm sure we can find something to keep you busy."

After Angela leaves I stare out of my window for several minutes. Today, basketball guy's office is empty. From the position of his door, I can't even tell if his hoop is still there.

Susan Trevor interrupts my reverie. She wants to warn me about Judd. She wants me to know he's got Henry duped. She wants to inform me he had a one-on-one breakfast with Jack last week. She wants to reiterate that he doesn't know anything about our business, that he's picking our brains one by one, that if we tell him everything we know he'll end up smarter than any one of us.

"Plus, he's already told Sally he's planning on being around for a while. He thinks Henry might hire him full-time."

I nod and make a small huffing sound. I've no idea why Judd would share this information with Sally, but I don't want to get into any long discussions with Susan.

She leans forward just enough to show some cleavage and reminds me that we've all looked at the D-SAW project before. We already know it makes no sense. It's a waste of time for everyone.

Worse, she reminds me, bringing an outsider like Judd in creates more work for everyone, especially her. We have to lead him by the nose, hold his hand, wipe his ass the whole way.

Worse still, we now know he's trying to dress up all the information we give him to sell Henry on the project, to create a full-time job for himself.

And then, if he does get the project approved, God help us. We'll be the ones who have to do all the work. We'll all be held accountable because we've all had input. We'll be expected to make the project succeed even though we know in advance it's doomed to fail.

"That's the art of Rainbow Painting," I remind her, glancing discreetly at my watch, wondering if I'll have time to complete and email my weekly report to Henry before catching another lunchtime movie.

Judd comes in five minutes after Susan. He's concerned she's not fully invested in the success of the D-SAW project. That she doesn't realize how committed Henry is to making this work. That perhaps she doesn't quite "get it."

I wonder what Henry has told Judd about each of us—and what personal observations Judd will be delivering back to Henry once the project is over.

"Susan likes to speak her mind," I tell him. "She's got strong opinions. But she's been doing this a long time. She's definitely committed to the best possible outcome for this project. Trust me."

Half an hour later, I check in with Angela, who's crying in her cubicle. Her face is puffy. I realize there's a bruise on the left side of her face. She's tried to hide it with makeup, but it's starting to show through.

"Is everything OK?" I ask.

She tries to compose herself, straightening in her chair, wiping the snot from her nose with a pink tissue.

"Yes, Mr. Wiley."

"Russell."

The cell phone on her desk starts to play a loud, jingly tune.

"Do you think you could email me that spreadsheet by eleven thirty?"

"Yes, Russell."

"That's great," I say and walk away.

"I'm at work," she whispers into her cell phone. "I told you to stop calling me here."

At eleven thirty, Angela appears at my door. She's still visibly upset. Nervous. Vulnerable.

"I just wanted to check that the spreadsheet I sent you was OK."

"Oh yes," I say. "The spreadsheet was fine."

She hovers in the doorway, needing something more. She's taken off her sweater. The white top she's wearing has half sleeves that reach just below her elbows, so her dark-caramel forearms are bare. I realize I have no idea about her family history, no knowledge of the ethnic combinations that have produced her.

"I'm sorry about before," she says. "It was unprofessional."

"I'm not sure what you mean," I say, thinking this will set her mind at ease. "There's certainly nothing to apologize for."

I wonder for a moment how she has constructed this six-week internship in her mind. How much it means to her that she's been working at such a well-known company. Perhaps for the past five weeks she's drawn something meaningful from her walk-on part as an office worker.

If I were playing my own role better, I would have discovered more about Angela's goals and aspirations. I would have taken her under my wing, imparted some adult wisdom, guided her toward her most appropriate career choices.

But I've been distracted. I haven't taken the time to get to know her. After five weeks, my knowledge of Angela begins and ends with her supple body and her glowing brown skin.

"Angela," I say, "are you interested in photography?"

I open the email Angela sent me. I download the spreadsheet onto my desktop and print out two copies. I study the numbers on the page, feeling strangely excited. Angela and I have arranged to meet in the downstairs lobby at twelve thirty.

The data it contains may be suspect, but the spreadsheet Angela has created looks highly professional. I turn back to the open document on my computer, changing a number randomly and watching all the totals recalculate. I'm impressed. Angela has formatted the file as expertly as an accountant. I try again. It's perfect.

Dave Douglas knocks, walks into my office, and closes the door behind him. No doubt he wants to vent about the D-SAW project and tell me again what a pain in the ass Judd is.

"Hold on, Dave," I say. I re-input the original numbers and save the file before I screw anything up.

Dave's here to tell me that Judd has asked him to cost out the whole project again based on a new set of assumptions. He's red-faced, spitting vitriol. He wants me to know he's got better things to do than take orders from some arrogant fuck-pig who doesn't know a thing about production.

"Why not just work with him?" I say. "He'll be out of here soon enough."

"Don't be so sure," says Dave. "I heard he was having breakfast with Jack last week."

Two minutes after Dave leaves, Judd walks in to offer his own complaints. He's getting frustrated that Dave isn't taking his project seriously enough, that he's already missed one of his deliverables.

"Why not just work with him?" I say. "He has his own way of doing things. But he knows his stuff."

"Don't be so sure," says Judd. "I'm starting to think he's coming at this with a different agenda."

"Hey," I say. "Don't forget that Dave's under a lot of pressure already. But he's trying to help. We all are." As if to prove it, I hand him a copy of the freshly minted spreadsheet and promise to email him the file too.

I get to the lobby at 12:25. I don't want Angela to be there first. She'll only attract attention.

She steps out of the elevator bank wearing dark glasses and a tan raincoat cinched around her waist.

She smiles and waves at me. I nod at her discreetly and wave back with a hand that stays glued to my side.

I start walking toward the revolving doors slowly, hoping she'll fall into stride with me in a way that will look super casual—the way that it looks when two colleagues of the opposite sex, with a significant difference in age and responsibility, just happen to be leaving the building at the same time.

It's all perfectly innocent, I tell myself. We're just having lunch. It's not as if I called an escort service and asked them to send a dusky, barely legal teen dressed in a Cold War–era spy outfit.

"Hey, Angela," says a youngish, balding guy on his way back into the building.

"Hi, Bryan," she says.

"Who's he?" I ask.

"Bryan? He works in corporate finance. He helped me one day when I was lost on the seventh floor."

"Let's go," I say.

We head to the International Center of Photography on Sixth Avenue. My company ID gets us in free, without any pressure to make the suggested contribution. The main exhibit is a retrospective of a well-known and highly perverted German fashion photographer.

We stand in the middle of the main floor, surrounded by twelve-foot-tall images of seminude blonde women striking aggressive poses. There are a lot of nipples and high-heeled leather boots on display. It makes me wonder how different life would be if the Germans of my grandfather's generation had succeeded in their plans to dominate the world.

Angela stands quietly in the midst of it all. She's about five-three in her own buckled-but-flat-heeled leather boots. She has taken off her sunglasses. A strand of her long black hair is caught in her left eyelash. I reach out my hand to gently disentangle it. She flinches.

"It's OK," I say softly. I lift the single hair with the tip of my finger and let my hand fall back to my side.

We eat lunch at a deli near Times Square, sitting at a table in the upstairs seating area. Even though we're at the "crossroads of the world," this is a low-traffic spot. The room is large and spare, with the feel of a bus station. I come here occasionally when I want to read the paper and not be disturbed. It's not the kind of place where I'm likely to run into anyone else from the office. Now, at the tail-end of the lunch hour, there are only five other people scattered around the room.

We set our trays down and take off our coats. There's a lone guy by the window who has put down his plastic fork and is watching Angela's every move. She folds her coat over the back of a chair and sits down opposite me.

"So what did you think of the exhibit?" I say.

"I loved it," she says. "I love everything to do with fashion." She smiles at me. It's the sweet, innocent, trusting smile of a young woman who knows she's safe in the presence of a highly professional—and happily married—authority figure.

Either that, or she's waiting for me to suggest we take the afternoon off and check into a room at the Novotel.

"I'm sorry," I say. "I didn't realize there was going to be quite so much skin on display. I thought the models would be wearing a few more clothes."

She laughs.

"That's OK. I thought they were beautiful."

It has been several days since I said good-bye to "Erika Fallon." Now, looking into Angela's round brown eyes, a whole different fantasy plays out. I can't help imagining a simple yet visually vibrant life that involves beaches, sunshine, energetic sex, adequate sleep and abundant quantities of fresh fruit to consume. In this world, there are no arguments, no responsibilities, no deadlines, no household chores to perform. It's just me and Angela, cut off from the world, ensconced in a happiness cocoon. Fantasy Angela always dresses seductively. She laughs at all my jokes. She craves the physical contact that only I can provide. But she also knows instinctively when to leave me alone.

"What kind of music are you into?" I ask.

She mentions the names of a couple of different rappers and hip-hop artists.

I've heard of one of them, I tell her. "I hear he's pretty good."

She picks at her salad with her plastic fork.

"What kind of music do you like?" she asks.

I mention a couple of the Britpop bands Sam and I fell in love with when we were in London. Angela pushes out her lower lip and shrugs. I tell her the names of the singers from those bands who went on to solo careers. Some of them are still big in England. When they pass through New York, Sam and

I faithfully join the small crowds who gather to see them play. I mention a couple of the young, New York–based retro-new-wave-pseudo-punk-rock bands I've been listening to recently. She hasn't heard those names either.

We talk about movies and TV and books.

"So your favorite movie is *The Fast and The Furious*?"

"Yeah. You really should rent it." She stabs at her food, teasing it around the plate without picking anything up.

"And you've never even seen *The Godfather*?"

"I think my boyfriend had the DVD once," she says. "I fell asleep."

"And what do you do on the weekends?" I say.

"I don't know. The usual. Dancing. Shopping. Church."

"And how did you get that bruise on your face?"

She turns and looks out the window. Her eyes fill up and her lower lip trembles.

"It's OK," I say. "You don't need to say anything."

But it's too late. In an instant, we've switched from the gauzy, soft-focused world of the Playboy Channel to the brightly lit set of an afternoon talk show. Angela spills out the story of her troubled home life, her jealous boyfriend, the depths of her religious convictions, the grandmother she loves, the anguish she feels over breaking her personal vow of chastity. She started having sex with her boyfriend. Then, soon after, one of his friends saw her talking to some other guy in the park. It was completely innocent. Now someone keeps calling her cell phone and shouting that she's a shameful sinner, a disgraceful slut. The story gets jumbled, grows more complicated. I'm baffled by all the twists and turns, breakups and reconciliations. I've lost track of who's who. But I nod sympathetically at what I think are the appropriate moments.

"You can hardly blame yourself," I say softly.

"I thought he was the one," she says.

"The one who was calling you? Or the one who hit you?"

"The one I'd be with forever."

We walk back to the office in silent reflection. Angela's puffy eyes are hidden behind her dark glasses.

Most people think they bury their true selves—that they compromise their essence, give away part of their soul—when they enter their generically designed, monotonously systematic workspace. But maybe some people's true selves are more compromised, more rigidly controlled in their lives outside of work.

Maybe Angela's one of those people. Maybe she needs the safety and structure of an office to allow her true self to surface. Maybe we're the only ones who get to see her as someone confident, playful and relaxed. If she's lucky, she'll find a career path that makes her feel empowered and not simply exploited.

Angela and I ride the elevator back to our offices on the twenty-fifth floor. We pass through the doors and pause by the wall where the *Chronicle* logo still hangs. From here, we will be heading in different directions, me to my office and Angela to her cubicle.

She takes off her sunglasses.

"Thanks for lunch," she says. "And for listening."

My sense is that, more than anything, Angela needs a hug right now. But I'm not the person and this not the place to do it.

"No problem," I say. "I hope it all works out."

CHAPTER TWENTY-TWO

Greg Witchel arrives. He brings wine and beer. He hugs Sam and kisses her on both cheeks, European style.

"You look fantastic," he says to her, and she smiles sweetly in her new outfit, her face framed by the honey-like glow of her recently highlighted hair.

He turns to look at me. "It's great to meet you, Russell," he says. His handshake is cool and firm. He has the confident air you'd expect from an envelope salesman.

He and Sam sit on the couch. I sit on the armchair. We each drink a beer.

Sam asks Greg about the conference, and he starts talking about an interactive multimedia demonstration he saw.

"The technology's really amazing," he says.

"Those are neat looking sneakers, Greg," I say. "Did you get them here in the city?"

Sam asks Greg how things are in Springfield, and he starts talking about the three-bedroom house he's renting and his new Mazda and Nate Murray's near-fatal motorcycle accident last year.

"He broke everything," says Greg. "But I saw him last week. He's looking great."

"You're looking great too, by the way," says Sam, returning the compliment she received earlier. "It looks like you've been working out."

Greg talks enthusiastically about his workout regimen and the dietary supplements he favors. Sam seems interested even though I'm sure she knows that some of the products he mentions make unproven and controversial health claims.

"I don't like the way those things are sold," I say. "With those dubious multilevel marketing operations."

"It's funny you should say that," says Greg. "Because in addition to my day job, I'm a part-time distributor for Nature's Strength. I have the rights for three separate zip codes."

"Well, whatever you're doing," says Sam, "it looks like it's working."

We go out to dinner and order different kinds of salad and different fish entrees. We all drink a couple more beers. Even Sam, which is unusual for her.

We go to a bar and Greg tells me more about the envelope company he works for. He tells me how lucky I am to be with Sam. He tells me that his company has a patented paper technology. He pulls an envelope out of his pocket and demonstrates both its non-tear tensibility and its easy-opening design features. He drinks two more beers and goes to the bathroom.

"You two seem to be hitting it off," says Sam.

"He certainly knows his envelopes," I reply, trying unsuccessfully to rip his product sample in half.

"You know what, Russell?" says Greg, returning from the bathroom. "I'd love to get a meeting at Burke-Hart Publishing. We've been shut out for years. You guys should know our latest envelopes are proven to lift response rates at least ten and up to fifteen percent. I told my boss I was going to meet you socially tonight. He said to let you know we'll be happy to extend you guys a thirty percent discount on your first order. You can't lose."

"Thanks, Greg," I say. "I'm not really the person who does that, but I'll pass it on if I can."

We go home and Sam puts sheets and blankets on the couch for Greg. We decide to drink the wine Greg brought earlier. Sam and Greg sit on the couch, on top of the sheets and blankets. I sit on the armchair again.

Sam tells the story of how Greg dumped her in high school senior year to go out with Karen Barbash, who had bigger tits and loved giving blowjobs. Greg tells us about his bitter divorce from Karen. How he moved to Seattle for a couple of years. Dropped out of sight for a while. He had to move back to Springfield, though. He missed Greg Junior and Paul so much.

We finish the wine, and Sam and I go to the bathroom to pee and brush our teeth and wash our faces. We say good night to Greg and go into the bedroom, and even though it's after midnight on a weeknight, Sam immediately puts her arms around my neck and kisses me. We fall onto the bed, kick off our shoes, and unbuckle, unbutton, unzip, unclasp, and shed each other's clothes. Sam tells me she loves me and wants me right now. She's not usually vocal during sex, but tonight when I enter her she groans loudly and shouts, "Fuck me!" She wraps her legs around me and screams "yes" and "harder." And

I thrust harder. And the bed bangs against the wall. And Sam's groans and shouts grow louder and louder.

I'm in what's called the Empire Room on the thirty-fourth floor watching Judd present his recommendations for the D-SAW launch to Jack and a few other onlookers—finance types mainly, along with Tyler Milken, who's here to take notes and report back to Connie Darwin.

Henry is seated next to Jack, watching Judd like a proud father. Only Jeanie is seated with the grown-ups at the main table. Susan, Dave, Martin and I are relegated to chairs against the wall.

Judd is in his element. He's abandoned all dubious fashion choices and is wearing a straight-down-the-middle blue suit, white shirt and solid red tie. It's the uniform favored by the execs who ride the New Haven line—Jack and Henry are similarly attired.

"This presentation is about the future of a brand," he begins. "It's a great brand. A powerful brand. It's a brand that has helped Burke-Hart Publishing grow into what it is today."

It's familiar stuff, but he delivers it well. I count three beats during his meaningful pause.

"At the same time," Judd goes on, "the *Daily Business Chronicle* is a mature brand. With an audience that has declined more than fifty percent over the past ten years. With a readership that's aging twice as fast as the general population. And with an advertising base that's down forty percent since the year 2000. Everyone in the newspaper industry is struggling to capture the next generation of readers—and the *Chronicle* is no different. But the truth is, these younger readers have grown up on the internet. It's how they get their news and their entertainment. It's where they explore their interests and meet new people. The internet is home to these consumers. It's where they *live*. And increasingly, it's where advertisers go to reach them."

I realize why this intro is so familiar. I wrote it for Henry two years ago. At the time, it was the foundation of our argument that the *Chronicle*'s print and online divisions be merged as soon as possible. Of course, the argument was rejected on the grounds of being too logical. As long as the idiotic Mark Sand runs our online unit, doing things logically is not an option.

"At the outset of this project," says Judd, "I was purposed to find ways to restore growth to this great brand. To open up new revenue streams. To enhance our bottom-line profitability. This great brand is not going away. But we need to restore it to growth. Because in business, as they say, growth is the only sign of life."

I get stuck on the "I" part of Judd's phrase "I was purposed." Having set up the rationale for our new brand extension, he's positioning himself to take credit for this whole new direction. There's not one word of acknowledgment for the input the rest of us have given him.

I watch in silence as Judd zips through slides talking about the new metrics this project will give to our business. How *he*'s streamlined the cost base and leveraged economies of scale in production and distribution. How *his* marketing plan relies more on efficient upselling through our customer database than expensive awareness advertising.

Judd's pumping up this opportunity as if his entire future depended on it. It doesn't even matter that the content he's delivering is like a warmed-up plate of yesterday's refried beans. He's selling it hard. Jack and Henry are lapping it up.

Clearly, it's not only Judd's future that depends on the D-SAW project. Jack and Henry need it too. They've been stuck in "slow-growth/no-growth" land for way too long. They've sat idle as Yolanda Pew and Barney Barnes—in just three years—have rolled out one new magazine launch after another. Meanwhile, even as he trails his online competitors, Mark Sand can still point to double-digit advertising growth.

Now Jack and Henry are not just feeling the heat. They're desperate. Before they get restructured out of their jobs, they need to sell a new idea to Connie Darwin and gain her support in selling it on to Larry Ghosh.

Unfortunately, this tired, lamebrained project—with Judd at the helm—is the best they've come up with. This time around, the *Daily Edge* has been reimagined as a free tabloid targeting young urban commuters, with a design that's based more on the *Huffington Post* than the *Daily Business Chronicle*. Multiple stories will appear on every page, with quick-read summaries of all the major news and business stories. Judd's plan also calls for the *Daily Edge* to be included as a supplement to the *Chronicle*, delivered each day to all our home subscribers. The hope is they'll pass this dumbed-down version of the news along to their kids. There's no plan to increase our subscription price because research has shown that *Chronicle* subscribers don't want anything more to read. That means the project's success or failure will hinge entirely on advertising revenue. Right now, Judd is furiously painting a rainbow that imagines advertisers actually accepting the value of—and paying a premium price for—this unwanted product and its unproven distribution model.

I look over at Tyler Milken, Connie Darwin's executive assistant. Despite his seemingly innocuous job title, he's the person Judd has to sell to the most. Like Judd, he's an ambitious MBA-type who wants to be running the world one day. What Tyler reports back to Connie will make or break the launch plan. Tyler's taking copious notes.

On the wall behind Tyler are a series of rather menacing black-and-white art portraits. Each one captures an animal's face in close-up. I gaze at them for several seconds before I realize the animals I'm studying are all sheep.

Susan Trevor digs me in the ribs and points at the screen. Judd is taking the audience through his project P&L, detailing the investment required for the launch and the long-term profit potential which, if deliverable, would justify the upfront investment. This is where this project always falls down. The risk is too big and the reward too small. In our division, we can't afford to spend years losing millions on a project that's never been seen as a surefire success.

"What's remarkable about this plan," says Judd, "is that, unlike most launches in our industry, we're looking at a profitability right from the outset. The risk is small and the reward is potentially huge. Even using conservative revenue estimates, we're looking to add three million dollars to the bottom line in year one, growing to fifteen million by year three."

"What the fuck?" Susan whispers loudly in my ear.

"What the fuck?" I say loudly to myself.

I'm studying a hard copy of Judd's presentation, alongside the spreadsheet Angela created. The numbers we gave Judd showed a seven-million-dollar loss in year one, but the arrogant shitheel has cut the marketing budget from twelve million to two million dollars. He's doctored the numbers, butchered the plan I gave him. The little bastard is out to create a job for himself. This is not going to stand.

I jump out of my chair, march toward Henry's office. I'm ready to take Judd down. I have the evidence in my hand.

Just past Angela's cubicle, I turn around and march back to my office. I open up the spreadsheet I saved on my PC. It won't hurt just to check one thing.

"Fuck. Shit. Fuck."

I fucked it up myself. That day I was playing around with Angela's spreadsheet. I didn't re-input the numbers properly before I re-saved the file. I hit the "save" button when I should have hit "don't save." I'm the one who gave Judd the bogus ingredients to bake into his plan.

Now what do I do? Who can I tell about this? I look down at the cover of Judd's presentation and there's one obvious answer.

Don't say a word.

CHAPTER TWENTY-THREE

Henry calls me to his office. He's nervous. He, Judd and Jeanie have been summoned to a meeting next Monday with Connie Darwin and Tyler Milken. This is the meeting that will determine the fate of the D-SAW project and whether or not we move forward with the launch of the *Daily Edge*. I know Henry's nervous because he keeps telling me how calm he feels.

I'm nervous too. If Connie approves the P&L Judd presented, I'm screwed. Henry is still unaware that the marketing budget I gave Judd is one-sixth of the size it needs to be.

I balance the pros and cons of telling Henry my mistake. I figure if I come clean now, it's a hundred percent certain I'll get fired. On the other hand, I estimate there's only a twenty-five percent chance of the project getting approved. Which means there's a seventy-five percent chance no one need ever know.

I email my Unicorns article to Fergus on Sunday morning and kiss Sam good-bye before she heads to work at Artyfacts.

I'm flying to Miami this afternoon for a media conference the *Chronicle* is sponsoring. While I'm out of town, Sam has decided to spend a few days in Hartford with Beth-Anne, her pregnant younger sister.

From the airport in Miami, I take a cab to the Biltmore in Coral Gables. Erika and Sally flew down earlier in the day to get everything set up. I find them in the room adjacent to the main ballroom, arranging product information and promotional items on the table in front of our booth. Erika, hair pulled back, is wearing a white T-shirt under a half-zipped hooded sweatshirt.

"Looking good," I say.

"We're getting there," she replies.

"Anything I can do?" I ask.

"I think we've got it covered."

Sally says, "I'm just going to get rid of these boxes," then heads behind the booth and through a door.

I pick up one of the zero-gravity pens we've been handing out for the past three years. They're bulkier than a normal pen, but with the added advantage that they write upside down.

"These still popular?" I ask.

"You'd be surprised."

I look around the room. A few other people are at work on their displays. A couple of companies have finished setting up and left for the evening. Some other booths are still packed in their crates.

Sally reappears. "So, what are you guys doing this evening?" I ask, casual but businesslike.

"We're going to eat here," says Erika. "Early start tomorrow. Got to be fresh."

"That's good. I might just eat in my room. I've got some work to catch up on."

"We thought we'd wait till tomorrow to go wild at South Beach," says Sally.

"Really? Not too wild I hope."

"We're just going for dinner," says Erika. "Why don't you join us?"

I sit through the first sessions of the conference worrying about what to wear for dinner and checking for emails on my BlackBerry. I'm hoping to get word from Henry that the D-SAW project has been abandoned.

During the midmorning break, I stroll through the expo area to look at all the booths. People are grabbing up the *Chronicle*'s zero-gravity pens and cramming them into *New York Times*–branded shopping bags. Erika is talking to a steady stream of scavengers posing as potential advertising customers. She encourages everyone to put a business card into a plastic fishbowl to enter our special prize drawing.

Now that I'm viewing Erika purely as a staff member, I am able to appreciate the poise and grace she brings to all her interactions. She is clearly an asset to my team—approachable and highly attentive to customers without being overly flirtatious. She exudes a maturity that Sally, busy demonstrating the upside-down writing abilities of our giveaway pens, clearly lacks.

I watch as a tanned, brightly dressed male executive drops a business card into the bowl, then leans toward Erika, says something quietly to her, and hands her a second card.

I glance at my BlackBerry screen and see the heading "Message from Henry," sent by his assistant, Ellen. I click it open and get the news displayed on my tiny, handheld screen:

> *D-SAW project approved. Press release going out this afternoon. This is exciting for us all. EOM*

My skin suddenly feels sensitive to the cold blasts of the air-conditioning. I loop around to the coffee station and prepare myself a cup. I wait till I feel the color returning to my cheeks before walking back to our booth.

I grab a handful of business cards from the fishbowl to see the kind of names we're collecting.

"Who was that George Hamilton–looking guy with the hair plugs?" I ask Erika.

When the conference breaks at four thirty, I call Fergus on my cell phone. I want to get his reaction to my article.

"We're good to go," he says. "I fixed your typos. I'll let you know if it's running long when we get the layouts back."

"That's good," I say. "So, did you hear the news?"

More than my article, I want to talk to Fergus about the D-SAW project. We'll be going into full launch mode, and no dissension will be allowed. He's the only person I can talk to truthfully about the disaster that lies ahead. It's a disaster that the Ghosh Corporation is big enough to recover from. But that doesn't mean it won't hurt the *Chronicle*'s reputation or destroy individual careers.

He searches the internet to find the press release and reads it while we talk.

"'This is an exciting day for one of America's best-loved brands,' said Jack Tennant, president of Burke-Hart Business

Group and publisher of the *Daily Business Chronicle*. 'The *Daily Edge* edition will not only broaden our customer base and open new streams of revenue, but unlike most launches, it will also be accretive to earnings from year one.'"

"That's what they think," I say. "But I didn't tell you the best part. Some idiot made a ten-million-dollar mistake in those projections. No one caught it. Jack thinks he's going to make three million dollars in year one. In reality, he's going to lose at least seven."

"Fuck," says Fergus. "Was it that asshole consultant?"

"Actually, it was that asshole me."

I call Sam to confirm she got to Hartford OK. She sounds happy, pleased to have some time with her sister before the baby comes.

"You should see it," she says. "The nursery's all decorated. Beth-Anne and Steve are so excited."

When we hang up, I roll off the bed and head to the shower with the lingering sound of Sam's voice in my ear. I conjure up a memory. We're dancing in our living room. She's wearing a black dress and her vanilla perfume. There are silver hoops in her ears. She's moved the coffee table closer to the wall so we can twirl around the imitation Persian rug. I hold her close to me. She rests her head on my shoulder. I move my left hand down to the small of her back. Despite the difference in our heights, we've always found ways to fit our bodies together.

She tilts her head and we kiss. I feel her tongue in my mouth immediately. We abandon any pretense that we're dancing. I lift the back of her dress, grab the cheeks of her ass. She's not wearing underwear.

She steers me back toward the couch and starts unbuckling my belt. I push her hands away. I can do it faster. I start to remove my pants and underwear, but she forces me back. I bump into the couch and collapse into a sitting position, pants still around my ankles. She straddles me, guiding my cock inside her.

She starts riding me, but I cling to her, pulling her down, restricting her movements. I want to make this last.

I gradually loosen my grip, and she moves on me slowly. I lean back on the couch and look at her. In the flickering light she looks peaceful and menacing.

I lift her dress over her head and drop it on the cushion next to me. She's wearing only a black bra. I run my hands over her thighs, her stomach, up and down her arms, feeling the softness of her skin, the muscles beneath.

I reach around and fumble with her bra, unclasping it on the second attempt. I press my face against her chest.

She bounces on me faster, making pleasurable, encouraging sounds. She wants to feel that we're really fucking. My mouth is glued to her breast, my hands are on her butt, assisting each upward motion, not resisting as she pushes back down.

I groan as I come. The image of Sam disappears. I lean my hands against the shower wall and let hot water rain down on my head for a couple more minutes.

CHAPTER TWENTY-FOUR

I meet Erika and Sally in the lobby. Erika is wearing a red silk shirt and blue jeans. Sally is in a more revealing, semitransparent top and tight black pants.

"Am I overdressed?" I ask.

"You're the boss," Erika reminds me. "But this is Miami."

"You can always leave the jacket in the car," says Sally.

We head out in their rental car to Miami Beach. Erika drives. I take the passenger seat, with Sally in the back. Erika steers us through the streets of Coral Gables, past the stores along Miracle Mile. I take care to intersperse my glances at Erika's profile with concentrated stares at the road ahead and frequent looks out of the side window.

"So," says Sally, leaning in between our seats, "how involved are we going to get with the launch of the *Daily Edge*?"

"I guess you heard the news," I say.

"Judd called me as soon as he found out," says Sally. "He's really excited."

"He called you?"

"Sure. Why wouldn't he?"

"I guess you haven't heard," says Erika. "Sally has a new boyfriend."

"Really?" I say.

Sally gives me her mischievous Drew Barrymore smile.

"Of course, I advised her against it," says Erika, pulling up at a stop sign. "You know I don't approve of office romances."

We valet park and head into the restaurant Sally selected. It's called Point. Sally told us it would be unforgettable. As soon as we walk in, I understand why. Point takes the concept of can't-hear-yourself-think restaurants way beyond the natural limit. A DJ in the corner is spinning Latino electro-pop music at a level that makes the floor vibrate and my body feel assailed. Tables on the far side of the room are circled around a large dance floor. Erika points to a bin full of sani-wrapped ear plugs, and she and I each grab a pair. Sally dances ahead of us and enters Erika's name onto an ATM-style screen to confirm our reservation. The hostess spins the screen round, jabs at it a couple more times, then signals us to follow her.

We're seated in a loud corner and handed laminated menus with pictures of food on one side and drinks on the other. Our waitress switches on a floodlight-style tabletop lamp so we can see what we're looking at and points out the various switches that allow us to dim or increase the light. We can signal her to come back by using a flight-attendant call button that lights a separate red bulb above our table.

We point to the drinks we want. A large bottled water, plus a cosmopolitan for Sally, a Virgin Mary for Erika and a Corona for me.

Finally the waitress hands us each a notepad and marker to write with so we can exchange notes during the meal.

I write: *Judd?*

Sally writes: *He's kewl.*

Our drinks arrive, and we point to a selection of appetizers. Sally points to the screen above the DJ booth that has been showing images from old black-and-white movies. Every minute or two the videos stop and words appear on the screen. Right now it reads: *Let's Dance!*

Sally jumps up and heads to the dance floor. Erika and I signal that we'll stay put.

I hold up my *Judd?* note again.

Erika writes: *Not my type.*

I write a new question: *So what do you do for fun?*

I see her laugh, then write: *Birdwatching!*

We sit quietly, sipping our drinks, watching Sally bop around the dance floor, making new friends along the way. The music washes over us. Lights are flashing all around. A random series of photographs is flashing against a nearby wall. We look everywhere except at each other. My hand grips the Corona bottle. Erika's caresses the stem of her glass. Our knees are just inches apart.

Sally comes back to sit with us a minute, drinks more of her cosmo. Suddenly she's pointing at both of us and then at the sign that now reads: *Everybody Dance!*

We all head to the dance floor. Sally spins away from us and into the crowd. I'm left shuffling my feet hesitantly opposite Erika. I try to mimic her. She moves sinuously, eyes half-closed, a thoughtful smile on her face. I wonder if it's obvious to the other dancers that we're just colleagues dining out on a business trip, not a real couple.

The sign above the DJ reads: *Wave Your Arms in the Air.* We dutifully wave our hands.

Erika points back to our table. I give her a thumbs-up sign. We wave to Sally, then sit back down. Our appetizers have arrived. We watch the dancers as we eat. Every minute or two, they respond to new instructions from the DJ:

Hug Someone

Show Your Tattoo

Touch a Stranger's Nose

After a while Sally joins us again, and the three of us finish eating. We're waiting for our plates to be cleared. Under the table, Erika puts her hand on top of mine. My body tightens, but she doesn't move her hand. I look at her, and she nods toward the screen, which now reads: *Take Your Partner by the Hand.*

I turn my hand slowly under hers until our fingers are entwined. I sit frozen, holding my breath until the screen switches back to an old Laurel and Hardy movie. Erika takes her hand away from mine. She picks up her drink and sips it without looking at me. Sally seems not to have noticed anything.

By the time we've finished our entrees, Sally is working on her third cosmopolitan. The three of us are dancing again. Sally is shimmying with a dark-haired guy who looks and moves like a professional salsa dancer.

Erika and I maintain a professional distance, even as the dance floor grows more crowded. Suddenly she beckons me toward her and cups her hand toward my ear. I glance up at the screen, which now commands us to *Whisper a Secret in Someone's Ear*. I sense Erika's lips close to my earlobe, but because of the music and the earplugs I'm wearing I can only feel the breath from her mouth. I can't hear what she's saying.

After she steps away, I signal that I have a secret to share too. I position my lips close to her ear and whisper, "I dream about you."

I'm not sure how loud I'm speaking. But I'm suddenly aware that there's been a break in the music. I step away from Erika as the beat resumes. She starts dancing again, moving her body in the same effortless rhythm as before.

We drive back to Coral Gables with Sally, who exchanged numbers with the salsa dancer before we left, talking loudly between us the whole way.

We ride up in the elevator. Erika and Sally get out first. They're sharing a room to save on expenses.

"OK, guys. Have a good night," I say.

"I feel tipsy," says Sally, stepping out first. "And my ears are ringing."

Erika takes Sally's arm to steady her. She turns to me and says, "Good night, Russell. Sweet dreams."

In my room, I throw my jacket on the back of a chair and lie down on the bed, still clothed. One floor down and three doors down the hall, Erika Fallon is undressing. The phone rings. I was dozing. I roll over and see that several minutes have passed. I press the receiver to my ear.

"Russell. I wanted to tell you something before I went to sleep."

"What is it?"

"I dream about you too."

I pause to consider the appropriate response.

"I have to go," she says. "I think Sally's throwing up."

At 3:17 a.m. I wake up again. Still clothed. The phone is in the cradle. I head to the bathroom, not a hundred percent sure if that conversation happened or if I dreamed it.

By morning, Pete has emailed me his draft of the Livingston Kidd presentation. I print it out at the hotel's business center to read on the plane home.

I'm on an earlier flight than Erika and Sally. My plane sits on the tarmac for forty-five minutes. I grip the armrest next to me, trying to remember the sensation I felt when Erika first put her hand on mine. Slowly, I turn my palm upward. My fingers wriggle in the air like the legs of a dying bug. I stare back out at the tarmac until we taxi for takeoff.

Pete's done a good job with the Livingston Kidd proposal, but I feel something's missing. I decide to look at it again later and compare it to the samples of my best work I keep at home.

"Hey, how's it going?" I keep my voice casual. It's not the voice of someone who held hands with—and whispered inappropriate things in the ear of—a female colleague last night.

"It's good," says Sam. "How was your trip?"

"Not bad. The usual media conference stuff. Everyone predicting things that won't come true. Like this new thing Twitter that's supposed to take over the world. I don't see it. Hey, what happened to that box in the hall closet? The white one. With my work stuff in it."

"The one I kept asking you to put in the basement?"

"That one."

"I put it in the basement."

"Great. Where's the key?"

"Right here. On my key ring. So I won't lose it."

"That's OK. You can give it to me tomorrow when you get back."

"Ooooohh. That's the thing. I just told Beth-Anne I might stay till the weekend if you said it was OK."

"Well, I need my stuff. Maybe the super can cut the lock."

"What if I mail it to you? I'll do it tonight. You'll probably get it by Thursday. Would that work?"

"I guess I can wait. When are you coming back?"

"Maybe Sunday night. Or Monday. What do you think?"

"That old I'm-staying-till-Sunday-so-I-might-as-well-stay-till-Monday routine."

"So it's OK?"

"I'll miss you," I say.

"I'll miss you too."

"I don't want to institute a ton of process," says Judd as he hands out new three-ring binders to the project team gathered around the table of the small conference room. "But remember, I'm a process kind of guy."

"What is this?" asks Susan Trevor, flipping through the photocopied forms and charts in her binder. "*Project Management for Dummies*?"

Judd doesn't address her point directly. For the first time, though, he seems slightly rattled. Most Rainbow Painters don't stick around after their concepts are approved. But Judd's been given the role of project manager on the *Daily Edge* launch team. Even aside from having to deliver against his rosy financial projections, I'm guessing he's nervous about keeping this fractious group motivated and his idealized process on track. He stands at the head of the table and refers to a page of notes as he speaks.

"Welcome to our first planning meeting as we move toward the successful launch of the *Daily Edge*. I think we're all excited about the prospect of working on such a major new initiative for the company. And we all know how much work needs to be done if we are going to launch our new edition successfully. Every one of you has to manage a team that will contribute multiple deliverables to this project. And it's my job as project manager to help clear your path of obstructions and ensure we meet all our critical path objectives. Does that make sense to you all?"

He looks up from the paper trembling in his hand, searching for some sign that his team is buying into this notion. All he gets is hostile silence until Hank Sullivan nods his head almost imperceptibly.

"Great!" says Judd. "One of the most important things we need to do today is to identify our interdependencies. Because even though we're all owning our own department's deliverables, we have to be aware of each other's deadlines so the whole project can come together seamlessly. The last thing we need is for a delay in one aspect of the project to cause a delay in another area. Are we all good with that?"

Dave Douglas clears his throat.

"Excellent!" says Judd. He turns to the easel he has set up next to him and flips the cover to reveal a grid he has drawn with eleven rows, representing the weeks until we launch, and six columns, each labeled for our separate departments.

"We're eleven weeks from launch," he says. "And frankly, that scares me. I just want to make sure we map out everybody's role so we can parallel-process most effectively. Susan. Let's start with you. What do you see as your key deliverables over the next few weeks? What are the interdependencies that we need to be aware of?"

"I don't think my deliverables are going to fit into those little boxes you've drawn," says Susan. "Do you have any idea what I'll be doing the next few weeks?"

Judd is thrown for only a second. "I don't want to get too granular here. This is the thirty-thousand-feet view. Right now, I just want to get our schedule agreed so Jeanie, Hank, Russell, Martin and Dave know when to expect their pieces from you and vice versa."

"OK," says Susan. "As long as you remember I'm leaving at four thirty today."

And so it goes. Somehow we get through the session, sharing enough information, taking the appropriate level of responsibility for meeting the deadlines we each need to meet. All the while, my head grows heavier and my body starts aching a little more.

"Good meeting," says Judd. "I'm calmer. You guys should know by now, I'm all about process."

Martin and I walk four blocks to a Chinese restaurant we've discovered on Forty-sixth Street. It's a place that meets the three basic needs for a candid lunchtime conversation: The food is good. The service is fast. And Henry wouldn't be seen dead here.

We're seated at a small table next to a mirrored wall. Tea, crunchy noodles and duck sauce appear before us. Within sixty seconds we've ordered our favorites from the lunch specials menu.

"So," I say. "What's new?"

"It's official," says Martin. "Barney made the offer this morning. I accepted."

"Fuck," I say, dipping a noodle into the sauce, popping it into my mouth and chewing. "So that's why you were so quiet in Judd's meeting. Congratulations, I guess. Has anyone told Henry yet?"

"Not yet. Barney worked it out with HR. There's nothing Henry can do."

"Fuck," I say again. "He's going to have a cow when he hears."

Two hot and sour soups are deposited in front of us.

"So what happens after you're gone?" I ask. "If Henry's looking to cut staff, he's not going hire someone to replace you. He's going to have to promote from within."

"That's one reason I don't feel so bad. Rachel's obviously ready to step up."

I slurp at my soup while Martin tells me all the reasons Rachel is right for his position. How incredibly organized she is. How she sees the big picture. How she used to manage three people in her last job. He's wearing a brand new denim jacket designed to look like he's been sleeping rough in it for years. Tufts of hair are sprouting from his ears.

"You don't think Liz can do it? She's been here longer. Everybody likes her."

"Liz? Your old flame? No. She wouldn't be right. She's a good designer. But she's not a leader. I can't see her running the department. Plus she just had the kid and all."

The waiter returns with our food. I pick up my fork and attack my plate of prawns and mixed vegetables.

Martin fumbles with his chopsticks and works on a mouthful of chicken and broccoli before saying, "I'm getting out just in time, Russell. You should think about it too. The newspaper business is in the toilet. Barney thinks the *Chronicle* is fucked. If this new project doesn't work out, Larry Ghosh will probably fold the paper and take it all online."

We talk more about the reasons why I should follow Martin's lead and jump ship while I can. But somewhere in the back of my mind, I hear Henry whispering, "Loyalty's important." And I do feel a loyalty. If not to Henry, at least to the *Chronicle* and to the people who work for me. I can't leave now. I can't leave my team at the mercy of Judd. Plus there's that little matter of my ten-million-dollar mistake. Sometime soon, I'm going to have to own up to that. It's my mess. I'm a hundred percent responsible. One way or another, I need to clean it up.

Martin and I are quiet for the first three blocks as we head back to our building. I feel chilled. I need to lie down.

"Just for the record," I say, "nothing ever happened between me and Liz. And despite that, I'd still promote her over Rachel any day of the week."

CHAPTER TWENTY-FIVE

I'm running for a train. I know it's leaving in sixty seconds, and I'm about three minutes away. But I run anyway. Quickly, I'm out of breath. I can see the train in the distance, about to pull away. I'm gasping for air. There's no way I can make it, but I keep running. Everything is heavy. I'm moving in slow motion. I want to collapse and die. Instead, I wake up. I'm breathing heavily through a dry, bitter-tasting mouth. I'm alone in the bed. My nose is stuffed with congestion. My whole body feels sore, beaten up. It's 3:17 a.m. I caught a cold coming back from Miami. I need to pee, but I don't want to get up.

I call in sick and lie in bed watching TV. I ask Mike, my doorman, to buzz me when the mail comes so I can at least look for the files I want to crib from for the Livingston Kidd project.

Midafternoon, Mike calls and I put on shorts and sneakers to go get the mail. I've been feeling sorry for myself, drinking red zinger tea and eating cereal. My head is still foggy.

I sort through the mail. The usual bills and fundraising solicitations. And a handwritten envelope from Sam. Like her voice, I've always liked Sam's handwriting, as if she curls her pen around words the same way she does with her tongue. This script is hurried-looking, more angular than normal, but it's still recognizably hers. I can feel the key inside.

The elevator door closes, and I try to slide my finger under the envelope flap. The flap's stuck tight, so I turn the envelope on its side to rip off the end instead. The elevator bumps to a stop, the door opens, and I step into the basement. Something's not right. The envelope won't tear. My fingertips send an urgent message to my brain: they've felt this kind of envelope before. I spin round and kick my leg forward to make the closing elevator door slide open again.

I inspect the envelope as the elevator glides slowly up to the sixth floor. The postmark is Enfield, Connecticut. Not Hartford where Beth-Anne and Steve live. The paper feels lighter but slightly thicker than a standard business envelope. I didn't notice at first, but there's an easy-open tear-off strip. It's the kind of feature that makes opening envelopes fun, that increases direct mail response rates from ten to fifteen percent. I pull the strip, tilt the envelope, and let the small metal key slide into my palm.

I don't know Connecticut well, so I check it on the internet. Enfield's easy to find. Just south of the Massachusetts border. Only a few miles from Springfield, Massachusetts. The town where Sam grew up. The town to which high school sweetheart/envelope salesman/natural foods entrepreneur Greg Witchel has recently returned.

"Hi, Beth-Anne. Is Sam there?"

"Hi, Russell. Not right now. Can I have her call you?"

"That's OK. I just wanted to ask her if we had any cold medications."

"You have a cold? That's too bad."

"When do you think she'll be back?"

"I don't know. Did you try her cell?"

"No. Maybe I'll do that. You guys having a good time?"

"Yes. It's been great to see her."

"What have you been up to?"

"Not much. Just the mall and back. The doctor wants me to take it easy till the baby comes. We've mainly been sitting around chatting."

"Just the two of you?"

"And Steve when he's around. Which isn't often."

"That's nice. When do you think Sam will be back?"

"I don't know. She borrowed the car. Went for a drive. I think she was getting a bit stir-crazy."

"OK. I'll try her cell then. Can you tell her I called?"

"OK. Feel better, Russell."

"OK. Good luck with everything, Beth-Anne."

"You too."

I leave a message on Sam's cell phone. Casual. Asking her to call me. Telling her I'm home sick. Just running downstairs, but otherwise I'll be here.

I go to the basement, fetch the box I need, and sit with it by the phone. Half an hour goes by. I open the box. This was supposed to be my best work. But now it seems average and uninspired. I compare it to what Pete has done for me on Livingston Kidd. I can't quite figure out what parts of his presentation I was hoping to fix. Today, his stuff looks better than I thought and mine looks worse than I remember.

Another half hour goes by. I try Sam's cell phone again but don't leave a message. I email Pete and tell him the Livingston Kidd presentation looks great. He should get it to Randy Baker. If it's OK with Randy, then send a copy to Henry and we're good to go. I tell him he should be the one to email Henry with it. I don't tell him that the effort is worthless. All along, we've just been going through the motions. It doesn't matter how good the presentation is. The Livingston Kidd account is already lost.

I call Beth-Anne again.

"Hi, Russell. She's not back yet."

"Yeah. I tried her cell a couple of times. Should I be worried?"

Beth-Anne hesitates, then says, "I just think she loves to drive. She said she doesn't get much chance in the city."

"You have no idea where she went?"

"She didn't say."

"Maybe to meet an old friend?"

"I don't know, Russell."

"It wasn't me who wanted to sell the car," I say. "She was the one who didn't want to deal with the alternate-side parking."

Later when I try Beth-Anne's number again, it rings four times and the answering machine picks up. I don't leave a message. I try a couple more times, in case Beth-Anne picks up while her recorded message is still playing. After that I start hanging up on the fourth ring, before the machine picks up.

I call Fergus at home. Julie tells me he's working late, closing the new issue of *Vicious Circle*. I try his office, leave him a message. Ask him to call me back no matter how late.

The apartment is quiet. I pad to the kitchen in my thick hiking socks. I fill the electric kettle and sit at the kitchen table waiting for it to boil. I rinse out the mug I've been drinking from all day. My favorite mug. The one with the red London bus on the side. I sit in the corner of our kitchen at our glass-topped table. In the time it takes the water to boil, I realize how easy it would be to lose my grip completely. Slipping into insanity would be as easy as walking through the wrong door. Insanity is the chair next to mine. Because I sat in this chair, I can stare at the kettle, the mug, the colorful box of Celestial Seasonings tea. I can stand up and pour the boiling water. I can sit back down and wait for the phone to ring or the tea to brew. It was just luck I sat in the sanity chair. If I had sat in the other one, I would be mad already.

The herbal tea is meant to soothe, but I grow increasingly agitated. I try a different flavor. I sit on the couch. I watch TV with the sound turned down.

The phone rings. It's after midnight. It's Fergus. I need to tell him about Sam. But he's talking first. He's excited. He has news he needs to tell me. He wants me to hear it from him before I hear it from anywhere else.

"Is this about Sam?"

"Sam? No. What's wrong with Sam?"

"It doesn't matter. Tell me your thing."

"Brace yourself."

"I'm braced."

"I really hope this won't ruin our friendship."

"Why would it?"

"It's this article I've been working on." And then he stops talking. As if he's hesitant to reveal something really bad. I turn off the TV and toss the remote onto the coffee table.

"Just tell me what the fuck it is."

"You know how much I hate Larry Ghosh."

"Yeah?"

"Well, a few weeks ago I pitched my editor a story idea."

"About?"

"We were looking for a new angle. We had that torture-porn article last month. We wanted to follow it up with something different. And not just the usual right-wing nutjob stuff."

I lean forward on the couch, the phone pressed to my ear. "And you came up with…?"

"It was just meant to be this tiny, small, inconsequential little piece about how Ghosh is screwing up the *Daily Business Chronicle*. You know, the kind of stuff you're always telling me about."

"You mean the stuff that has nothing to do with Larry Ghosh?"

"Well, anyway, when Ghosh Media announced the launch of the *Daily Edge*, we suddenly had a news angle to run with."

A chill runs through me. "What kind of news angle?"

Fergus tells me all about the story he's written. The inside story of Project D-SAW. How Larry Ghosh has been pressuring the *Chronicle*'s management to improve our financial results at any cost. With me as his unnamed source, he has concocted a story of corporate desperation, executive ineptitude and financial mismanagement. He thinks he's blowing the whistle on how the Ghosh Corporation is putting the final nail in the coffin of one of America's most respected newspapers. And what's the big news he's breaking? Where's his smoking gun? I think I've already figured it out, but I want him to tell me.

"You know that screwup on the business plan?" he says. "The ten-million-dollar mistake? How you told me the project would have never been approved without the fake numbers?"

"You motherfucking cocksucker."

"I'm sorry, Russell, I had to put it in."

"You fucking asshole."

"I'm sorry. I'm a journalist. This is news."

"Did you use my name?"

"Of course not."

"So how bad is it going to be?"

"I don't know. But I had to warn you. My editor has it in for Ghosh too. He decided the story was so big he's put it on the cover. Our publisher wants to make as much noise as possible with it. We're sending press releases everywhere. She's tripled the print run."

"You fucking shit fucker."

"I'm sorry, Russell," he says again.

I resist the urge to call him a backstabbing Judas. I can't tell Fergus this, but there's a part of me that's glad he's done what he's done.

"Whatever." I hang up the phone and rest my chin on my chest for a while. I'm shivering, sitting all alone in the empty apartment. I never did get the chance to tell Fergus about Sam.

I don't sleep. And then I do. I dream the Twin Towers have magically reappeared. I leave the Burke-Hart Building after dark, look downtown, and there they are. Lights twinkling on all hundred and ten floors as if they'd never been away. People around me are rejoicing, but I start crying instead. Even in my dream I understand this is a mirage, a falsehood—something even sadder than the empty sky.

Eventually it gets light outside. There's no point trying to sleep. I shave and shower. I get dressed. I sit on the bed. I feel too tired to think, to feel, to function in the world. I go to work.

I rub Lucky Cat's paw. I try Sam's cell phone number again. I check my email and the corporate intranet. I call Christine Lynch in HR to tell her that I'm about to meet with Jeremy Stent. Barbara comes into my office with a manila folder that conceals the good luck card she wants me to sign for Angela, who is leaving today. I study the card, the bland words that others have already written. I can't think of anything appropriate to say. I ask Barbara to leave it with me. I open the other manila folder on my desk. The one that contains Jeremy's severance letter.

"Hi, Russell. You wanted to see me?"

The best way to handle these things is to get right to the point. No pleasantries or chitchat. No pretense that this conversation is anything other than what it is.

"Sit down, Jeremy," I say. "I have some bad news."

He looks at me blankly. I bite my bottom lip to let him know how hard this is for me. "I'm sorry, Jeremy, but we're going to have to let you go."

"What?"

"I said I'm sorry, Jeremy, but we're going to have to let you go. We recognize that you're an extremely intelligent and talented individual, but we've come to the conclusion that maybe this isn't the right fit for you and maybe it would be better for all involved if you maybe left to pursue a different career path."

"What do you mean, maybe?"

"Well, not just maybe. I didn't do a good job phrasing that. Each time I said maybe, I probably should have said actually instead."

"You're firing me?"

"We'd prefer to announce that we've come to a mutual agreement. You are still within your probation period. We will set your exit date for two weeks from today, but we won't need you to actually be here during that time."

I slide the severance letter across the desk. He reads it quickly.

His face collapses. "What have I done wrong?"

"You haven't done anything wrong. Like I said, you're obviously smart and talented. It's just that maybe this isn't the right fit for you. Actually."

"Just tell me what I've done wrong. I can fix it."

"Jeremy, I think we've decided that actually your talents will be better suited elsewhere."

He tells me he doesn't want to leave because he loves it here and he loves the people and everyone has been so nice to him and says, "Please, Russell, don't do this to me. I need this job." His voice cracks and he starts sobbing.

I stare at the colorful spines on the book jackets on the shelf behind his left shoulder, aware of the type but not reading the printed words, and say, "Sorry, Jeremy. It's nothing personal. There's nothing I can do. We just think it's better for all concerned if you leave immediately. Please hand your ID and company credit card to Tony from security, who is waiting in the corridor and can help you carry any boxes you might have down to the street."

Jeremy stops sobbing and still doesn't move, so I say, "Or maybe we can ship them to your home address in a day or two if you prefer."

"I want to talk to Henry," he says.

"I'm sorry. That won't be possible."

"And what about the fire drill?"

"What fire drill?"

"There's a fire drill today. I'm filling in for Roger as fire warden. I'm supposed to check the bathrooms."

"I think we'll manage."

A minute later I get up and open the door and ask Tony if he could help escort Jeremy out.

Jeremy says, "I'm OK." He finds a tissue in his pocket, blows his nose, and walks out of my office and down to his cubicle with Tony following a few steps behind.

I shut the door, sit down, grip the arms of my swivel chair, close my eyes, and breathe slowly. My brain feels like a bowl of mashed potatoes. Someone knocks at the door, but I don't say anything and the person goes away. I hear a siren in the street and the blaring of horns. I imagine an ambulance trapped in midtown traffic as a heart attack victim lies dying on the sidewalk two blocks away. I concentrate on my breathing and start counting each breath. I tell myself to count from one to fifty. To block out the world. To focus only on the numbers in my head. I wonder if Jeremy learned anything useful here. I wonder if I could have helped him more. I wonder if I should have told him how annoying he was. I stop wondering and focus only on my breathing and counting. By the time I reach thirty-five, my body has stopped trembling. I am calm. And Jeremy is someone else's concern.

I stand up and notice a slip of paper that someone has slid under my door. It looks innocent enough. But it still feels ominous. It's a two-word message from Randy Baker. *Call me.*

He picks up immediately.

"It's official," he says. "My year is in the crapper. Livingston Kidd's agency just called. They've done a deal with the *Times*. Print. Online. Events. You name it. Sucking up their entire budget. They've been working on it for weeks. We didn't even get a look in."

"Shit," I say. "Fuck. That sucks."

"Yep," says Randy. "Do you think this day can get any worse?"

I hang up, spend a few minutes gazing over at the empty office where basketball guy used to spend his days.

I didn't say it to Randy. But to me this doesn't feel like a day when the market opens down and bounces back. This feels like a day when the bottom falls out.

CHAPTER TWENTY-SIX

By ten thirty, Fergus's *Vicious Circle* story is being picked up, analyzed and interpreted by business websites, bloggers and irate investors, all the way from wsj.com to the Yahoo! Finance message boards.

On mediaweek.com, the story is the day's main news item, complete with a PDF of the magazine cover. The *Vicious Circle* art director has had fun with this. The cover art shows a picture of a battered grocery cart sporting a *Daily Business Chronicle* license plate. The magazine's headline reads, "EXCLUSIVE: Ghosh Pushes *Chronicle*, Wheels Fall Off."

Barbara knocks on my door, holding an orange fire-resistant vest.

"Jeremy asked me to give this to you," she says.

I ask her to leave it on my chair, then turn to the article on my screen.

"Can I take Angela's card?" Barbara is still hovering near my desk.

I look at it again. We—the people saying good-bye—are depicted as a sad-looking bunch of cartoon animals. The messages inside are variations on the usual entreaties to "Stay in touch!" and "Come back and see us!" Though maybe they seem a little more heartfelt this time around. Angela has made friends throughout the building. I can't send Barbara away again, so I scribble, "Thanks for all your efforts! Best wishes for a successful future." As soon as I sign my name, Barbara snatches it away. She's in a hurry to whisk it to its next signatory.

"Just a second," I say. I take the card back.

I write, "P.S. Don't forget to rent *The Godfather* sometime soon."

Barbara reads what I've written, gives me a worried look, and is gone.

I turn to my computer and begin to read.

> "*Chronicle* Crisis: New Revelations May Push Struggling Title Over the *Edge*. Burke-Hart insiders are already panicking amid steep readership and advertising declines at the *Daily Business Chronicle*. Latest hopes to impress new boss Larry Ghosh are pinned on upcoming launch of tabloid dubbed the *Daily Edge*. New edition to be distributed as a supplement for current subscribers and as stand-alone newspaper for commuters in top twenty metro markets. Free distribution ploy marks last-gasp effort to connect with 'lost generation' of eighteen- to thirty-four-year-old readers. As *Chronicle* rushes *Daily Edge* to market, *Vicious Circle* quotes 'well-placed Burke-Hart source' who reveals devastating flaws in business plan. Among the prob-

lems: Prototypes of *Daily Edge* fail to excite current or prospective readers; advertisers refuse to commit additional funds; and most devastating of all, *Chronicle* insiders presented *wrong* version of business plan to management. Contrary to optimistic statements by *Chronicle* publisher Jack Tennant, *Vicious Circle* asserts the *Daily Edge* will be a financial drain on money-losing *Chronicle* for three-plus years. New revelations unlikely to please investors or impatient management at Ghosh Corporation. Meanwhile, Burke-Hart spokesperson claimed to be unaware of either *Vicious Circle* magazine or specific problems cited."

I leave another message on Sam's cell phone. As I'm doing that, my other line starts ringing. I cut my message short and pick up.

It's Susan Trevor. "Turn on your TV. Right now. CNBC."

I reach for the remote. Fergus's face fills the screen. He's being interviewed about his article.

"What I think is most sad," says Fergus, "is that before Ghosh took over, the *Daily Business Chronicle* was one of those rare brands that actually stood for something."

"Can you believe this shit?" says Susan. "Just when I thought things couldn't get any worse."

"Susan, I'll call you back. That's my other line. I'm expecting a call." I hang up on Susan. As I pick up my other line, the fire alarm starts sounding.

"Hi." It's Sam.

"Hi."

"How's it going?"

"You tell me."

"What's that noise? Is this a bad time?"

"It's just a fire drill."

"Do you have to go?"

"I can wait a minute."

"I can call back."

"Just tell me one thing."

"Let me call you back."

"Are you and Greg fucking up there in Springfield?"

The fire alarm keeps ringing.

"I get the sense you don't like Larry Ghosh," says the CNBC interviewer to my best friend, Fergus Larner.

The fire alarm stops. A muffled voice starts giving instructions over the sound system.

"...destroys everything he touches..." says Fergus.

There's a knock at my door.

"...polluting our culture..."

It's Erika Fallon, wearing her orange fire warden's vest.

"...in the event of a real emergency..." says the disembodied announcer on the building's intercom.

"...the consequences could be devastating..." says Fergus.

"I've come to rescue you," says Erika.

"I'll be right there," I say, one hand over the receiver. I pick up the remote and mute my TV. The fire drill announcement stops. The alarm stops ringing. Suddenly everything is silent.

"Are you still there?" I say to Sam.

"Yes," she says. "And yes."

There's one last close-up of Fergus, then the CNBC show cuts to a commercial. I'm holding the phone to my right ear. I pick up the remote with my left hand, turn off the TV. My chest feels tight, but I'm not feeling any emotion. *Is this shock?*

I wonder. And then I stop thinking. My head feels heavy but hollow.

"That's it?" says Sam. "You're not going to say anything?"

"What is it you want me to say?"

I hang up the phone, put on the bright fire warden's jacket, and head down the hall to make sure no one's trapped in the men's bathroom.

At her good-bye party, Angela is wearing a white hooded sweatshirt with a glittery red letter A over her left breast.

The conference room table is covered with a paper tablecloth. On top of that are plastic cups and a selection of sodas, along with an ice cream cake that most people will try not to eat. Next to the cake are plastic plates and napkins. Plastic forks are also provided. But it will take at least twenty minutes for the ice cream cake to melt sufficiently for these forks to serve any useful purpose.

Angela may not know it, but this is the standard setup we use for every office party. I've instructed my team to make sure that all birthday and farewell celebrations are equally lame. It's the best way to ensure we don't play favorites—that no one gets upset when their own celebration comes around. Only gifts under twenty-five dollars are allowed, along with any suitable premium items we can dig out from the storage closet.

Kelly Gardner helps Angela cut her ice cream cake and distribute pieces to the assembled group. A couple of guys from the mailroom have shown up, as well as that bald guy Bryan from corporate finance. Jeanie and Judd are nowhere in sight. They've been keeping a low profile all day.

Sally Yun presents Angela with a bag filled with *Chronicle* merchandise. There's a baseball cap, a T-shirt, a sports bottle and a zero-gravity pen. People don't usually get emotional at these events, but Angela seems close to tears as she opens and reads her card.

"Thank you all," she says, and the room goes quiet. "I've really enjoyed working here. I can't believe my time here is over already. I've learned so much. Everyone's been great. Thank you so much for your help. It was especially great having such a friendly and understanding boss. Thank you, Mr. Wiley. Sorry—Russell."

She smiles at me sweetly, and everyone waits for me to say something. I'm expected to sound enthusiastic, steadfast and bland. While saying good-bye to one person, I'm supposed to reassure the rest of my team that life goes on, the work routine continues, it's OK to be left behind.

"Well, Angela. It's been great having you," I say a little louder than I'd intended. "Be sure to come back and see us! Stay in touch!"

I'm pouring myself some more ginger ale when Barbara appears at my side and informs me that I'm wanted in Jack Tennant's office immediately.

CHAPTER TWENTY-SEVEN

I enter Jack's office. He's sitting behind his desk with the Project D-SAW business plan, a copy of *Vicious Circle*, and assorted printouts of the day's news reports spread in front of him. Jack's always been known for his energy and enthusiasm. But today he seems subdued.

There are two empty chairs to choose from. I sit in the one on the left. I sink into it a little, realizing immediately the other one might have been a better choice. Because this is the moment I finally start losing my grip.

"Well, Russell, this has been quite a day," he says.

I hear wind rushing in my ears. I close my eyes. I'm about to be fired. I always wondered if I could handle my own execution with dignity, but I fear I'm about to fail the test. I open my eyes. I realize I've been holding my breath. I exhale slowly.

"Are you OK?" says Jack.

"No," I say. Even though it's only a single syllable, I can't say it without my voice cracking. Then suddenly I'm sobbing. My body's shaking and I'm clinging to the arms of the chair, tears running down my face, trying not to look like too much of a baby in front of the publisher of the *Daily Business Chronicle.*

This is embarrassing. But I can't help myself. I've been betrayed by my wife. And by my best friend. I've screwed everything up at work. I'm a failure. I'm a traitor. And a sham. Plus, I'm scared. When Jack is done firing me, I'll walk out of this office all alone in the world. With no job. No one to turn to. And nowhere to go.

"This...hasn't...been a...good day...for...me," I manage to say.

Jack pushes a box of tissues across his desk. I don't want to let go of the chair, but there are bubbles of snot emerging from my nostrils. I grab some tissues and blow.

I start to feel a little calmer. I stuff the wet tissues into my pants pocket. I need to explain myself, confess all I've done wrong, make Jack understand why I've been reduced to this blubbering mess.

"I'm sorry."

"It's OK," says Jack.

"No," I say. "It's all my fault. The mistake in the business plan. It wasn't Judd who screwed it up. It was me. I told my friend at *Vicious Circle* all about it. I didn't know he was going to write an article. But I should have kept my mouth shut. And the one about Unicorns. That was me too."

"Unicorns?"

"Yes. I wrote it. I'm Christopher Finchley."

"Let me get this straight," says Jack. "You're saying you made the ten-million-dollar mistake that *Vicious Circle* is writing about?"

"Yes."

"But after you made the mistake, wasn't the plan reviewed by Judd Walker?"

"Yes."

"And then Jeanie Tusa?"

"I guess."

"And then Henry Moss?"

"I think so."

"So three people signed off on your mistake?"

"Uh-huh."

"And how did you come to make the mistake?"

"I was helping Judd with a spreadsheet. I typed a number wrong."

"Why wasn't Judd doing the spreadsheet himself?"

"He asked me to help."

"So yours was an honest mistake?"

"Yes. But I could have owned up to it sooner."

"Do you normally prepare the spreadsheets your finance department presents?"

"No."

"So you weren't the one responsible for any of Jeanie Tusa's previous errors?"

"No."

"Well," says Jack, "let's assume this article in *Vicious Circle* is correct and there was a mistake in the business plan as it was presented. Who should I hold accountable? You, the typist? Or the consultant who presented the plan? Or maybe the financial director whose job it was to verify the numbers? Or should it be the financial director's boss? And for the purpose of this discussion, let's say that this boss had been alerted by corporate finance to an ongoing problem of serious budgeting errors coming out of his department."

"Well," I say, "when you put it like that."

"Russell, I applaud your honesty. But this was not your project. And verifying the numbers was not your responsibility. And neither was ensuring the necessary fail-safe mechanisms were put in place. Henry had been warned about this. Your mistake was a test of the system. The system should have been fixed." Jack looks over at his credenza, where various mementos, awards and pictures from his long career at the *Chronicle* are on display. "Perhaps if Henry hadn't been so busy plotting…" He trails off, shakes his head, then refocuses his gaze at me. "Regarding this article." He picks up the copy of *Vicious Circle* that's lying on his desk and waves a hand over the printouts of online articles from CNN, the *New York Times*, even the BBC. "The good news is that it's given us the kind of publicity money can't buy. The whole world is now talking about our plans to launch the *Daily Edge*."

"They're not saying very nice things, though." My voice sounds nasal. I reach for another tissue and blow my nose again.

"As I told Larry Ghosh this morning, I'm used to being abused in the press and to being underestimated by others," says Jack. "Even by those who claim to be my most loyal lieutenants. Anyway, Russell, as for this alleged mistake, the official word from me, the *Daily Business Chronicle* and from the Ghosh Corporation is that there was no mistake—there *is* no mistake. We are standing behind the numbers we announced to Wall Street. The launch of the *Daily Edge* will proceed as planned. We will simply need to find a way to launch successfully with ten million dollars less than we might normally have spent."

"I'm not sure that's possible," I say.

"You may be right," says Jack. "Unfortunately, given the level of scrutiny this project has generated, we can't go back and adjust the numbers. But let's put that topic in the parking lot and deal with it later. I want to tell you the real reason why I called you here this afternoon."

Jack stands up and walks around his desk. I look over my shoulder as he walks past me. His assistant, Nora, heavily pregnant, has entered bearing a tray of tea and cookies.

"I've got it," he says to her. "Russell, why don't you join me over here?" Jack sets the tray down on his coffee table and waits for me to walk over and sit on his couch before he lowers himself into his armchair. He pours me a cup of tea.

"Milk or lemon?" he asks.

"Milk, please," I say. "Thank you." It was Sam who got me into the habit of drinking tea the English way, but I push that thought aside. I drop a sugar cube into my china cup and stir the tea Jack has handed me. I look over at his desk, which now seems far away. I blow on my tea and take a sip. It's Earl Grey. I realize how large Jack's office is, even compared to Henry's. I count fifteen windows as I wait for him to prepare and taste his tea, then place his cup and saucer down on the table.

Jack leans forward, hands clasped together, fingers interlocked. "As of one o'clock this afternoon, Larry Ghosh and the board of Ghosh Corporation have asked me to succeed Connie Darwin as CEO of Burke-Hart Publishing. I have accepted the offer."

"Er, congratulations," I say. I'm starting to feel even more foolish about my crying jag.

"As of two o'clock this afternoon, I have asked several people to leave the company. Among them, I am sorry to say, are Henry Moss and Jeanie Tusa. I have also terminated, effective immediately, the contract of the consultant on the D-SAW project, Judd Walker."

"Oh, wow."

"At the same time, I have asked Yolanda Pew to assume the title of publisher of the *Chronicle* and president of the Burke-Hart Business Group, and I have promoted Barney Barnes to become the president of the Lifestyle Group. Both Yolanda's and Barney's new responsibilities will include all the print, online and offline brands that they control."

"It sounds like the new structure makes sense."

"It would have made even more sense two years ago when you first proposed it."

"I guess we allowed history to get in the way of logic."

"That has been a problem of ours, hasn't it? But hopefully we are now in a position to change all that. Which brings me to you, Russell Wiley."

I don't say anything. I'm hoping that the fact that I'm not only still in the building but also sipping milky, sweet tea in the office of our new CEO means I'm not getting fired. But I don't want to take anything for granted.

"You're one of the few people in the building no one says a bad word about. Your value to this organization was probably the only thing Henry and Barney agreed on lately. Did you know Barney tried to hire you to run his conference division two years ago? Henry hit the roof. I had to play Solomon on that one."

"I didn't know that."

"Well, Russell. We've got some big challenges ahead. Are you ready to take on some new responsibilities?"

Five minutes later, I leave Jack's office and head back down to twenty-five. Lucky Cat is there to greet me, the new vice president of marketing for the Burke-Hart Business Group.

CHAPTER TWENTY-EIGHT

Six Weeks Later

I shave quickly, cutting through the foam with a disposable triple-bladed razor. I shower, lathering my hair in a nettle shampoo that makes my scalp tingle. I towel myself dry and walk into the bedroom naked. The lights are on, the curtains closed. I disconnect my iPod from my laptop and insert it into the dock of my speakers. I dress myself while Lloyd Cole sings about young idealists. I pack all my devices—computer, BlackBerry, cell phone—into my messenger bag, then clip my iPod to my belt and plug in my headphones. Lloyd's no longer angry, no longer young, no longer driven to distraction, not even by Scarlett Johansson. Then I'm riding down the elevator, heading out into the cold, gray January morning, listening to a song about New York City sunshine.

The downtown 6-train is crowded. There's no room to read my *Chronicle*-wrapped *New York Times*. Clinging to a pole, I pull out my iPod and call up my latest downloaded episode of Roger Jones's video podcast.

The opening graphics are slick, professionally produced. With accompanying music and sound effects, the words "The Daily Diary of the Incredible Shrinking Man" appear on-screen, followed by an animated photomontage that shows Roger melting away before our eyes. A title slide announces, "Day 61, Weight Loss 42 lbs." Then Roger appears, sitting on a chair in his bedroom. He starts talking to the camera. On his slimmer face, his moustache looms larger than ever. The woman next to me looks over my shoulder at the screen. She nudges her friend, and through my headphones I hear her say, "Have you seen this guy? He's hilarious."

I watch the three-minute episode, chuckling at Roger's deadpan observations about everyday life. Today he notes a surprising coincidence: just one day after Oprah featured a medical discussion on the benefits of farting, Mayor Bloomberg called a press conference to reassure the public about strange smells wafting over New York City. I wince a little when Roger starts describing the physical realities of his post-surgery life, such as the pungency of his own emissions and the strange places he finds loose flesh hanging. But I know that his scatological openness and self-deprecating style are part of his appeal. His videos are generating more than 275,000 downloads each day. And he's getting email and marriage proposals from fans all over the world.

When Roger started posting his daily musings on YouTube, he was just an anonymous fat guy with a camera he'd borrowed from the office. He didn't tell anyone at work what he was doing. He didn't tell anyone watching what he did for a living. The subtext of his first video, recorded the night before his surgery, was the fear he might not survive his operation. Dizzy and nauseous from his liquid diet, I think it gave him strength to know that, whatever happened, he was leaving this message behind.

During the first few days of his recovery, Roger's sister was on hand to videotape his progress and document the speed with which his sense of humor returned. Within a week, he was alleviating his medical-leave boredom by posting more and more of his video updates online. With category tags like "diet," "fat" and "surgery," his postings quickly found an audience. In another two weeks, an episode of his diary became a featured video on the YouTube home page. At that point, Roger: a) really took off; b) got busted by his boss; and c) became a cornerstone of my vague and still-underfunded marketing plan to get advertisers interested in the launch of the *Daily Edge*.

I didn't change much of what Roger was already doing. Apart from the souped-up opening titles, Roger's YouTube videos retain the DIY aesthetic he's known for. But I did give Roger complete freedom to talk about work. Regular viewers now know that Roger is employed by the *Chronicle*—a paper he says is just like him, "shrinking but not disappearing." For the past several weeks, viewers have shared in Roger's anxiety as he sat helpless at home reading the negative news and dire prognostications concerning the launch of the *Daily Edge*. One day he dressed up in a cape and tights and fantasized about saving the *Chronicle* from the launch of the "Daily Disaster." The next day he confessed he had spent six hours updating his résumé in an effort to switch industries at the first opportunity. The day after that, he told viewers he was going to keep his day job for a while longer—and that the *Chronicle* was giving him the time and resources to create his own *Daily Edge*–sponsored website.

The day Roger returned to work, his office was overflowing with cards, gifts and flowers sent by his online admirers.

Last week, his website attracted 1.7 million unique visitors. Along with all its exclusive Roger Jones content, it also features promotional content from twelve different corporations. Advertising on the site is free. But the only way for an advertiser to be featured is to book a campaign in the *Daily Edge*.

I walk across town from the Fifty-first Street station and pause at the light to look up at the Burke-Hart Building. I cross the street, then cut across the mini-plaza. Two police officers are joking with the crowd gathered behind the barricades: a mix of college-aged tourists, high school girls playing hooky and middle-aged men trying to look inconspicuous. The presence of a few paparazzi-types feeds into and enhances the communal anticipation. Everyone in the crowd, amateur and professional, is clutching some kind of digital or video camera, or multifunction cell phone. I walk unnoticed past the throng, making sure to display my company ID as I get close to the revolving doors.

A cheer goes up, and I look back as a white stretch limousine pulls up to the curb. A chauffeur steps out and opens the passenger door. Then, with the assembled onlookers capturing every moment, a pair of glittery platform boots appears. Chunky, six-inch heels connect with the sidewalk, and then, a split second later, Kiko Soseki has pivoted herself upright, wobbling slightly in her boots as if she were on a spring. She straightens the cubic-zirconia-studded sunglasses that half-cover her face and waves to the cheering spectators.

Kiko takes a couple of halting steps forward. Part of her morning ritual includes speaking to the hyperactive Japanese

TV crew that waits for her each day. For the benefit of the TV cameras and her fans, Kiko opens her pink fake fur jacket to reveal the outfit underneath. It's a tight sweater dress with what looks like a large splatter of green paint across the front. Prominently printed within the splatter is the now-ubiquitous slogan, "Everybody Needs an *Edge*." More than anyone, Kiko has risen to the challenge of publicizing the launch of the *Daily Edge*, often by turning herself into a billboard using clothes she has designed herself.

Behind Kiko, Sally Yun and Angela Campos—a.k.a. the Me Soseki Crew—emerge from the limo and start striking poses for the crowd. Lately, Sally has adopted a Mohican hairstyle in homage to Annabella Lwin of Bow Wow Wow. Along with black thigh-high boots, tight green shorts and a red-and-white floral jacket, she has a designer-punk T-shirt that reads, "I Want Candy…But I Need an *Edge*." Completing the multicultural tableau, Angela Campos is dressed as a dandy highwayman, an updated version of the Adam Ant look, complete with white stripes across her face. Angela's version of the outfit retains the ruffled collar and sleeves, but the jacket is cut short to expose her taut stomach.

"Hi, Russell!" she calls out. Heads in the crowd turn my way, then quickly lose interest. Of the three Crew members, Angela is still the most likely to break character and utter phrases that are not preapproved. But I don't worry about that. Breaking character has become part of her character's charm.

Liz Cooke steps out of the limousine's front passenger seat, talking into her Bluetooth headset. She circles behind the TV crew, taking care to stay out of the shot. Apart from a baseball cap that bears the slogan "Everybody Needs an *Edge*," she's dressed inconspicuously. Liz gives the rolling finger signal to Kiko, who wraps up the interview. Kiko, Sally and Angela head over to their fans to sign a few autographs. I notice several members of the crowd holding the new issue of *Posse*, which has a picture of the Me Soseki Crew on the cover. The boots Kiko is wearing will be featured in the next issue of *Heel*.

Liz sees me and smiles. She's having fun playing the role of Svengali to the online and, increasingly, real-world phenomenon she has created.

Six weeks ago, before I promoted Liz to Martin's old job as creative director, Kiko was just a regular, moderately popular MySpace user. Her few hundred online friends included Japanese and American art students, graphic artists, New York club kids, plus a few dozen sexual predators who'd chanced upon her provocative photos and blog entries.

But then, everything changed. It wasn't only my world that got turned upside down.

After I promoted her, I told Liz I wanted her to make as much noise as possible to promote the launch of the *Daily Edge* brand. Don't think of it as a newspaper, I told her. If we act like we're launching a newspaper, advertisers will come down with hives. I gave her a shoestring budget, access to some resources of the Ghosh Corporation and another copy of Christopher Finchley's article on creative anarchy.

Have fun, I told her. And don't worry about failure. Failure, after all, was all but guaranteed.

The plan Liz came up with had nothing to do with newspapers. And even less to do with selling advertising. Instead, she presented ideas that were outrageous, illogical and ridiculously cheap. I approved her plan immediately. Then, like a good Unicorn, I got out of the way.

Within the first week, Liz worked with Kiko to refine and relaunch her online identity, mixing fact with fiction to create a persona with maximum global, cross-generational and multimedia appeal. The new MySpace Kiko was a blank slate of a woman: uncensored yet mysterious, she represented a bridge between American and Japanese cultures; she was shy, but she didn't mind blogging about her most intimate secrets; she loved Japanese tradition but sang songs in English that, if they were ever translated, would shock her parents; and of course, MySpace Kiko—just like her real-life counterpart—loved to party.

Through her new page and profile, Kiko introduced the world to her new BFFs, Sally and Angela. She posted dozens of photos, videos, plus a few homemade acoustic MP3 demos of her sly, confessional songs.

Meanwhile, Liz let Kiko and the Crew loose on the New York club scene, with a paid group of paparazzi always in tow and trendy club kids blanketing the city with promotional material. Quickly, the members of the Me Soseki Crew were added to everybody's "must-have" list—both as MySpace friends and guests at VIP events. Pictures showed up everywhere—from Style.com to DailyCeleb to Go Fug Yourself. When word got out that the Me Soseki Crew had signed a deal with Ghosh Music, they graduated instantly to the gossip columns and tabloid press, providing relief for weary writers—and readers—desperate to break their Paris-Britney-Lindsay addictions.

Everyone wanted interviews. But Liz restricted access. She didn't want Kiko and the Crew's popularity to peak too soon. Instead, she used exclusive fashion shoots with selected Burke-Hart magazines to build credibility and feed the frenzy.

Between shoots, she took the Me Soseki Crew into the Ghosh Music studios. Along with Kiko's original songs, the group recorded *Daily Edge*–inspired versions of several eighties classics. Thanks to the efforts of leading music and video producers, session musicians and additional, uncredited backup singers and dancers, the Crew proved to be a surprisingly listenable, provocatively visual, instantly downloadable musical phenomenon. When their first single—"Edgemusic"—was released last week, it became the most-requested song on U.S. radio and entered the Japanese, British and Swedish record charts at number one, based on download sales alone.

Today, Kiko has more than 1.5 million MySpace friends—second only to the legendary Tila Tequila—and she's racking up seventy-five thousand new adds each day. Sally and Angela aren't far behind, signing up new friends at a similarly frantic pace.

By the time I get to my twenty-sixth-floor office, the pictures now being taken will be popping up on screens all over the globe. By the end of the week, Liz will conclude negotiations with the editors of *People*, *Star* and *Us* magazines. If she times it right, she'll get a guaranteed cover for Kiko and the Me Soseki Crew, along with a live appearance on Letterman, just one week before the *Daily Edge* launches.

I smile back at Liz, then turn and pass through the revolving doors of the Burke-Hart Building. I stride through the lobby, past the gauche corporate logo and toward the elevator bank. The headlines in the elevator confirm what I already know: the world has gone mad. Thankfully, I've realized the only sensible way to respond is by acting crazy.

CHAPTER TWENTY-NINE

I sit in the executive chair in the corner office I've inherited on the twenty-sixth floor. I look at myself in the large antique mirror that hangs on the north wall. From where I'm sitting, I see my own reflection, with Lucky Cat waving from the windowsill and, behind him, the clamoring lights and billboards of Times Square.

I log on to the Ghosh Corporation intranet to make sure the new world disorder is holding. There's a countdown clock built into the home page that informs the whole company the *Daily Edge* is launching in twenty-three days. Beyond that, there's nothing new to worry about.

I open my email. A few friends and colleagues have remembered my birthday and sent messages or animated greeting cards. Martin's is headlined, "Remember: Thirty-eight is the new twenty-five!"

There's also a note from Sam. From a new email account. I have to press the "Not Junk" button before I can open it. It's a simple birthday wish, delivered by email, our now-preferred form of communication.

This is the first birthday I've celebrated without Sam since I turned twenty. I'm not used to being a grown-up without her. Most days, I'm not even sure I'm a grown-up at all.

Sam's living with Greg in his rented house in Massachusetts. Together, they see his kids on weekends. Maybe Sam and Greg's ex-wife Karen reminisce about their carefree high school days during the awkward moments when the kids are exchanged. I try not to think about that. And I try not to think about sex, or my lack of it. These days I sleep alone.

Instead of adding up days without sex, I'm focused on counting down to the launch of the *Daily Edge*. I'm keeping busy, working long hours, spending nights in a Burke-Hart suite at a hotel in the East 70s. I'm even using the fitness center a few times a week. Neither Sam nor I go to our apartment in Park Slope without telling the other. There are many issues we still have to deal with, but right now, we're being polite.

And today I'm thirty-eight. Which is somewhat different from being twenty-five. In my late thirties, I'm a single, unattached adult for the first time in my life. Meanwhile, Sam's already making bold career decisions. According to her email signature, she's the person "Delivering Nature's Strength to West Springfield, MA!"

"Something funny?" asks Ellen, bringing in the daily schedule and meeting folders she prepares for me. Having my own full-time assistant for the first time is another adjustment I'm trying to make.

"Nothing," I say. "Just someone I know has finally got themselves a job."

"Good for them." She lays the details of my day across the desk. "You've got Barbara at nine thirty. You're meeting with Jack at ten. Oh, and I moved your two thirty with Susan up to two because Hank says he needs to review bookings with you at three."

"Right," I say. "That old 'three-o'clock-meeting-on-your-birthday' trick."

Ellen looks surprised. "It's your birthday? No one told me." But then she winks and is gone.

Alone in my office, I start thinking of the birthday messages I could send myself.

> *Congratulations, Russell! You're thirty-eight. You've survived the meltdown of your company and the collapse of your marriage. If you avoid any more fuckups, this could be the best year of your life!*

Or:

> *Holy shit, Russell! You're thirty-eight. What the hell are you doing, sitting there with that dazed expression, alone in the world, surrounded by someone else's stuff?*

When this was Henry's office, the furniture made sense. Dark wood. Leather. It felt comfortable, lived-in. Now it unnerves me. It isn't mine. I don't want it. But I haven't had time to think about replacing it. And I don't have anything to replace it with. One day soon, if I survive the launch of the *Daily Edge*, I'll figure it out. Swap the old for the new. Find a modern, high-tech style I like. I won't care what anyone thinks. Just nothing secondhand. That's the first furnishing rule of my new adult life.

Ellen sticks her head around my door.

"Are you in for Fergus Larner, calling from *Business Week*?"

"Sure. Put him through."

Within two days of Fergus's *Vicious Circle* cover story hitting newsstands, he was weighing three new job offers. He started at *Business Week* three weeks ago. With Jack's approval, he took his favorite columnist, Christopher Finchley, with him.

"Hey, birthday boy. Good news. We're making *The Finchley File* the featured blog on our home page this week." Fergus is really enjoying his new job. He tells me he's grateful for the security he feels as part of McGraw-Hill's flagship, billion-dollar brand. I'm glad for him too. He's finally landed at a publication that offers him some real long-term security. "You were our most viewed last week. People are linking to you from all over the world. We're getting hundreds of emails and comments. Our book division wants to do a deal with you too."

"I told you that being Kiko Soseki's number four friend on MySpace would help," I say. "So are you still buying me that birthday drink tonight?"

"Have you done something different with your hair?" I ask Barbara as she hands me this morning's printouts. She blushes but doesn't reply. Since I promoted her to manager of online auctions and digital rights management, she's been taking fashion advice from Liz Cooke and one or two of the female sales executives. In addition to a sizable raise, Barbara now has a windowed office for the first time in her thirty-plus-year *Chronicle* career.

"This is amazing," I tell her, scanning the list of current bids for all the *Daily Edge* ad units we're auctioning online. The "jewel box" square on the corner of our front page is now generating offers as high as $123,000. Full-page ads on our back cover are up to $212,000. These are more than double the standard prices in our rate card.

"Supply and demand," she says with a smile.

It was only five weeks ago that Barbara came up with the idea of limiting the number of ads in the *Daily Edge* and auctioning a portion of them online. "You have to understand supply and demand," she told me. "That's how it works on eBay. Why is the 1957 water-carrying boy worth more than any other? You just can't find one."

I took Barbara with me to a series of meetings, allowing her to sell her plan to Hank Sullivan, our new VP of sales, then Yolanda, and ultimately Jack. Within two days we had a plan to: a) cut the number of pages in the *Daily Edge* to a maximum of forty per day, helping us reduce our annual print budget by eighteen million dollars; and b) allocate seventy percent of the available advertising to clients who were already in the *Chronicle* and sell the remaining thirty percent exclusively by online auction.

While online media auctions aren't new, no other national newspaper promises its advertisers that it won't print more pages to accommodate new ads as they are sold. In the *Daily Edge*, every page a client buys leaves less space for its competitors. Plus, the *Daily Edge* is the only national newspaper with secret weapons like Roger Jones and Kiko and the Me Soseki Crew. We're offering our newspaper advertisers extra promotional opportunities they can't get anywhere else, such as ad banners on Roger's website or product placements in the Me Soseki Crew's much-photographed lives.

"Randy Baker just closed a twenty-six-page schedule with BlackBerry," says Barbara. "He says the client and agency are really excited. We've made them the sponsor of the official Me

Soseki Crew gallery on Flickr. And we're guaranteeing that we'll post at least two new photos of Kiko, Sally or Angela using their BlackBerrys at every event."

Before my ten o'clock meeting with Jack, I take a stroll through the sales department.

Things are quiet, but I can sense the intensity. For the first time in years, our salespeople are getting their calls returned. There's no time for chitchat in the corridors. They're competing with each other to lock up the best positions for their clients.

Before I turn the corner, I hear the sound of someone banging the large gong Hank Sullivan has set up outside his office.

Booiiinnnnggggg.

Every time one of the salespeople closes a deal, he encourages them to pick up the hammer and give it a loud bang. For the past few days, we've started hearing that gong echo through the halls several times an hour.

Georgina Bird passes me on the way back to her office.

"Kenneth Cole just came in," she says. "Twelve pages. Can you believe it? Two months ago I couldn't even get an appointment."

Hank Sullivan pops his smiling face out of his own corner office.

"Have you heard? The launch issue is completely sold out," he says. "And I've got North Face ready to commit a million and a half if we can get the Me Soseki Crew to wear their jackets in their next video."

"No problem. I saw the storyboards last night. Tell them we'll guarantee a minimum of twenty seconds screen time and exclusivity in the apparel category. But we'll need a signed contract by end of day—otherwise we're taking it to Nautica."

I ride up to the thirty-fourth floor and head over to Jack Tennant's office. Tyler Milken is posted outside Jack's office. He waves me in.

"Good morning, Russell!" Jack shouts, leaping up from his chair and pumping my hand. Jack's a head shorter than me. His handshake is crushing, his smile broad. "Sit down, sit down. Hot chocolate, right?"

"That would be great."

I sit in one of Jack's antique guest chairs as Jack steps outside to ask Tyler to fix our beverages.

"I've asked Yolanda to run up with the updated prototypes," says Jack, coming back into the office and sitting behind his huge desk. "Is it too bright in here?" He jabs at a few buttons and three large, semi-opaque blinds start lowering along his southern wall of windows. "Have you seen the dashboard?"

The dashboard is a daily email our corporate finance group sends out filled with our latest revenue information. As a VP, I've been added to the distribution list. I usually skim it for the *Chronicle*'s advertising and circulation figures—and for the data tracking how well the *Daily Edge* is doing.

"Not yet," I reply. "How's it looking?"

"See for yourself," Jack hands me this morning's printout.

"Wow," I say.

"Look at the results from our latest circulation test."

I scan the numbers. We're testing a new bundled offer where readers are being offered the *Chronicle* plus the *Daily*

Edge plus their choice of any of our lifestyle magazines all at one low price.

"These numbers are great."

"Barney tells me that we're getting response rates ten to fifteen percent higher than our best estimates."

"Well, it's a great offer."

"He says you came up with the idea—and that you discovered some amazing new envelope."

"That just fell into my hands," I say. "A friend of my ex-wife's is in the business."

"Well, I just gave Barney the go-ahead to mail another ten million pieces. He says his budget can handle it because of the special discount you were able to get us."

"It was a team effort," I say. "The new corporate structure certainly helps us get things done."

Tyler appears at my side and places two cups and saucers on the desk. I thank him. Tyler's not such a bad guy. He's still a bit shell-shocked by Connie's sudden firing, but I think he'll be OK. Jack's keeping him around at least while Nora is on maternity leave. I sip my hot chocolate.

"Ad revenue's holding up well in the *Chronicle*," I say. "Most of the spending in the *Daily Edge* looks incremental."

"You haven't heard the best part," says Jack. "I just got off the phone with Ken Millard, the new guy at Livingston Kidd. They're switching out of the *Times* and coming back to the *Chronicle*. Plus, they're putting an additional million dollars into the *Daily Edge* so they can sponsor the Me Soseki Crew's mall tour. Ken says he loves what we're doing to attract younger readers."

"That's great," I say. "You really saved us on that one, Jack."

"You gave me the ammunition, Russell. I just pulled the trigger."

Yolanda Pew arrives with boards showing some new layouts for the *Daily Edge*, as well as screenshots for the companion website. As the *Chronicle*'s new publisher, Yolanda is working directly with our editors on product development—everything from the print edition to the website, to all of our audio and video podcasts and mobile news updates.

For the most part, Jack and Yolanda are handling the serious side of our business strategy and giving me and my team free rein to pursue all forms of creative anarchy. Because I'm not spending much cash, it doesn't matter whether the things we try actually work or not. If one idea flops, we simply try something else. Only after a concept takes hold virally and builds significant critical mass do we look for ways to link it to the launch of the *Daily Edge* and connect it to the packages we're offering advertisers.

While Jack and Yolanda review and discuss the new layouts, I hang back a step. Yolanda recaps the rationale for the latest changes in typefaces and graphics. Jack turns to me, puts his arm around my shoulder, and pulls me forward to join the discussion.

CHAPTER THIRTY

Erika Fallon appears at my doorway. She's wearing a beige cotton turtleneck, dark brown corduroys, soft leather boots. It's a low-key, conservative outfit. On her, it seems incredibly provocative.

"Russell, can we talk?" she says.

I clear my throat. "Sure. Come in."

Since we held hands and exchanged whispered secrets in Miami, an air of self-consciousness has hovered over our interactions. We haven't spoken about what happened. Some days I wonder if Erika attaches as much meaning as I do to the moments we shared. Then, in the middle of a meeting, I'll realize I'm gazing at her a little too much. She'll realize it too and smile at me across the room. Those are the moments that sustain me.

Erika knows Sam and I have split up. But that doesn't create permission for anything. We still work together. I'm still her boss.

Besides, we've both been working nonstop, combining our day-to-day *Chronicle* responsibilities with preparations for a major product launch. Erika has gotten us through Hank Sullivan's holiday party and planned a series of road shows where Yolanda and our editors preview the *Daily Edge* for advertisers. When Sally Yun was co-opted by the Me Soseki Crew, I gave Erika the OK to use outside vendors wherever necessary. She's hired the Benjamin Shapiro Company, Ben's new event marketing firm, to produce the New York launch party for the *Daily Edge*.

Erika sits across the desk from me. I gaze at her. In the mirror behind her I can see the reflection of her lustrous hair. The aura I used to see around her in the late afternoon is now present throughout the day. She smiles, studying my face.

"I'll just come out and say it," she says. "Ben's offered me a job. He's got a lot of interesting clients. More work than he can handle. I told him I needed to talk to you first. I wouldn't feel good about leaving before the launch."

I purse my lips, breathe deeply through my nose, feel my stomach expand. I exhale slowly. My mind is jumping ahead to the day when Erika and I no longer work together. We're hosting our launch party for advertisers in twenty-four days. I start imagining all kinds of possibilities for Erika and me, starting the morning after that.

I take another breath and choose my words carefully.

"Professionally speaking, you know I will hate to lose you. You bring a style and flair to the *Chronicle* that we desperately need. You're extremely talented, exceptionally well organized. You've got huge fans throughout the sales department. And, of course, a huge fan in me. But for all those reasons, I would never want to hold you back if you truly think this is a better opportunity."

"I know it will be very different. But it's exciting. I would like to give it a shot."

"I'd appreciate it if you could just get us through the big New York event."

"Of course. And thanks, Russell. I knew you'd understand."

She gets up and walks toward the door. My heart contracts with every step she takes, every squishy squeak of her soft leather boots. I could commend myself for the way I handled that. Or I could curse myself for blowing an opportunity to ask her out.

At the door, Erika hesitates. Then turns. "Just out of curiosity...what would you have said if you were speaking unprofessionally?"

She gazes at me, waiting for an answer.

I smile, give it my best shot.

"Perhaps that's a conversation we could have over dinner sometime."

"Sure," she says, smiling back. "There's no rule against dinner with an ex-boss."

"I hate this," says Susan Trevor, clicking the pause button on the MP3 file we're listening to. "You're such a bastard for making me do it."

"Maybe I am," I tell her. "But I couldn't keep your talent hidden any longer."

For the past month, Susan has been heading to the Ghosh Radio studios once a week to record a podcast called "Don't Push Me ('Cause I'm Close to the Edge)." As long as she doesn't start bashing people by name, I've given her complete freedom to rant about anything that's on her mind. Which means an average episode veers from: a) her thoughts on the stupidity of our senior management, to: b) the impossible expectations that are being put upon her and her department, to: c) her fiercely protective responses to the negative press the *Daily Edge* is still generating, to: d) her humorous reactions to the *Wall Street Journal*'s plans to run scratch-and-sniff ads.

"I hate my voice. I sound so whiny."

"Everybody hates their own voice," I reassure her. "But everybody loves yours." It's true. People, it seems, can't get enough of Susan complaining. The fact they are not a hundred percent sure she's for real adds to the appeal. We're promoting the podcasts with filler space in the *Chronicle*, sponsored by the behavioral care division of Cigna. Last week Susan cracked the iTunes top one hundred.

"Have you lost weight?" I ask her. I've heard she is back on some kind of grapefruit diet.

"Maybe a couple of pounds."

"And where are you on the charts this week?"

"Twenty-seven." She smiles.

"Top thirty! Tell me the truth. You love it, don't you?"

"Yeah, I guess I kinda do."

"OK," I say. "Just don't let any of this cheer you up too much."

I walk into the large conference room on twenty-five at exactly three o'clock.

"Surprise!" comes the shout from a few overeager members of the group.

Everyone is here. My eyes are drawn to Erika first, who smiles at me from across the room. The Me Soseki Crew is still in full garb. Liz is here with rest of the creative department. Hank is here with Randy, Georgina and several more members of the sales team. Susan and her advertising services department are in the far corner mingling with Dave and his production group. Barbara is already taking flash photographs with her digital camera. Ellen is smoothing the edges of the paper tablecloth. Martin and Ben are both putting in guest appearances. Meg, Pete and Kelly have torn themselves away from their client-presentation treadmill. The only obvious absentee is Roger, but Meg whispers in my ear that he's on his way. Things in my old department have been running a whole lot more smoothly since I promoted Meg to director and delivered her a thirty percent raise and the promise of a special bonus tied to the successful launch of the *Daily Edge*.

For my birthday celebration, everything is as cheap and cheerful it should be. The plastic plates and cups on the conference table. The selection of sodas. The ice cream cake with the personalized icing. At the far end of the conference table, past the end of the red paper tablecloth, three white boxes are stacked—one small, one medium, one large. It's an impressive presentation, especially if the gifts inside adhere to my twenty-five-dollar rule.

"Wow!" I say, opening my arms and taking in the scene with an expression of mock surprise. "I can't believe you guys went to all this trouble!"

We go through the usual rituals of cake cutting, soda drinking, and chitchat. Then Hank Sullivan claps his hands and calls the room to attention.

"Listen up, people," he says. "The time has come to say a few words about our man of the hour, our marketing visionary, not to mention our birthday boy, Russell Wiley.

"Just a few weeks ago, the *Chronicle* was being written off as yesterday's news and people were predicting that the *Daily Edge* wouldn't even get out of the gate.

"Six weeks ago we hadn't sold a single ad into the launch issue of the *Daily Edge* and the *Chronicle*'s biggest advertiser told us they were pulling their entire schedule. Today, our launch issue is sold out and Livingston Kidd is not only back in the *Chronicle*, they're spending more with us than they ever have before.

"Of course, we in the sales department would love to take all the credit, but the truth is we couldn't have done it without Russell here and all you crazy marketing people. I don't understand a single damn thing that you're doing. But keep it up. It's working."

Hank enthusiastically leads the assembled group through a spontaneous chorus of "For He's a Jolly Good Fellow," then segues into the obligatory off-key rendition of "Happy Birthday."

He hands me my birthday card, which I open and scan quickly. Erika has added an X and an O by her signed name.

"Thanks everyone," I say, catching Erika's eye again. "I'll study all these comments later."

Then the gifts begin.

Meg steps forward and hands me the small package from the top of the pile. I set it down on the table. It's a plain white box with a lid that lifts off. There's tissue paper inside. I unwrap it carefully to reveal the gift.

Beneath all the folds I find a furry black caterpillar. I pick it up and hold it in front of my face for the whole room to see. It's a fake mustache. I press it to my upper lip. People are snickering, nudging each other, whispering comments to the person next to them. Then Roger Jones—still huge, but noticeably slimmer—walks into the room.

"Hey, that's mine!" he says. And everyone starts laughing. Roger is clean-shaven. It's the first time any of us have seen him without facial hair. He walks over, shakes my hand, then pulls me into a big, hearty hug. Barbara's digital camera flashes from five feet away.

"You're always telling me to shave it off," he says, loudly for the room. "It was the only gift I could think of that came in under your twenty-five-dollar rule."

"Roger, this is priceless," I say, matching him for volume. "But watch out. The marriage proposals will only increase from here."

Barbara poses us for two more photos, with Roger and me taking turns with the fake mustache.

Then Hank steps forward again. "All right. Let's move on to box number two."

Kiko steps forward and hands me the medium-sized box.

Again, I set the box on the table and lift off the lid. Inside, there's a plastic Lucky Cat. It's identical to the black one I have in my office, only this one is pink. I hold it up to the room.

"I noticed you kept your first cat in the office," says Kiko. "It brought you luck at work. Now you can take one home too. Pink is to make you lucky in love."

"Thanks so much," I say, posing with Kiko for Barbara's photographs. "I hope this works as well as my first one did."

Barbara instructs Sally and Angela to get into the shot too. She knows the value of every photo op that involves the Me Soseki Crew.

"All right," says Hank. "I hate to break the party up, but some of us have clients to call and insertion orders to process. Let's get to the final gift of the day."

"Well, hello everybody," says Ben, standing with both hands on top of the large box that remains unopened. "For those of you who don't remember me, I'm Ben Shapiro. And I used to work here. Until I was eliminated by the former regime. For those of you who were worried about me but forgot to call, I just want you to know I'm doing just fine. In fact, getting fired was the best thing that ever happened to me. You'll all be hearing much more about the Benjamin Shapiro Company in the weeks ahead. But apart from what's in this box, I do want you all to know I had *nothing* to do with planning this lavish affair. So what's in here? Let's see." He lifts the lid of the box himself and pulls out a large, fluffy, impossibly expensive bathrobe. "Well folks, this is the bathrobe that got me fired. In fact, it's the one you, Russell, asked me to put aside for Jeanie Tusa. Oops. Sorry, Jeanie, wherever you are. Didn't quite get it to you. But, Russell, just lose a few more pounds and I'm sure this will look great on you."

"Ooohh," I say. "That hurt."

Barbara takes some photos. Then Ben calls Erika over. "You should really be thanking her for the robe," he whispers to me. "She's the one who dug it out of the storeroom."

Ben steps discreetly out of the frame, and Erika and I hold the robe up for the camera. Then, with nothing more to look at, some people get back to their ice cream cake and interrupted conversations, while others start drifting back to their cubicles and offices. Erika helps me fold the robe so I can place it back in the box. We're both silent, even for the few seconds when, unnoticed by the others, she traces a fingertip across the back of my hand.

Back in my office, I sit alone at my desk. I pull the head off my new Lucky Cat. There's a small package of crackers inside. Fresh. Not only edible, but quite tasty too. I eat two, then leave the packet open on my desk for future visitors to enjoy.

I play with the cat for a while, removing and replacing its detachable head. Then I look at the countdown clock on my computer screen. Twenty-three days to launch. Twenty-four days till our big party. I put my hand on the cat's pink head, close my eyes, and make a wish that involves Erika Fallon—a wish that I hope will start coming true twenty-five days from now.

I open my eyes and see an instant message pop up on my screen. It's from Erika. *Did you see what I was pointing to? The note in the bathrobe pocket?*

I type: *A note? BRB.*

I step quickly to the coffee table, open the large white box, feel in the pockets. There's a folded piece of paper, closed with a circular seal.

I read: *Russell, I know you already have one of these. But, speaking unprofessionally, you never know when you might need two. XO Erika.*

I hurry back to my desk.

I type: *Found it—thanks! Speaking unprofessionally, how about dinner on...* I double-check my calendar and type in the date.

Erika shoots back: *Can't wait...sweet dreams till then!*

I look at my smiling reflection in the wood-framed mirror; the lights of Times Square are getting brighter in the fading light of a late January afternoon. I place my two Lucky Cats a few inches apart on my desk. They smile at each other. I start moving them closer. When their faces are almost touching, I angle their heads so they can whisper in each other's ears. Both cats take a half step back. They're grinning at each other, savoring the anticipation of what comes next. Finally, they tilt their faces and lean forward again. And this time they kiss.

THE END

ACKNOWLEDGMENTS

Thank you to the hundreds of colleagues I met and friends I made during my years at *Adweek*, *Time* Magazine and the *Wall Street Journal*. This book wouldn't exist if we hadn't experienced together the highs and lows of print publishing, or sat through the Powerpoint presentations and training sessions, or lived through the takeovers and mergers that have defined the recent history of the media business.

A grateful shout-out to all the teachers who encouraged my youthful writing dreams or, when necessary, gave me a shove in the right direction, especially Fr. Alfred Thomas and Con O'Halpin, and the exceptional authors and writing instructors Susie Mee and Carol Emswhiller.

A big smile to all the writers I met through the Amazon Breakthrough Novel Award contest in 2009, in particular Kerry Dunn, Sheryl Dunn, Dwight Okita, Jarucia Jaycox Nirula, Steffan Piper, Brandi Lynn Ryder, Sofia Samatar and Robert Leland Taylor. And huge thanks to Alex Carr and Sarah

Tomashek at AmazonEncore for their valuable advice and support throughout the publication process.

Finally, a very special note of appreciation to Martine Bellen, Heather Chase, Jennifer Cohen, Lloyd Cole, Catherine Cusset, Randy Dwenger, Ken Foster, Shelley Griffin, Philomena Hine, Lee Klein, Hilda McVeigh, J.B. Miller, Ben Neihart, Karen Quinn, Alessandro Ricciarelli, Victoria Skurnick and, most of all, the ever-inspiring Amanda Filipacchi.

Amanda Filipacchi, 2010

ABOUT THE AUTHOR

London-born Richard Hine began his career as an advertising copywriter. After moving to New York at the age of twenty-four, he held creative and marketing positions at *Adweek*; *Time* magazine, where he became publisher of *Time*'s Latin America edition; and the *Wall Street Journal*, where he was the marketing vice president responsible for the launch of the *Journal*'s Weekend Edition. Since 2006, Hine has worked as a marketing and media consultant, ghostwriter, and novelist. His fiction has appeared in numerous literary publications, including *London Magazine* and the *Brooklyn Review*. He lives in New York City with the novelist Amanda Filipacchi.